Invaders

Book 1

Edited by Diana Cox

Created with Atticus

CONTENTS

1. TIM 1
2. TIM 6
3. TIM 9
4. TIM 12
5. TIM 18
6. TIM 21
7. TIM 28
8. TIM 32
9. TIM 37
10. TIM 40
11. TIM 44
12. TIM 47
13. TIM 51
14. VERONICA 55
15. TIM 60
16. VERONICA 64
17. TIM 67
18. VERONICA 70

19.	TIM	78
20.	TIM	81
21.	VERONICA	85
22.	TIM	89
23.	VERONICA	95
24.	TIM	99
25.	VERONICA	105
26.	TIM	111
27.	TIM	117
28.	TIM	121
29.	TIM	127
30.	TIM	131
31.	VERONICA	135
32.	TIM	138
33.	TIM	142
34.	VERONICA	146
35.	TIM	150
36.	TIM	156
37.	TIM	160
38.	TIM	166
39.	VERONICA	174
40.	TIM	181
41.	FELIX	189
42.	TIM	194

43. VERONICA 198
44. FELIX 201
45. TIM 206
46. FELIX 214
47. TIM 225
48. FELIX 231
49. VERONICA 236
50. TIM 240
51. VERONICA 245
52. TIM 249
53. FELIX 253
54. VERONICA 258
55. TIM 261
56. HELENA 266
57. TIM 273
58. HELENA 277
59. TIM 279

1

TIM

HE'S DRUNK THE NIGHT they arrive.

Not "out-of-your-mind" drunk. Just regular old "it's-Tuesday-so-let's-keep-it-nice" drunk. Half a bottle of vodka will do the trick. Even to a guy his size.

It happens on his way back from town.

Living alone, at the end of a narrow gravel road, halfway up a hill, definitely has its advantages. For instance, you can drive home drunk without anyone noticing.

He's singing along to some lame country song, when Buddy begins whimpering from the backseat.

"Yeah, I know it's bad," Tim says, grinning up at the mirror. "Anya was right when she told me I'd never become a rockstar."

Buddy isn't looking at him, though. The German shepherd sits with his back turned, staring out the rear window, shackles raised.

"What'd ya spot? A deer? I didn't see nothin'."

Some animal probably crossed the road behind the car. The forest is right on the other side of the hill, and Tim will often meet rabbits, foxes, deer and even the occasional badger when driving to and back from town. If he'd bother to take up hunting, he'd never have to pay for meat again.

But he's done enough killing for one lifetime.

Buddy gives a shrill bark, causing Tim to jump.

"Will you cut that out? The deer is gone!"

But already as he utters the words, he realizes it wasn't a deer or any kind of animal that has roused the dog. Buddy's simply too agitated. He's rarely heard Buddy bark like that before. And he keeps staring fixedly out the window.

So, Tim slows down and checks both mirrors, squinting to see if there's anyone following the car. He sees nothing but darkness.

"The hell you caught sight of out there, Buddy?"

He needs to take a piss anyway, so he stops in the middle of the road. Yanking the handbrake, he opens the door and stumbles out.

The night is cold, the air clean and crisp. It's January, the Month of Broken Promises, and it will begin snowing any day now.

"Hey there!" he calls out, going to the back of the truck. "Anybody out here?"

His voice rings out over the hill. It's mostly meadows, with the occasional shrubs. Some of the farmers keep sheep here in the summer, but the landscape is too steep and bumpy for any agriculture. Way down below is the pool of light from town, embers in the darkness.

Tim peers around. His eyes have adapted to the lack of light. But still, he doesn't see anything or anybody out there.

From inside the car, Buddy is still complaining, giving off low barks.

"Wonder what's gotten into him," Tim mutters, unbuttoning his pants. That's when he catches a glimpse of the dog's face through the foggy car window, and he finally notices Buddy's eyes are turned *upwards*.

He cranes back his neck.

And there he sees it.

A green bulb, moving across the night sky. It's too bright to be a plane, too slow to be a comet. It's also silent, at least as far as Tim can tell over the hum of the truck's engine.

He just stands there, mouth and fly both open, staring stupidly at the thing crossing overhead. It seems to be descending, because it grows slowly bigger. He still can't make out any details—no wings, tail or propellers. If it's an aircraft of some kind, he's never seen one like it before.

Perhaps a falling satellite? He's heard of foreign governments now and then retiring older models by letting them drop and burn up in the atmosphere. But this one isn't burning; not exactly. It's more like it's *glowing*. And by the speed of it, it doesn't seem to be falling. It strikes him more as a controlled descent.

He loses it from sight behind the hill.

Ten seconds pass by. Ten more.

Tim holds his breath, waiting, although not sure for what. Buddy whimpers anxiously from inside the truck.

Tim decides the show's over and resumes what he originally stepped out of the truck to do. Just as things start flowing, there comes a low, deep boom. A brief, violent rumble shakes the ground. Tim feels it in his feet. There's also a push against his chest, causing him to take a step back, sucking the air from his mouth. He gasps as he regains balance, narrowly avoiding getting piss on his shoes.

The truck's lights blink once, then go out. The engine coughs and dies.

The silence that follows is deafening. All he can hear is his pulse thrumming away in his skull and Buddy barking louder than ever before inside the car.

"Holy shit ... what was *that*?"

Did the thing just explode on the other side of the hill? Was it some sort of drone bomb sent by terrorists?

No. A bomb would send up lots of smoke and dust. On a windless night like this, he should be able to see it rise over the hill. But the sky is still clear and black.

Besides, Tim knows what a bomb feels and sounds like. He's experienced mortars and roadside bombs. This was different.

An EMP then?

An EMP wouldn't send out an actual shockwave like the one he'd felt. Not unless it was accompanied by a nuclear explosion. In which case he wouldn't still be here, and neither would the hill.

Tim checks his phone. It's been shut off.

Definitely some kind of electrical discharge. What the hell would cause that if not a bomb?

He suddenly doesn't feel like standing around here like an idiot. So, he hurries back inside the truck. Buddy yelps from the back.

"I know, I know, Buddy. We're going. Okay? Hold your horses."

He turns the key, expecting the ignition to click and the engine to stay dead. Whatever shut off the truck probably did it by frying the circuits. To his surprise, though, the old girl starts on first try.

He drives the rest of the way home, keeping an eye on the hilltop the whole way.

Pulling into the dirt lot which serves as his driveway, he parks the car and gets back out. The night is still quiet like a graveyard. The cabin looks just as he's left it: windows intact, door locked, nothing out of place.

He lets Buddy out of the truck. The dog immediately starts for the hill.

"Nope," Tim tells him firmly.

Buddy stops and looks back with an obvious question in his eyes.

Tim shakes his head. "We're not going over there. We'll get ourselves lost. I'm not spending the night freezing my ass off in the middle of the woods."

Buddy gives an impatient whine, as though calling his bullshit. Tim wouldn't get lost, not even in his drunken state. For one thing, the effect of the alcohol would quickly wear off in the cold night air. Second, he knows the forest like the back of his hand.

"Come on, we're going to bed."

He strides to the front door, pulling the key from his pocket.

The truth is, he doesn't *want* to go looking. For some strange reason, he's scared.

And Tim never gets scared.

2

TIM

THAT NIGHT, TIM DREAMS of strange, glowing objects falling from the sky.

He wakes up the next morning to a mean hangover.

For a brief moment, he's lost in time. He reaches out to feel for Anya, but his hand finds nothing but the sheets. Blinking his eyes open, he sees daylight filtering through the curtains. The messy state of the bedroom brings him back to the present reality. A reality in which he's the only human sleeping in the bed.

By his feet lies Buddy, already awake. His head resting on his paws, his dark eyes are fixed on Tim.

He rolls onto his back with a groan. "Watching me sleep again, huh? I told you, that's kinda creepy."

His mouth feels like he's eaten a fistful of sand. He sits up slowly, careful not to set off an avalanche of pain in his skull. His elbow gives off the familiar stab of pain.

He glances at the alarm, wanting to know how much he's overslept. But the display is black.

Damn thing must have broke again. Gotta get a new one.

He rubs his eyes with the base of his palms. "I had this crazy dream. Something came dropping from the sky and landed in the ..." He looks at Buddy, who stares back at him, knowingly. "Holy shit, that wasn't just a dream, was it?"

The dog jumps to the floor and goes to the door. He sits down, looking intently up at the knob.

"Hold on one moment, Buddy."

Tim grabs his phone off the nightstand. Tries to activate the screen, but the phone is still out. He turns it on. As he waits for it to boot, he frowns, recalling the strange incident with the truck dying. He reaches over and flicks the switch for the reading lamp mounted on the wall. It's dead.

Damnit. Whatever it was, it fried the generator.

He hadn't noticed last night. Not even bothering to turn on any lights, he'd just kicked off his clothes and gone straight to bed.

As the phone starts up, a message ticks in. It's from the company who delivers his groceries once a week, telling him this Wednesday's delivery is on its way.

He checks Facebook. He has a pseudo-account just to be able to snoop around. It's business as usual. Jokes. Gossip. Shit for sale.

He checks the national and the local news sites. Nothing about a strange object dropping from the sky.

So either it didn't happen, or no one else noticed.

He hopes for the former, still clinging to the possibility that it has all been some sort of drunken hallucination. That the power outage is caused by something unrelated. Like a simple wire malfunctioning, or the generator running out of propane.

But judging from the way Buddy is burning the door, willing it to open, Tim can tell the dog remembers something happening, too.

He takes a deep breath. The thought of going out there now, in the daylight, sober, is not quite as scary, though still not exactly how he hoped to spend his morning. But whatever that thing was, it basically landed in his backyard. And despite himself, he can't help but feel a responsibility to find out what the hell it was.

"All right," he says with a sigh. "Let's go and check, then."

3

TIM

HE GRABS A HAIR-OF-THE-DOG before leaving the cabin.

Both to fight the headache, but also to stiffen his resolve.

The can is warm, since the fridge is out like the rest of the power. His place is heated only by a wooden stove in the living room, but he didn't bother getting a fire going before he left. He generally doesn't mind the cold.

Instead, he went outside to the steel cabinet next to the overhang where he keeps the firewood. The generator had shut off, just like he expected, for no discernable reason. Plenty of propane left in the tank, it started willingly as soon as he reset it.

Now, as he's trudging along the path used mostly by deer and the occasional hiker, he chugs down the last of the beer, then throws the can away.

If he hadn't been hungover, he might have appreciated how beautiful the meadow looks this morning. A

thin layer of freshly fallen snow covers everything, making the grass all glittery. The sky is overcast, the sun trying desperately to break through.

He hears rhythmical footsteps up ahead and sees a female jogger. Buddy has already spotted her and comes to his side. The woman is wearing earbuds and is clearly lost in thought, and she doesn't see them until she almost bumps into Tim.

"Jeez," she exclaims, swerving to avoid them. She glances back once, but doesn't stop to apologize.

"People nowadays," Tim grunts. "Completely wrapped up in their own shit."

Buddy gives him a look of agreement.

They walk for another ten minutes when the dog reacts to something up ahead. Stopping, he raises his head and gives a low bark.

At first, all Tim sees is a light-brown bundle writhing on the frozen ground. It appears to be a hare, lying on its side, doing some kind of weird dance.

"Heel," he tells Buddy. "Stay."

The dog obediently—though reluctantly—puts his butt to the ground, and Tim steps closer to study the hare, trying to figure out what the hell it's doing. It looks like it's running. Or that it *thinks* it's running. In reality, it's only spinning in circles. Foam around its mouth, its eyes rolled back. The poor guy produces a strained whimpering.

He's having some kind of seizure.

Whatever is going on with it, it sure looks unpleasant. Tim gives it half a minute, just to see if it will snap out of it.

It doesn't.

So he does the kind thing and places the heel of his boot on its neck, grabs its hindquarters with one gloved hand, then yanks upwards hard enough to snap the little guy's neck.

It immediately stops moving. A few last spasms, but that's only nerves.

The animal smells oddly. A sharp, sour smell. Like limes. He notices something else then. The hare looks as though it's been rolling around in mud. Its paws are all dark from dirt, and some has gotten in its ears, too.

But as Tim crouches down to have a closer look, he realizes it isn't dirt at all.

He takes the tiny front paw and presses it with his thumb, making the toes spread apart. Some mossy stuff is growing in there. It's black and shiny. Some sort of eczema, probably. Not scaly like psoriasis, but fuzzy. It's growing everywhere. Around the mouth and snout, below the eyes, on the belly and in the crotch.

"Poor guy," Tim mutters. "Musta been itchin' all over."

He hasn't seen this particular rash before, but he knows wild animals carry all kinds of nasty diseases. For one thing, they're riddled with fleas and ticks, but they're also prone to bacterial infections like salmonella and Q fever.

He stands back up and sniffs as his nose begins to run.

Buddy takes it to mean he can come closer.

"No, you stay away from him," Tim tells him firmly. "Don't you go getting yourself sick now. I just paid a fortune to have you vaccinated, remember?"

Buddy reluctantly slinks in an arch around the hare, eyeing it all the way, clearly eager to get a proper sniff.

Tim steps away, bends over and wipes his glove in the frosty heather. He isn't too worried about bringing spores home with him; he knows they wouldn't be able to live in this cold without a warm host. But still, just to be on the safe side, he makes a mental note to wash the glove when he gets back.

4

TIM

SINCE TIM DOESN'T KNOW exactly where the thing landed, he keeps to the path that he thinks of as the main one as they enter the forest. It will take them through the center and all the way to the other side.

Buddy seems to agree this is the right direction. He runs about twenty yards up ahead, nose to the ground, sniffing eagerly.

In the summer, mountain bikers come up here to ride around with their stupid, colorful helmets and tight outfits. This time of the year, though, Tim rarely meets anyone, which suits him a lot better. He moved up here to get away from people, not to be greeted by clowns from the city every time he goes for a walk. In fact, walking in the forest is one of the only activities that allows him to truly unwind.

Today, however, he feels uptight. His mind keeps circling around Anya, even more so than usual. Close to four years dead now, she still occupies his thoughts most of the time. Then again, is that any wonder? She was his one shot at happiness in this life.

He'd never been with a woman before Anya, had never even dated. He wasn't supposed to be a husband, much less a father. Him meeting Anya and falling in love was a glitch in the Matrix. He knew that, even when she was still alive and healthy.

So when the stroke came and took her from him, he was barely surprised. It was simply the universe correcting things back to how they were supposed to be. Tim, alone. Miserable.

Buddy is probably the only reason he hasn't ended things. That, and Helena. Not that his daughter would give a damn. He's not suicidal, he's simply at peace with the fact that he's just running out the clock. He'll keep his job, so he has something to do. He'll keep drinking because it makes living hurt less.

But happiness? That's for other people.

It was always in the cards, really. Dad split before he was born, Mom died when he was five. In school, he was bullied, ostracized. They called him a half-wit—which is true in more than one sense.

It wasn't until Tim hit puberty and outgrew his bullies by several inches and pounds that they finally stopped picking on him.

He left school as soon as possible. Took up different kinds of work before joining the army to get away from everything. His years abroad were some of the most meaningful. Grotesque as it may seem, killing people in a foreign country gave him a sense of purpose. Finally something he was good at.

Then, at the age of twenty-five, he met the woman who changed the course of his life forever.

Fourteen years he had with her. Not a bad run. Most people don't get to be happy for that long.

As he's walking along, immersed in dark thoughts, he suddenly becomes aware of a change in the air.

He stops and looks around, trying to discern what exactly is different. He can't put his finger on it.

Buddy slinks around him in a restless manner.

"You feel that too, boy?" he whispers, his breath forming puffs of white smoke in front of his face.

It's like the pressure has dropped slightly. His eardrums feel like they need to pop. There is also a very subtle vibration in the air. Like what you'd expect just before an earthquake. It tickles the tiny hairs in his nose. He figures that's why Buddy is growing more anxious; aren't dogs said to be more sensitive to things like that?

He then notices something else.

All sounds have stopped. No birds are chirping. The breeze has died down completely. The rustling of the dead leaves, the clicking of the branches touching each other overhead, the squeaking of the tree trunks swaying gently. It's all gone. Like someone has muted the world.

"What the hell is this?"

Even his voice seems to be swallowed up as soon as the words leave his mouth. Like the air is too thick for the soundwaves to move properly.

"You know, maybe we better just turn around and—"

That's when he sees it.

It's right there, less than thirty paces off the path. He almost walked right by it.

He's not exactly sure what he expected. A burned-up satellite, maybe. Piece of a broken plane. Or even something as exotic as a meteorite. Whatever the case, he expected the object to be in a crater.

It isn't in a crater.

It is just sitting there. Like someone gently placed it on the ground.

No longer glowing, it looks like a boulder. Big as a van. Around it, while not a crater, is a perfect circle, maybe twenty feet across. No snow has fallen within this circle. Not a single flake. Almost like the rock has been giving off heat. It looks kind of natural, but at the same time very much like it doesn't belong. Like it's masquerading as a rock.

Why would that word come to mind? Tim thinks to himself, growing still more tense. *"Masquerade." Like that thing is trying to fool me. Like it has conscious intent. It's obviously just a rock ...*

But he can't really convince himself that that is true, and he doesn't feel like going any closer. So for a few minutes, he just stands there, his thoughts debating with each other.

Come on, you fool. It's just a boulder.

Yeah, a boulder that dropped from the sky.

If it'd dropped from the sky, there would be a crater. You felt the impact, remember?

So, this isn't the thing I saw landing last night? Then why haven't I seen it before?

He has no answer to that one. Theoretically, he could have passed by the boulder every time he'd walked this path without noticing it. But that's highly unlikely. If nothing else, Buddy would have picked up the—

"Buddy?"

Tim blinks as he realizes the dog has left his side.

"Hey, Buddy?"

He sees him next to the boulder—or whatever it is. Buddy is skulking around it, sniffing it carefully, shackles standing on end. He's alternating between whining and growling. The sounds are way too faint, as though the dog is very far away.

Something's really wrong here.

"Buddy!" he calls out, starting forward. He can sense the words not reaching the dog. "Buddy, get away from—"

He steps on something mushy and looks down. A hedgehog. Lying on its back, its tiny legs splayed out. The naked part of its belly is overgrown with the shiny black stuff he saw on the hare too.

"Aw, Jesus," he mutters, stepping around the poor thing. "*Buddy!*"

This time, he shouts loud enough that the dog actually hears him. To his horror, he sees Buddy now standing on his hindquarters, one front paw resting on the boulder, his snout scanning the air. He reacts to Tim's call, jumps down and comes back to him.

"Damnit, why'd you have to go near that thing?" Tim scolds him. "It could be radioactive for all we know. Come on!"

He's about to turn, darting one last glance at the boulder, when he notices something really strange about it. "What the hell ...?"

Crouching down, he lets out a gasp. The rock isn't actually touching the ground; it's sitting two inches above it.

It isn't leaning or standing on anything. There aren't any trees or anything else nearby to support it.

It's simply *hovering*.

"Oh, come on," Tim croaks. "This is too messed up. We're getting out of here right now."

He turns and strides back, Buddy on his heels. Just as they get onto the path, something gray and feathery drops from above and lands right in front of Tim, causing him to shout and Buddy to jump and bark.

"It's okay," Tim tells him, forcing his heart back down his throat. "It's just a dead pigeon. Don't touch it."

He steps over the bird, making sure Buddy doesn't go near it. He acts like it's perfectly normal that birds die and fall from the sky. He also pretends he doesn't see the black stuff around the bird's eyes and beak.

He's not really sure who he's trying to fool. All he knows is, he wants to get as far away from that rock as possible.

5

TIM

SHOULD HAVE NEVER GONE over there. Should have stayed home.

The thought keeps haunting him, even after they return to the cabin. His mood is even darker than before.

He tries to act normal, tries to get on with things as though it is any other day. He fills Buddy's water bowl and pours him his breakfast with robotic motions. All the while, his mind is somewhere else, arguing with itself.

Should I call someone?

Who would you call?

I don't know. The cops. Anyone.

What would the cops do about a boulder in the forest? Arrest it?

He finds himself standing by the windows in the living room, staring out over the meadows.

He keeps thinking of dead animals. If that thing out there is emanating some form of radiation, the authorities need to know about it. As far as he knows, though, radiation poisoning doesn't cause black, moss-like growths. And would it even happen so fast? Doesn't radiation sickness take days to kill someone? Besides, Buddy has touched the thing, and he is all right.

As though the thought summoned him, Buddy comes into the room. He licks his mouth, then walks to his usual spot next to the fireplace, dropping down on his blanket with a sigh.

"You seem okay," Tim remarks.

Buddy looks up at him without lifting his head.

Seeing the dog makes Tim feel a little better. Of course that thing out there hasn't caused the dead animals. It's some kind of fungal infection going around.

He gets a fire going. The familiar activity calms him down a bit. Just as the flames are growing, his phone rings.

He pulls it out and sees Benny's name on the display—his colleague down from the factory. Tim remembers he promised to take a look at Benny's car this morning—the fuel filter is blocked and probably needs changing.

He answers the call. "Hey, Benny."

"You sick? Boss says you haven't called in."

"Yeah, I know. Tell him sorry. It completely slipped his mind."

"Huh. Slipped your mind? Boss isn't gonna like that. You went drinking last night?"

"No more than usual."

"So, I take it you won't come check out the car?"

"No, no, I can do that. When are you getting off today?"

Benny says something Tim doesn't hear. His gaze has been caught by something outside the window. A hare comes jumping across the meadow. It stops to nibble at the still-green leaves of a blackberry bush.

Tim stares at it.

It looks just like the one he killed. Of course, all hares look alike. But even from this distance, Tim can see the mossy stuff still stuck in its fur. Except it's noticeably grayer now. More dull. The hare stops chewing. Perks its ears and listens.

"Tim?"

The hare shakes its fur, and the gray stuff drizzles to the ground. Then it hops on, disappearing out of sight.

"Tim? Hey, Tim? You there?"

He clears his throat. "Yeah."

"You all right, man?"

"I'm sorry, I … I guess I'm not really feeling right after all. I'd better stay home."

"Sure. I'll take it to the shop. Don't worry about it."

Benny disconnects without saying goodbye. Probably pissed off that Tim went drinking, forgot about him and then blew him off. Tim can't really care less.

That wasn't the same hare. It wasn't.

There are dozens of hares around here. This one has also caught whatever disease is going around. But unlike its cousin out of the trail, this one has kicked it and survived. That's the explanation.

Still …

They did look awfully alike.

6

TIM

HE HAS A HARD time focusing on anything.

He drifts around the cabin aimlessly. Doing unimportant stuff just to keep his hands busy. He eats a bowl of oatmeal despite having no appetite. But save for the pretzels last night, he hasn't eaten in almost twenty-four hours.

His mind keeps circling around the boulder, the hare, the black stuff.

The rational part of his brain tells him he needs to call someone. Tell them about what he's seen.

But something holds him back. For some odd reason, it feels like a private matter. He knows it's silly. But calling the authorities—assuming they'd even believe him—and having them arrive would mean a lot of unwanted attention. He'd have to answer a bunch of questions. Would have to lead them through the forest. What if they take one look at the boulder and laugh? What if this is all in his head?

For now, he isn't going to stir up anything.

He's cleaning the dishwasher's filter—something he's been putting off for weeks—when Buddy comes to the kitchen, his claws clicking on the old wooden floor.

"How you feelin', pal? All right?"

Buddy replies by sitting down and scratching away at his ear with his hind leg. He then saunters over to his water bowl and takes a drink.

Tim continues rinsing the filter, brooding as he stares out the window above the sink. A murder of black crows is flying across the steel gray sky. The sun has come up and is already headed for the horizon again. This time of year, daylight is a rare commodity. No wonder everybody gets depressed.

He thinks of Helena. Debates whether to call her. Check in. It's been, what, four months this time? Half a year? He can't even recall.

Last time they spoke, she was living with her boyfriend. Dennis or Teddy or something. A law student. Helena is studying to become a therapist.

It makes him proud, having a daughter with such a bright mind. The thought of him ever finishing an education is ridiculous. Luckily, Helena hasn't inherited his condition. Even though the risk of that was miniscule, he was still weary of putting a child into this world knowing it could potentially suffer the same fate as he.

Anya talked him into it. She really wanted a kid.

He glances at the pictures on the fridge. Anya, wearing a silly hat while holding up a giant ice cream cone. From their trip to Egypt.

"You got what you wanted," he mutters. "You always did."

Another picture of Anya and Helena standing next to a snowman, laughing at the camera.

"Should I call her? Whaddya think?"

Anya's eyes tell him yes.

"Okay," he says, breathing deeply. "Okay, honey, I will. Just to check in."

He looks around for his phone, noticing the dog's bowl is empty. That gives him pause. It's a big bowl. Almost half a gallon when it's properly full. And he just filled it up this morning. Didn't he?

Probably not. Just thought I did.

Buddy has gone back into the living room. Tim can hear the fire crackling in there, can feel the heat already reaching the kitchen. He fills the dog's bowl, then remembers his phone is in the charger in the bedroom.

There are no missed calls, no messages.

He slumps down on the bed, scrolling through the short list of contacts. Most of them are practical acquaintances. The plumber. The vet. His boss. Only a handful of social contacts. They are sorted by most recently used, which means Helena's name is at the very bottom.

He gathers his resolve, then calls her up.

She picks up on the third ring.

"*Hello*?" Her tone is guarded right away.

"Hey," he says in what he hopes is a casual tone. "It's your father."

"Yeah?"

"I, uh ... just wanted to check in on ya."

"I'm a little busy, Dad."

"Oh. So now's not a good time?"

"That would be the implication, yes."

"Sorry, Helena. I'll—I'll let you go, then."

She sighs. "*No, wait. It's fine. We can talk for five minutes.*"

"You sure? I don't wanna bother you."

"It's fine."

"Okay. So, what are you doing?"

"We're playing tennis, me and Freddie."

Freddie. That's right.

He makes a mental note.

"Tennis?" he asks. "Isn't it a bit cold for that?"

"It's indoors."

"Oh. I didn't know that was a thing."

"Yeah, well ..."

He chews his lip. His back is prickly with sweat. "Sure I'm not interrupting? I can call back later, if that's—"

"It's fine, Dad. Freddie went to the changing room. His racket needed a new grip, so we're just waiting around."

"We? It's not just you and Freddie then?"

"We're playing against this other couple from university."

"I see. Are you winning?"

Helena scoffs. "*We're down two sets.*"

"Well, you can always make a comeback. It's never too late."

Helena doesn't answer.

"You there, honey?"

"Look, Dad, why are you calling me?"

"Like I said ... I just wanted to check in."

"You always say that. I don't know what it means."

"Well, I just want to hear how you're doing. That everything is fine, you know? Is that such a bad thing?"

He means for it to sound lighthearted, but it comes out defensive. He immediately regrets it.

"It's not bad, it's just ... weird. I'm not a kid anymore, Dad. You don't need to check up on me."

"Well, you're kind of a kid to me, honey. No offense. I know you're a grown woman, but you'll always be *my* kid, you know?"

Helena doesn't answer. He can hear sounds in the background. People playing, shouting.

Tim is rubbing his thigh like he's trying to start a fire. "So, how's school?"

"*Look, Dad.*" She takes a deep breath. "*Can we stop doing this?*"

"Doing what?" he asks stupidly.

"*You calling me from time to time. I just ... I don't feel like it, okay?*"

"Oh. Okay. Sure. If it's inconvenient, I'll just—"

"*It's not inconvenient, Dad. It's awkward. And it's unnecessary. I'm sorry, but who are you fooling?*"

His face starts to burn. "I'm not trying to fool anyone."

"*But this is how it always goes. I'm having a great day. I needed this time to blow off steam. To hang out with friends. This semester is killing me, and me and Freddie are ... well, we're going through a rough patch, I guess ... and we finally get the time to hang out and do something together and not worry about school. And then you call me up, and we chat for five minutes. Then we hang up again, and you go on with your life and feel a little better about yourself. Meanwhile, the rest of my day is messed up. I keep thinking of Mom, I feel guilty for never seeing you, all this shit from the past ... I don't want to stir it up anymore. I just want to get over it, you know?*"

She stops talking. He can hear her breathing fast.

Tim blinks several times. "I ... I had no idea you felt that way, honey."

"*Well, now you know.*"

He nods slowly, as though she could actually see him. "If it's what you want, I'll stop calling."

"*It's not what I want! Jesus, Dad. Stop putting it on me. It's not my fault we don't have a relationship, okay?*"

"No, I know. That's *my* fault. My condition—"

"*Oh, cut it out, please. That fucking excuse again.*"

It feels like a slap. He actually gets a little angry. "Now, listen. It's certainly not an excu—"

"Freddie's uncle, he's got cerebral palsy. He's in a wheelchair. He's got three kids, Dad. We just spent Christmas with them. And guess what? They all love each other."

Tim gapes, unsure how to reply. And then he says something really damn stupid. "Well ... I'm glad Freddie comes from such a loving family. Not all of us are that lucky."

*"**Lucky**? Dad, are you listening? The guy's got CP. You call that lucky? He's made his own happiness. He's **trying**."*

Tim realizes he's clenching his jaw and wills the muscles to relax. "I get your point, honey."

"You do? Well, then do you also see why I don't want you to call anymore?"

"Look, like I said. If you want me to back off, I'll respect that. But this is me trying, okay? I loved your mother very much, and I never wanted our family to get torn apart like it did. Not a day goes by where I don't miss her. If she was still around ..."

"Just stop, Dad. Please."

"What?"

"I can't listen to you talk about her."

He sighs. "I'm sorry. I know you miss her too."

To his utter surprise, Helena laughs. It doesn't sound like happy laughter, though. More like she is on the verge of tears. "*Christ, you really don't get it, do you*?"

"Get what?"

"It's not about her. It never was."

He throws up his hand. "Then what? Help me understand."

She scoffs. "*I'm not your therapist, Dad. You can't just dump your grief on me and then ...*" Someone says something in the background. A guy's voice. "*No, it's fine*," Helena tells whoever is there. Then she addresses Tim again. "*I gotta go, Dad*."

He shrugs. "I don't … I don't know what to say."

A brief pause. "*That makes two of us, then*."

She ends the call.

7

TIM

HE SITS FOR A long time in the bedroom, staring at the phone in his hand.

There's a hollow feeling in the pit of his stomach. A torrent of emotions swirling around below his Adam's apple.

He feels confused, hurt, angry, guilty. He feels like getting drunk.

Should have never called her. Why do I always make it worse?

He expects Anya, or rather, the version of her that he keeps in his mind, to give him an answer. She usually chimes in when it's something about their daughter. But not today. Anya keeps quiet. Not because she wants him to stew—Anya was never like that. More likely, the message is that it's up to him to figure out how he messed up.

He broods for a couple more minutes until he decides it's a knot he can't untie.

He finally gets up with a sigh, goes to the fridge and gets himself a beer. There are only four left. Not enough to get hammered, which is what he needs.

He goes to the living room. The temperature has gone up considerably. He notices a faint smell of lime, which strikes him as odd, because he never buys any kind of fruit.

Buddy is asleep on his blanket. His front paws twitch, as though he was walking. He gives a low whimper.

"You're dreaming, Buddy."

The dog growls from deep down in his throat, but he doesn't wake up. Instead, it looks like he tries to get to his feet, his legs flailing. Tim has seen him sleepwalk once or twice before, back when he was still a pup.

"Hey," he says, walking over there. "Wake up, Buddy."

He stops as he realizes Buddy's eyes are already open. Staring pleadingly up at him. His mouth is open, too, and he's panting as though out of breath. His legs are still moving in spasmodic jerks.

Tim feels his gut drop as he sees the thin, black rim running around Buddy's snout. "Oh, no. No, no, no ..."

The dog gives off a pitiful whine. His neck spasms, twisting backwards. He tries to bark, but it sounds more like a hoarse wheeze.

Tim's mind starts reeling as a cold rush of fear sweeps through him. *He's infected. He caught whatever the hare had.*

"It's okay," he tells the dog, finally snapping into action. He scoops up Buddy, noticing the heat coming off him. He's practically burning up. The smell he noticed before, the limey scent, is coming from him. "It's okay, Buddy. I'm taking you to see Alan. He'll fix you up. Don't you worry."

He keeps talking as he strides through the cabin. He grabs the keys for the truck and leaves without bothering to lock the door.

Placing Buddy gently on the backseat of the car, he gets in behind the wheel while scolding himself for not taking things more seriously. Now Buddy might die, and it will all be his fault.

"You're not dying," he says out loud, turning on the engine. "No way. You're going to be fine. Just hang in there, Buddy."

He guns it out the driveway and heads down the bumpy road.

By the time they reach the foot of the hill, Buddy has fallen silent on the backseat.

Tim keeps darting glances at him over his shoulder. He can see his stomach rising and falling in uneven breaths.

He pulls out his phone and scrolls through the numbers, finding the one saying Vet.

"Andersen."

"Alan, it's Tim. I need your help. Are you at the clinic?"

A brief pause. "*It's five thirty, Tim.*"

"Shit, right. Can I come to your place then?"

"What's wrong?"

"It's Buddy. He caught something. Fungal, I think. It's bad."

"Sorry to hear it. Look, I'd love to help, but Lis and I are just about to leave. We're going on a couples' date tonight, and—"

Is everybody going on fucking couples' dates today?

"Please, Alan. I think ... I think he's seriously ill."

Alan speaks calmly. "*Maybe you should take him to Aalborg. They have the on-call vet. I can call them up for you, tell 'em you're coming.*"

"Aalborg's forty-five minutes away," Tim says, restraining himself from yelling. "He can barely breathe, Alan."

"Jeez, it's that bad? How long he's been ill?"

"Since ... I don't know. An hour."

"That doesn't sound like fungi to me, Tim. You sure he's not having an allergic reaction?"

"I don't know! All I know is this weird, black stuff is growing on his face. That's why you need to see him, Alan. Please!"

A few seconds of silence. Then, Alan sighs. "*All right, I'll take a look at him.*"

"Thank you, Alan. Thank you. I'm on my way to your place."

"No, come to the clinic. I'll head over and meet you there in five."

8

TIM

TIM PULLS INTO THE lot behind the veterinarian clinic and jumps out of the car before the rumble of the engine has died down.

He tears open the back door and picks up Buddy. The citrusy smell is more pronounced now. The black stuff has spread rapidly. It's filling up the dog's nostrils, running along his mouth, covering his eyelids. There's even some protruding from his ears.

Oh, God ... what the hell **is** *that stuff?*

Buddy is still breathing, but very faintly.

Tim's throat is all tight as he carries the dog to the building. "It's all right, Buddy. You'll pull through. We're here now. Alan will fix you. He'll make you better, you'll see."

The back door opens and Alan waves at him. "Come on. This way."

Alan is ten years his senior. Gray hair always combed back neatly. He's chronically dark around the eyes from working too much and sleeping too little. He's also a heavy smoker, and he flicks away half a cigarette as Tim comes to the door.

"Goodness," he says, raising his brows at the sight of Buddy. "Looks like he's been through a chimney."

"No, it's the black stuff I told you about."

"Right, get him inside."

Alan closes the door behind them. Tim carries Buddy down the hallway. The air smells like fur and cleaning products. The building is usually buzzing with sounds. Right now, it's quiet as a tomb.

"In here," Alan says, pointing to a door on the right.

They enter one of the exam rooms, the lights turning on automatically.

"Put him on the table," Alan instructs, going to the cabinet. He puts on a pair of rubber gloves, then begins examining Buddy.

He checks the dog's snout, his ears, opens his mouth and pulls back his lips. The inside of Buddy's mouth is a horrifying sight. The black stuff is growing all over his gums, in between his teeth, on his tongue. Glistening with saliva, it looks fresh and healthy. Like it's thriving growing in the dog's mouth.

"Goodness," Alan says again. "When did you first notice this?"

Tim can barely speak, barely think. "I ... I didn't ... he was fine just a few hours ago."

"You sure about that?" Alan asks, opening Buddy's left eye to examine his pupil. The dog is obviously unconscious now, for which Tim is thankful. "You're right that this is some kind of fungal infection, but it must have been in his system for days."

"I don't think so," Tim says, swallowing. "I'm pretty sure he caught it this morning."

Alan shakes his head. "No fungi grow that fast, Tim. Although, I gotta say ... this is something I've never seen before." He goes to the cabinet again, takes out a kit of some kind along with a stethoscope.

"Can you fix him?" Tim heard himself ask.

"Has he vomited?" the vet asks in return, listening to Buddy's lungs.

"No."

Alan lifts the dog's hind leg and checks the genitals. The moss is growing there, too. "Any blood in his pee?"

"Not that I noticed."

"Did he seem like he was in pain before the growth became noticeable?"

"No, like I said, he was fine. We were out walking, and he seemed completely like himself. Running around, sniffing things."

Alan takes out a large cotton swab and runs the tip along the inside of Buddy's cheek. Then he places it in a small plastic case and puts it aside. He then smacks his lips and turns around to look at Tim. "All right, I'm not gonna lie, Tim. This is bad. Frankly, I have no idea what he's got. But this far advanced ... I don't think there's anything we can do. You should have brought him in earlier, maybe I could have—"

Tim slams both fists down on the table. "How many times I gotta tell you, man? I couldn't have come in earlier, because he wasn't sick, damnit!"

Alan holds up his hands, surprisingly unfazed by Tim's outburst. "It doesn't matter anyway. I'll have to send a sample to the lab. Let them have a look."

Tim breathes heavily. "What about Buddy?"

Alan sighs. "I can give him something to put him to sleep."

"Good, then what?"

Alan goes to the cabinet again, taking out a tiny bottle and a syringe wrapped in clear plastic. "What do you mean?"

"Well, how will you treat him once he's under?"

"Tim, you're not with him here." Alan unwraps the syringe, fills it with the clear liquid from the bottle, then pauses to look right at Tim. "There's nothing else I can do."

Tim opens his mouth, then closes it again.

"I'm really sorry, Tim. I know how close you two were. But whatever this is, it's basically already killed him. It's in his lungs, his heart, probably his brain and every other organ, too. Even aggressive antibiotics wouldn't do any good at this stage."

Tim's lips feel thick and sticky. "But ... but if you don't know what it is ... how can you say you can't treat it? I mean, you don't know ... you haven't even run any tests on him!"

Alan shakes his head again. "I don't have to, Tim."

The resignation in the vet's voice fills Tim with dread. The way he talks about Buddy as though he's already dead. Everything is spinning. Things are moving way too fast. He can't get it through his head, can't process.

Except he can. The rational part of his brain works just fine, operating in the background of the emotional turmoil. He knew ever since he saw Buddy touch the boulder that this could happen. And the moment he saw the black stuff on his face, he knew he was probably gone.

He just can't accept it. Buddy is all he has left.

Worse still, he's all he has left of *her*.

"But ... but ..."

Alan gently grabs a handful of Buddy's scruff and is about to stick in the needle.

"Wait," Tim said. "Will ... will it kill him instantly?"

"It will," Alan says. "I'm sorry, but we shouldn't prolong it. Wouldn't be right. He's probably hurting. I can give you a few seconds if you need it?"

Suddenly, Tim is thrown back to that awful day four years ago. It was a warm afternoon. Spring was in the air. The world outside the hospital was full of hope. Ready to get on with things. Tim and Helena both stayed there until Anya slipped away. Then they'd hugged. Probably for the last time.

"Tim?"

Alan's voice pulls him back.

"You tell him goodbye now."

Tim looks at his friend lying there. His breathing is very rattly now, and so faint it is barely there. Tears fill Tim's eyes, and he swallows hard. "I'm sorry, Buddy. This is all my fault." He places a hand on his flank, stroking him. "I'll see ya, all right?"

Alan gives him a nod, and Tim turns away.

9

TIM

HE FINDS HIMSELF BEHIND the wheel of his truck. Not sure how he got there. Driving down the almost empty main street. He vaguely recalls speaking with Alan.

"At least let me take him home."

"I'm sorry. That would be against regulation, Tim."

"Why?"

"Because we have no idea what killed him."

"So what?"

"So, he'll probably have to be destroyed. To make sure the spores die with him."

"You mean, burned?"

"Cremation would be the way, yeah. I'll call SSI. They'll—"

"SSI?"

"The State's Serum Institute. They'll come take a look, decide what to do. You should go home and rest. Oh, and Tim?"

"Huh?"

"Take this."

"What's that?"

"Prescription for antibiotics. Drive by the drugstore on your way home. One now, one before bed, then three a day."

"You think ... I caught what Buddy had?"

"Probably not. But just in case, this will fry it."

Then Tim had staggered out of there, leaving through the backdoor.

And now he's driving through town, barely noticing the dark skies overhead, the empty storefront windows, the occasional pedestrian who's ventured out into the cold.

It's very strange, being alone in the car. Buddy always used to ride along with him, no matter where he was going. His eyes keep going to the mirror, checking the empty backseat. It's all furry from the hairs Buddy has shed over the years.

The reality of the situation still hasn't fully dawned on him. Buddy is dead. Gone. Never coming back. Just like that.

He pulls over as the pharmacy comes up ahead. Through the window, he sees an old lady with a walking cane talking to the pharmacist.

He fishes the crumbled prescription from his pocket. Just as he kills the engine, his phone starts ringing. He takes it out. It's Alan. Probably needs some more information about Buddy.

"Yeah?"

"*Tim? You home yet?*" There's something different in the vet's voice.

"Nah, I'm at the drugstore. Why?"

"Come back over here. You need to ... Goodness, I don't even know how to tell ya ..."

"What is it, Alan?" he asks. "Something wrong?"

"Yes. No. I don't know. It's Buddy."

"Well, what about him?"

"Just get the drugs and then get over here."

Tim is frowning now. "What is it, Alan? Tell me."

Alan is about to say something when there comes a bark from the background. It's one of excitement. One Tim has heard thousands of times.

His heart almost stops. "Who was that?"

"Come back, Tim. See for yourself."

10

TIM

BUDDY ALL BUT JUMPS in his arms as he bursts into the exam room.

Tim has trained him to never lift his front legs at anyone, no matter how excited he gets. But at that moment, he couldn't give a crap that Buddy is forgetting himself. He grabs him with both arms and squeezes him tight. Buddy whines happily and covers his cheeks and neck in sloppy dog kisses.

"Dear God ... Buddy ... you're alive!"

"Not just that." Tim looks up to see Alan by the counter. He's staring into the microscope, squinting one eye. "He's perfectly healthy, as far as I can tell."

"How ... how is this possible?" Tim asks, bursting into something that's part laughter, part crying, as Buddy almost tips him over. "Okay, easy, boy. Calm down a bit. I'm glad to see you too."

Alan turns away from the table, shaking his head. He looks at Buddy with a grimace Tim can't quite read. "I have no idea. I have never seen anything like this." He dips two fingers into his breast pocket and pulls out his packet of cigarettes. "You mind if I smoke?" Not waiting for an answer, he lights up a cigarette and takes a deep drag.

Tim studies Buddy a little closer as the dog begins to calm down. The black stuff is still in his fur, on his face, coming out of his ears. But it's gray now. Withered. Just like on the rabbit. It's also falling off in tufts. The floor is already littered with it. It looks like ashes.

"He just woke up," Alan says. He goes and opens the window. Leaning against the frame, he folds his arms over his chest. "I was just about to call SSI when he sat up on the damn table. He looked at me like he'd been napping. I'm telling you, I almost fell off the chair."

"But ... I don't understand," Tim says, shaking his head. "So he wasn't dead?"

"Oh, he was dead all right."

"Did you check? I mean, couldn't his heart just have been beating really slowly?"

Alan reaches the smoke out the window and gives it a tap with his index finger. "Believe me, Tim. The dose I gave him would have put down a horse. And I've seen enough dead animals in my life to know."

"So how can he be alive now?"

Alan takes another deep drag and lets the smoke seep out his nostrils. "Beats me. I checked his vitals, and he seems perfectly fit. No heart murmur, nothing in his lungs that I can hear. We need to run some more tests on him, but as you can see ... he seems just fine."

"He does," Tim smiles, patting Buddy on the head. The dog starts sniffing around the room, checking for interesting smells, acting like his old self. "So the shot you gave him, could it have killed the disease?"

Alan snorts. "It doesn't work that way. Two wrongs don't make a right."

"It does with cancer. I mean, you give cancer patients poison to get them better."

Alan raises one eyebrow. "This wasn't chemotherapy, Tim. It was pentobarbital. It shuts down your heart and your brain. I gave him twenty mil, which is way too much, but I wanted it to be over right away." Another deep drag off the cigarette. "I checked the bottle. I checked the syringe. I even checked the place I injected him. I didn't screw up. It all went into his vein like it should. It just didn't kill him. Not for good, anyway."

Tim nods towards the bottle still on the counter. "You sure it's the right stuff they put in there? Maybe the pharmacy messed it up."

"It wasn't a new bottle. I used it to put down a big old Rottweiler just yesterday. Worked like a charm."

Tim is about to ask something else, when the vet cuts him off, speaking now in a slightly raised voice.

"Listen, what do you think I've been doing for the last half hour, Tim? Just hanging out with your dog? I've gone over it. Again and again. Every damn possible explanation. I'm telling ya, there is none. In all my twenty years ..." Alan trails off, darting Buddy another look—almost one of suspicion.

Suddenly, Tim sees the hare jumping by outside the cabin. He hears and feels the snap from when he broke its neck.

It wasn't the same hare.

For some reason, he suddenly doesn't feel like asking anymore questions. He just wants to get back to his cabin.

"So, can I take him home?"

Buddy looks up, reacting to the familiar word.

Alan shrugs and flicks ashes out the window again. "I guess. I need to get back anyway. Lis already called me. I'm in for an earful for taking so long. Anyway, I'm still sending the sample to the lab, but I see no reason to call in the fire brigade for a healthy dog. Unless you notice him falling ill again, in which case you call me right away."

"Sure, I will."

Alan checks the cigarette, takes one last drag off of it, when he seems to recall something. "Did you get the drugs?"

"I did." Tim had run into the drugstore, all but shoving the old lady aside to get his prescription. On his way back over here, he broke the speed limit several times.

"Better take it," Alan tells him. "Just to be on the safe side."

Tim goes to Alan and holds out his hand.

Alan flicks the cigarette out the window, then looks at Tim's hand like he doesn't understand.

"Thank you, Alan. I really appreciate it."

Alan scoffs. "Don't thank me. I tried to kill your damn dog. You should thank God—He's the one who brought him back."

11

TIM

ALL THE WAY HOME, Tim can't stop eyeing Buddy in the rear mirror. Like he's going to drop dead any minute.

Not that there are any signs of that happening. The dog is just sitting there, looking like his old self, silently watching the open fields glide by. Now and then, he licks his lips, as though still tasting the remnants of the black stuff. Whenever he moves his head, more of it drizzles onto the seat.

The truck will need a thorough cleaning. Tim couldn't care less. His friend is all right, and that's all that matters.

"What a day, huh?" he sighs, sending Buddy a smile. "Don't know about you, but I'm starving. Whaddya say we treat ourselves to roast chicken tonight?"

Buddy perks up. Roast chicken is not just his favorite meal, it's also his favorite activity. He loves to follow every step carefully as Tim goes through the process of killing, scalding and plucking the bird.

It's a little past seven and completely dark outside. Which means the hens have gone to bed. All the easier to snatch one of the young roosters. They are getting to the age where they'll fight each other constantly, so he needs to thin out the herd anyway.

He swallows, noticing his throat is a bit scratchy. That usually happens when he visits Alan. Tim has never been good with smoke. The law that passed a few years back, prohibiting cigarettes in bars, finally made him able to sit and enjoy a beer without coughing.

He rolls down the window to get some fresh air in.

Driving up the hill, he can't help but recall the boulder. He'd successfully managed to put it out of his mind for a few hours, but now the thought of it makes him tense all over again. He still isn't sure what to do about it. He didn't mention it to Alan—not sure why. It still feels somehow like his private problem to deal with.

"Don't wanna think of that right now," he murmurs. "Can't do anything about it anyway."

Besides, the thing is just sitting out there, in the middle of the forest. It could go unnoticed for months. No one would likely happen upon it until spring, and by then it might very well be overgrown with moss and ferns. Perhaps that way the problem would even solve itself. Perhaps nature would simply swallow up the damn thing.

But there is the infection, of course. Tim can no longer pretend the strange illness doesn't come from the boulder.

On the other hand, is it even dangerous? Both the hare and Buddy kicked the infection. Perhaps the other animals will too. The hedgehog, the pigeon. Maybe it's just something that makes you really sick for a short while and then leaves again. Like a bad case of the flu.

That would make sense. And the thought makes him less uneasy.

The freezing air is making his eyes run, so he rolls up the window again.

Buddy gives a whimper from the backseat.

"What is it, boy?" Tim asks, turning his head slightly.

Buddy just breathes through his mouth, eyeing Tim like he wants to say something.

"You hungry? We're home in five. We'll get that chicken fired up."

This time, Buddy doesn't react with excitement. He just keeps staring at Tim.

If dogs can show emotions with their faces, what he sees on Buddy's face at that moment can best be described as concern.

As though he knew.

Even before Tim had caught on himself, Buddy knew.

12

TIM

A SPECK OF DUST must have gotten in his eye, because it keeps running even after he rolls up the window. He fights the urge to rub it. He works construction, so it happens fairly often that he gets sand in his eyes, and he knows how to rinse it properly. He has one of those salt water spray thingies.

Returning home, he heads straight for the bathroom and takes the eyewash bottle from the cupboard.

Leaning closer to the mirror, he pushes gently with a finger on the soft spot below his eye, turning the lower lid inside out.

What he sees in there makes him recoil with a gasp. He drops the bottle in the sink.

"Oh, crap ..."

He stares at himself in the mirror. His massive frame suddenly looks small. His face has gone from a forty-three-year-old war veteran to that of a scared kid.

He leans in again, checking once more.

It's still there: a thin strip of black, running across the red inside of his lid, right below the eyeball.

"All right, get a grip," he tells his mirror image. "You already took the pills. Alan said it would kill it. He said—" He breaks into a rattly coughing fit.

That's when it finally hits home. What had been circling just outside his consciousness all the way home from town. He's been through an emotional rollercoaster with Buddy, so he hadn't given his own health a second thought until now.

The scratchy feeling in his throat is still there, and it's worse. It has nothing to do with Alan's cigarette, of course; it's from the spore. It's already in his airways.

Looking himself up and down, he suddenly feels gravity very acutely. Like his body becomes exhausted in an instant.

How far advanced is it?

He tries to recall what Alan said. Something about the spore attacking Buddy's organs. His heart, his brain. Is the black stuff growing inside Tim's head right now?

Gotta call Alan. Just to let him know.

He goes to his pocket, finds it empty. He remembers taking out his phone in the car because he thought he got a text. Must have tossed it on the passenger seat.

Leaving the bathroom, he meets Buddy standing there, eyeing him.

"It's all right, boy," he reassures him, forcing a smile. "You kicked this thing and I will too. Don't you worry."

Tim goes back outside. The stars are lit, visible between a few drifting clouds. A mild breeze is stirring. Shaping up for a stormy night ahead.

He checks the door to the greenhouse—damn thing has a habit of blowing open when the wind is strong. He shuts the hatch to the henhouse, too. The fox seldom comes around—the smell of Buddy lets him know he's not welcome—but he doesn't want the birds to get sick from the draft.

The thought of the chicken reminds him of dinner. But his appetite is completely gone now. He has some leftover roast beef in the fridge. That will have to do.

He grabs his phone from the truck. Calling up Alan, he leans against the car. The cold air makes him cough again. Something comes loose and he spits it out. He can't see the gob in the darkness, but he can taste something sharp and sour.

I'll never be able to enjoy Mojitos again, that's for sure ...

As he waits for Alan to pick up, he hears a trumpetlike cry from above. He looks up to see a V-shape of big, white birds crossing the night sky. Swans. On their way to warmer parts of the world.

His call goes to voicemail

He clears his throat. "Alan, it's Tim again. I caught the thing Buddy had. I'm taking the antibiotics you prescribed. And I'm staying home like you said. Just wanted to let you know. Maybe you oughta ... you know. Anyway, call me back when you get this."

Just as he turns to go back inside the cabin, there comes a loud, metallic bang.

He jumps and stares at the truck. Something flops around on the bed. A soft sound, like fabric. He goes around to the back, staring in disbelief at the swan lying there. Its neck is obviously broken. So are both wings. One of them is still flapping. Then the bird stops moving.

Even in the darkness, Tim can tell the black stuff is everywhere on the poor thing. Around the beak, covering the eyes, under the wings, all over the legs and feet.

He moves away from the truck, not wanting to touch the bird.

Don't be stupid. You already caught it.

Still, he isn't going to move the dead swan.

Instead, he hurries back inside. Standing in the hallway, he breaks into another coughing fit, more violent this time, and he starts to feel dizzy. He runs the back of his hand over his forehead, and it comes away wet.

Buddy is there, looking at him.

"I'm spiking a fever," he tells the dog. "Gonna be a fun night."

He can't shake the thought of the swans migrating for the winter. If the one crash-landing on his truck carried the infection, the rest of them probably did too. How far will they bring it? How long before it's all over the world?

Can't do anything about it now. Even if you'd called the authorities the moment you saw the hare, they still couldn't have stopped it. This thing will run its course. Just focus on getting better. That's all you can do now.

So, Tim goes to bed.

13

TIM

IT'S THE WORST NIGHT of his life.

He's been ill before. He's been in pain. He's suffered pretty badly. Like the piece of shrapnel he caught in his elbow from the IED that went off. Not to mention the psychological effects of hearing your buddies scream for help with their limbs reduced to bloody stumps.

But nothing comes close to what the infection does to him.

The fever comes on like a freight train. He doesn't need a thermometer to tell it's critically high, higher than any fever he's ever had. He swallows a handful of aspirins, opens the bedroom window all the way to cool down the room, strips down naked and lies on the bed without a blanket. Still, it feels like he's burning up from the inside. Like his blood has been replaced with acid. More than once, he wishes for death, just to get some relief. Had he had a gun handy, he would very likely have blown his brains out. But he doesn't, and once it comes to that stage, he isn't able to get out of bed.

To begin with, the coughing keeps him awake. It gets quickly worse. He feels stuff clogging up his windpipe. Can hear it rattle in his lungs with each inhale. He can even smell it in his nostrils, that disgusting limelike scent. Both his eyes are stinging. He can't help but rub them. It does nothing to alleviate the itch.

And it's not just his eyes that are itchy. It's also around his lips, inside his ears, on his gums. Then the armpits, the scalp, the groin and the crooks of his elbows. Even his palms and the soles of his feet. It's enough to drive him mad, having every inch of his skin feel like ants are crawling on it.

To make it worse, when he runs his fingers over the itching places, he finds patches of the fuzzy growth. It's soft, yet rugged underneath. Like when an old, dry loaf of bread turns hard, then moldy. He swears he can feel the roots of it moving underneath his skin, digging deeper into his flesh.

Soon, he can't open his eyes anymore. The stuff is weighing down his eyelids like cakes of dried mud. When he shifts on the bed, he feels some of it come loose and drizzle onto the sheet.

Breathing becomes increasingly harder. His nostrils get clogged, and he can only pull in thin, wheezing breaths through his open mouth. Surprisingly, at that point, the urge to cough goes away. His throat feels less scratchy. It's almost like the growth down there decides to play nice just to make sure he can keep getting oxygen into his system.

He tries to stay calm. Tries to keep himself under control. To stay away from panic. But it's all but impossible.

He sees in fiery flashes the hare, the hedgehog, Buddy, all of them lying there, stone-cold dead.

And he keeps asking himself the question: *Will I have to die to fight this off? And if I do, will I come back, too*?

Outside the door, Buddy whines now and then.

Tim didn't let him into the bedroom. He didn't want him in here. He probably can't catch the infection again, but he shouldn't have to see him like this.

Then the pain set in, and it's horrible. It's like every fiber of his being is in agony. Like his body has been replaced with pure pain. Had he had the strength, he would have screamed. All he can do is give off hoarse croaking sounds while writhing.

And it's in his head, too. That's probably the worst part.

The most awful, horrendous shit flashes through his mind. Images, ideas, memories. Some of them false, some of them mixed with real stuff. These green figures with huge heads and glowing orange eyes keep appearing in his mind. He no longer knows who he is; he's not even sure he's a person anymore. He feels the most intense fear, panic, rage, guilt. He feels like he doesn't deserve to live. He has done horrid things to others, and horrid things have been done to him. He was both victim and perpetrator of the worst deeds the world has ever seen.

He feels insane. He literally feels his mind break apart and disintegrate.

And yet something makes sure he doesn't die. The infection keeps him alive. It needs him. Or maybe that's just some feverish figment of his imagination.

His thoughts at this point are way beyond his control. Like it isn't him thinking them.

In particularly, he keeps hearing two words: *Something's missing.*

They repeat inside of his head, over and over. Sometimes faint, sometimes loud like thunder. He doesn't know what they mean.

At one point, outside the window, he hears the trumpety cry from a swan. It could just be from his memory. Or, it could be the swan out on the truck. Waking back up.

Returning from the dead. Maybe it will catch up with its flock before they leave the country.

He slips into something which feels more like deep darkness than sleep. There are horrible nightmares. Images of giant, glowing boulders dropping from the sky. Green faces with glowing, orange eyes. Worms moving under his skin. Fire in his veins. Demons in his head.

And all the while, those words keep echoing: *Something's missing ... something's missing ...*

Then, he slips deeper into the darkness. It closes in, fills him up, pushes him down, drowns him from within.

It's horrifying. And it's a relief.

He lets go.

14

VERONICA

DRIVING BACK HOME, SHE decides not to tell Leo. At least not until she's broken up with him.

She's been trying to come up with a good reason for doing that anyway. And honestly, there are plenty to pick from.

Like how they hardly ever spend time together. How much younger he is. How his mom can't stand Veronica. Or how neither of them feels like working on improving things.

Basically, they never had a future together in the first place. They are little more than fuck buddies sharing a flat. How they'd kept it going for almost four years is pretty amazing to her now that she thinks of it.

She settles on telling him how she's not happy with her life and wants to start fresh somewhere else. He'll probably accept that. If nothing else, it'll be much less of a shock to him than the truth. That she's got cancer. That she won't be around for more than a few months.

Going up the stairs, she runs over the words in her mind, and when she locks herself into the apartment, she's surprised to smell shampoo and hear water running. She can hear him singing from the bathroom, and for a brief moment, Veronica hates him fiercely. She's furious with him because he's not terminally ill. That he's got plenty of time left and that he's wasting it singing Lady Gaga in the shower.

She swallows hard and sticks her head into the bathroom. "Hey, I'm back!"

Leo stops singing, yanks the curtain aside, and looks at her one-eyed, soap running from his hair. "Heeey, babe. Had a good run?"

Of course he assumes she went running. She always does. But not today. Today, she went to see her doctor. For a brief moment, she imagines what it would be like if she'd simply not showed up to the consultation. If she'd never gotten the biopsy results. If she'd just went for a run instead. She would still be dying, of course. But she wouldn't have found out yet. What she wouldn't give for just one more day in blissful ignorance.

"You're up early," she observes.

"Yep! Early bird gets the worm, you know." He grins and pulls the curtain a little farther aside, revealing his skinny, hairless body. "I've got a worm for you if you're in the mood?"

Veronica rubs her forehead and mutters, "Sorry, I've got a headache."

"Oh, that's too bad," he says, pulling the curtain back, then raising his voice: "It's probably best we get going anyway. Wouldn't want to miss the ferry."

Veronica was already headed for the kitchen to find some breakfast. Now she stops. "What ferry?"

"I spoke with my mom just now," he goes on. "She said it's already snowing over there, so we should bring warm clothes."

"Oh, fuck me," Veronica groans. "Is that today?"

She'd completely spaced on the trip.

It's this stupid tradition her in-laws have every January, bringing the family together in their vacation home on the

Isle of Hlér. It's only an hour and a half off the coast, but Veronica hates sailing, almost as much as she hates her mother-in-law.

Leo turns off the water and says something she doesn't catch. At that moment, she seriously considers springing it on him. If ever there was a valid excuse to opt out of a family gathering, terminal cancer has to be it.

Leo comes out from the bathroom, still dripping wet, drying his hair with a towel. He looks at her. "Why you just standing there? You OK?"

It isn't really a question of concern. But it still makes her choke up. "No," she says quietly. "Not really. Listen, Leo ..."

"Please, Nica," he cuts her off, looking at her earnestly. "Please don't use your headache as an excuse not to go."

She blinks. "No, it's not that. There's something else I'd better te—"

"Because you know, Molly texted me, and she's really looking forward to seeing you."

Somehow, the mentioning of Leo's niece makes Veronica change her mind. She likes the girl. To be honest, she's the only positive thing about these stupid family vacations. Only nine years old, she's still unspoiled, sweet, innocent. She and Veronica always play cards or give each other funny hairdos. And this will be the last time Veronica sees her.

What else am I gonna do today? she asks herself as Leo goes to the bedroom, chatting away, leaving a trail of wet footprints. *Sit around and stare at the wall? I might as well go.*

She realizes she's rubbing her hand against her hip because her palm is itching. She looks at it, but can't see any more of the black stuff. A phantom itch, isn't that what they call it?

Thin strips of it were running along the creases of her skin. When she saw it yesterday, she immediately recognized it: It was the same stuff that grew on the bird. She'd gone and washed her hand thoroughly in soap and hot water. The moss was really clinging to her skin; she had to use the nailbrush to get it off.

The bird had hit her out of nowhere. It happened right after she almost bumped into the big guy, the one with the German shepherd—the beast wasn't even on a leash. Veronica was jogging along the trail, breathing in the freezing air. Focusing on every step, loud music in her ears. When suddenly, something thudded against her shoulder. And—

"Ew!" Leo exclaims, reappearing in the bedroom doorway. "What the hell's this?"

He's holding a glove between two fingers. The smooth, crimson fabric is covered in the black stuff, making it all fluffy.

Veronica frowns. It hadn't been like that when she dropped it in the laundry basket. "Is that my glove?"

"Yeah! Did you, like, clean a chimney or something?" Leo asks, turning the glove over while wrinkling his nose.

"I ... I fell in some dirt," she mutters.

Leo goes back into the bathroom, flings the glove into the open washing machine, then turns to leave.

"Maybe wash your hands," she suggests as he passes her by.

"Sure, Mom," Leo grins. He plants a kiss on her cheek before going to the sink. "Hurry up and get your ass in the shower, will you? We're leaving in thirty minutes."

Veronica drifts off again. She sees the blackbird lying there on the trail, reduced to a ball of feathers. The poor thing was still alive. Some mossy stuff, all gray and black, grew all over it.

She considered stomping on the bird to put it out of its misery, but she couldn't bring herself to do it. Luckily, it stopped twitching just then.

Her hand went to her shoulder and brushed it. Some of the mossy stuff got on her glove, and she sniffed it. It had a distinct, sour smell. Almost like lemons. She wiped it on the frozen ground. And she didn't give it a second thought.

The glove had been at the bottom of the laundry basket for, what, twenty-six hours? The basket was right next to the radiator, and evidently, the stuff had thrived in the damp, warm fabric.

Veronica checks her palm one more time. Still no trace of it.

So, she forgets about it and starts getting ready for the trip.

15

TIM

DYING SUCKS.

Being dead, on the other hand, isn't too bad.

At least there's no pain. Just peace. Tim could have stayed there.

Except he isn't destined to. He's called back.

He opens his eyes, then closes them again with a grunt. The daylight is awfully bright. It must be close to noon, since the sun is blazing outside. He can hear birds singing and a plane going by.

Is it over?

He just lies there for half a minute, waiting, feeling every part of his body. There's no fever. No more itchiness.

He can't believe it. He's convinced that as soon as he wakes up properly and starts to move, it will all return.

He carefully blinks his eyes open once more. This time, he shields them with his hand. He finds himself splayed out on the bed, butt-naked.

Buddy must have managed to open the door to the bedroom at some point after he went out, because the dog's curled up at the foot of the bed. He's breathing through his nose, watching Tim with a curious expression.

"Still with the sleep staring, I see?"

To his surprise, he can talk just fine. His airways are completely free. Nothing clogging them. The bad taste and smell are both gone too. He sits up, inspecting his body. The sheets are still damp from sweat. But there is no sign of the black stuff. His skin is pink and smooth, like a newborn's.

"I'll be damned," he grunts. "Looks like I won the battle too, huh, pal?"

Buddy gives off a whimper. The sound hurts Tim's ears.

"Whoa, can you dial it down, please? My hearing's a little sensitive."

In fact, he seems to hear everything very clearly. Like someone has distilled the soundwaves. Or amped up his reception to ten. He rubs the base of his ear.

Whatever that mossy stuff did to me, it sure cleaned out my ear canals.

The thought of the mossy stuff makes him check the bed more thoroughly. He can't find a single trace of it. Which is a surprise, given how much of it he saw coming off of Buddy. The stuff had littered the backseat of the truck.

Another plane goes by outside. Except it doesn't really sound like a plane. It sounds like a car. He looks at Buddy. "We've got company?"

The dog tilts his head.

If a car had come to the cabin, Buddy would have gone to the front door right away and started growling. Which means there's probably no car outside.

Then what is it I'm hearing?

He gets up and goes to the window, noticing he feels lighter. Like when you've been sick for several days, unable to keep anything down. Except it doesn't feel like he's been emptied out. More like his body has become easier to carry.

He also notices absent-mindedly that his elbow isn't bugging him. Since the injury, he's been unable to fully extend his arm, and the joint will click and give off tiny jolts of pain, especially in the morning. For the first time in years, that isn't the case. It doesn't hurt, and he appears to have regained full range of motion in his arm.

He squints as he pulls the curtain aside. He's again surprised to find it isn't noon at all. In fact, it's close to dusk. And it isn't sunny, either. On the contrary, the sky is overcast with heavy clouds. Still, the light is painfully bright.

How long was I out?

He looks out over the meadows, and something funny happens to his vision. The focal point darts back and forth. It's a little dizzying. He blinks to try and make it stop.

The henhouse is visible from the bedroom. The birds are inside, settling in for the night. Tim can hear them shifting around on the bar, rustling their feathers, moving their—

*Hold on ... I can **hear** that?*

He listens.

Yes.

He can really hear the chickens.

He can hear a ton of other things, too. The tall grass moving in the evening breeze. Something stirring in the heather over by the blackberry bushes—a mouse, probably. And that car engine again. He realizes the sound isn't coming from the driveway, but miles away. It's not just one car, either. It's several.

I hear ... I hear traffic.

Even on the quietest days, he has never been able to pick up any noises from town. Not even a faint background hum. Now, however, he can practically hear the cars shifting gears as they drive around the streets down there.

Tim feels a surge of goose bumps run down his back.
What the hell happened to me?

16

VERONICA

THE TRIP TURNS OUT as bad as she feared.

They've hardly set out before she has to rush to the bathroom. After puking up the yogurt she ate in the car, she brings a plastic bag to the deck. The wind cuts right through her jacket and makes her eyes water, but at least the nausea subsides a little. She shivers like she's falling apart, and the tears are not just caused by the wind.

It's an emotional reaction, she figures. *My mind is starting to catch on to the fact that I'm dying.*

Leo texts her from the comfort of his cabin, asking if she's all right.

Her palm itches again, so she pulls off her mitten and groans. The black stuff has returned, growing in between her fingers now. And it's not just her hand. Now that she's aware of it, she can feel it in her armpits, in her groin, inside her mouth, even between her butt cheeks. It's not pleasant, but she can't really do anything to alleviate it because there are a few other passengers on the deck—mostly smokers who have to defy the weather.

When she finally spots the island coming up ahead, she goes straight to the car, buckles up and waits for Leo to join her. She's grateful for getting out of the wind. She's feeling a little better, but she gets quite the shock when she flips down the sun visor and sees her face in the mirror. The black stuff—which is now turning gray, just like on the bird—grows around her eyes, on her lips, inside her ears and nostrils. She looks like a coal mine worker who's just gotten off his shift.

"Jeez," she croaks, fumbling for the glove compartment—she keeps a packet of wet wipes there for when Leo has been to a drive-thru and left ketchup all over the wheel.

She goes to work cleaning herself. It turns out a lot easier than she thought. The moss is clearly dying, and it drizzles off willingly when she rubs it with the wipe. She unzips her jacket and pulls off her sweater to check under her arms. She finds the same: mostly gray and ashy. Whatever the nasty growth is, it can't survive on her body.

My immune system probably kicked it, she thinks, feeling a mild encouragement. *Guess I'm not completely dead yet.*

She's just finished up when Leo comes to the car. The skin where the moss sat is pink and flushed, but she doesn't need to explain anything, because Leo pays no attention to her face; he's babbling about some sci-fi movie he watched in the cabin.

They drive off the ferry and head for the cabin. It's snowing, and the landscape is picturesque. Veronica takes it in a lot more than she usually does. Despite the death sentence weighing on her mind—or, more likely, *because* of it—she feels like she's seeing everything for the first time, while knowing it's really the last.

The Isle of Hlér is very small. It has like three towns, but Leo's parents' cottage isn't in any of them. The only harbor is on the northwest corner, and the cabin is on the southeast, so they basically have to cross the island, which is only a fifteen-minute drive—when it's not snowing. Today, it takes them half an hour because it's really coming down, the roads are already covered, and for the first time, Veronica worries they might not be able to get back to the harbor tomorrow.

Of course, by then, she'll have much bigger concerns.

17

TIM

WHATEVER IS GOING ON with him, one thing is for certain: He feels ravenous.

Going to the kitchen, he grabs the bag of oatmeal and pours the whole thing into a bowl. He then adds half a gallon of milk and a cup of sugar, and he gulps it all down by the sink. When it's gone, he opens the fridge and looks for something else, something heavier.

He has a dozen eggs and a big rash of bacon. He fires up a frying pan and makes a huge pile of scrambled eggs. His mouth waters as he flips the bacon.

Tipping everything onto a large plate, he brings it to the living room. Forking down steaming mouthfuls of eggs, he drops down on the couch.

Something buzzes at the back of his head. It's like a slight vibration. He reaches over to scratch it, but it doesn't really help.

Then his phone rings. It's lying on the coffee table where he left it yesterday.

The name on the display says Petersen.

"Oh, crap ..."

He's all but forgotten he has a job. Bracing himself for an earful, he answers the call.

"Yeah?"

"Tim? Finally! Where the hell you've been?"

He winces and holds the phone away from his ear. He turns the volume all the way down. "I'm sorry, Frank. I've been sick."

"Too sick to call in? I could have pulled in a replacement. I have four guys here, sitting on their hands, still waiting for an operator."

"I know, I'm sorry. I meant to call you, but I slept in. Had a mean fever all night."

"Well, you don't sound sick to me. You feeling up for the night shift?"

"Not really."

"Come on, man. You owe me after that little stunt. You're really stiffing me for another whole day?"

"I might need to take tomorrow off too."

*"**What**?"*

"I'm sorry, Frank."

"Listen, if you don't show up here tomorrow morning—"

He disconnects and put the phone back down. He resumes eating.

He feels mild surprise at his own behavior. Normally, he would never miss work like that. But somehow, sitting in a crane, working the sticks and levers all night, it just doesn't seem all that important.

He gets the tingling sensation at the base of his skull again. Moments later, the phone rings a second time. Frank calling back. Tim lets it ring.

Not my problem. Let him fire me if he wants.

Watching the phone ring, he can still feel the buzz in his skull. It's almost like his brain is picking up the cell signal. Uncanny.

That fungus really did a number on me. Should probably go get checked out.

But to be honest, he doesn't feel like spending the night in the hospital, either. For one thing, he'll probably become hungry again soon—the plate is empty now, and the eggs and bacon have only served to dampen his appetite to a tolerable level. Besides, he's already laid plans for the rest of the night.

He feels better. Younger. Stronger. More clearheaded, even.

Part of him is freaking out. This could all be lingering symptoms of the infection. He might still need medical attention.

But a larger part of him is curious. This new state he finds himself in—be it temporary or not—he wants to explore it a little further.

So, he leaves the cabin.

18

VERONICA

SHE CAN'T HELP NOTICE how Leo keeps fidgeting as they drive. Running his thumbnail back and forth over his eyebrows. Tugging at his earlobe. Scratching first one armpit, then the other.

That's when Veronica realizes he caught the black stuff too.

Perhaps from her glove—even though she saw him wash his hands afterwards. Or maybe from the peck on her cheek as they went to bed last night. Or perhaps being physically close to each other was enough.

She watches him discreetly and sees thin, black rims under his eyes. It almost looks like eyeliner.

He senses her looking at him and turns his head. "Something wrong?"

"No, I just, uhm ... you feeling all right?"

"Sure, sure," he says, digging his nails into his hair. "Never better. Damnit, Hercules has been lying on my towel again. I'm itching all over from his hairs."

"Then don't throw your towel on the floor," she tells him automatically, feeling like a shit for withholding the truth. She knows of course their cat has nothing to do with it. "Speaking of, did you fill his bowl before we left?"

"No, I thought you did?"

She sighs. "No. We agreed that was your job."

"He'll be fine," Leo shrugs, rubbing his nose. "He'll go downstairs for a pity meal. Krestine always feeds him when he meows outside her door. It's not like we'll be gone for a week anyway."

Veronica keeps eyeing him as they drive on. She really takes in his face. He's handsome in a boyish, charming way. She can see why she fell for him.

"You keep staring at me," he grins suddenly. "I can feel it." He wags his eyebrows at her. "You itchin' for some dickin'? I'm sure when the others are asleep tonight, we can—"

"I'm on my period," she tells him—another automatic lie.

"Well, what is it, then?" he demands. "It's like you've never seen me before."

Veronica doesn't know what to tell him. Another point-blank question. Another chance to come clean.

She's saved by the fact that Leo spots the cabin up ahead just at that moment. He forgets all about her inquisitive looks and starts talking about how much he looks forward to his mom's food.

Leo's dad is busy shoveling snow in the driveway. He's a tall, heavy guy, and so out of shape, she can literally see steam rising from the collar of his sweater and pearls of sweat glistening in his moustache.

He pulls off his glove to shake Leo's hand, then Veronica's, then resumes shoveling. "It's really coming down, huh? Not sure I can keep it up."

"Well, we're all here, right?" Leo asks, throwing out his arms. "So I say, let it snow, let it snow, let it snow!" He laughs, then breaks into a coughing fit.

"I think Leo's right," Veronica says, squinting at Flemming through the heavy flakes coming down. "You should save your strength. At least wait until it stops snowing."

Her father-in-law relents and goes back inside with them. Veronica is glad to step into the warmth of the cabin.

Leo keeps coughing as they take off their jackets.

"You okay?" his dad asks, slapping him on the back. "Caught something?"

"Nah, nah, I'm fine. Think I just swallowed a snowflake. Man, I need to take a piss."

"Language, please," a cool voice tells him from the hallway.

Leo's sister, Alice—aka the Ice Princess, as Veronica dubbed her in her mind—is leaning against the doorframe, doing that thing where she sucks in her cheeks, making her face even thinner than it already is.

"Sorry, I mean I need to go potty," Leo tells her. "Heeey, Molly! My favorite niece!"

The girl appears from behind her mom's boney hip. She gives Leo a shy smile, then her eyes immediately go to Veronica. "Hi, Veronica."

"Hi, Molly. How're you doing?"

The girl ignores Leo's invite for a high-five—which probably saves her life, as Veronica will later come to think back and realize. Instead, the girl comes over and hugs Veronica. She's grown enough since the last time they saw each other that Veronica no longer needs to crouch to embrace her.

"You've gotten really big," she tells her, and for the first time since her diagnosis, she smiles. She actually tears up, and she's lucky she can use the cold weather as an excuse to wipe her eyes.

Molly has very dark hair, unlike her entire family. Leo, his sister, and both their parents, are reddish blonds. Veronica is an eighth Chinese, so her hair is black, and maybe it's because they look so much alike that Molly took to her early on.

Leo quickly hugs his sister—who looks like she'd rather not—then throws his beanie and scarf on the hanger and goes to the bathroom.

Molly leads Veronica by the hand into the living room. There's a half-wall separating the dining area from the kitchen. Leo's mom, Sylvia, is busy peeling potatoes. She doesn't look up from the pot, despite the fact that she must have heard them enter.

"Look, Grandma! Veronica is here!"

Sylvia carefully puts down the peeler, takes the dishtowel, dabs her hands gently, then comes around the wall and finally, when she can no longer avoid it, looks at Veronica with a smile that could have been used for cryotherapy. Had she only been able to freeze away the cancerous tissue on Veronica's ovaries, she'd have been happy to let her stare at her lower abdomen all day with those soulless eyes.

"Almost on time this year," she remarks, extending five skinny fingers full of rings.

To Veronica's surprise, her mother-in-law's attitude doesn't bother her. For some odd reason, she's even pleased that Sylvia, as usual, is being a bitch to her. Hopefully, she'll feel guilty when she learns about Veronica's death in a few months.

"Better late than never, right? Happy New Year, Sylvia." She shakes her hand firmly—hoping she's still contagious. Sylvia is a very petite woman, five inches shorter than Veronica. Still, the Ice Queen can easily make a room fall silent just with a mean look or a huff. She's definitely the ruler of Leo's family, and she hates Veronica for never bending the knee.

Her smile turns from self-assured to slightly sour when she realizes Veronica isn't taking the bait, and she pulls her hand away. "I could use some help with the roast."

"Sure," Veronica tells her.

She's about to join Sylvia in the kitchen when Leo pops up from behind and wraps his arms around his mom's skinny shoulders. "Hey, Mama!" he says, planting a kiss on her temple. "You look great as usual."

"Oh, will you knock that off?" she tells him briskly, freeing herself. "Aren't you too old for that monkey business? Why can't you just—" She cuts off her scolding as she turns and gets a look at Leo's face. "What in the world have you been doing?"

"What?" Leo asks innocently, sticking a finger in his ear.

"Your face. It's all dirty." She licks her thumb, and before he can pull away, she wipes the corner of his mouth.

"Aw, come on, Mom," he says, frowning. "That's disgusting."

"Talk about disgusting," she retorts, showing him her thumb which has some of the black stuff on it. "I'm not the one caked in mud."

"What the hell ...?" Leo mutters, touching the same place. He feels the mossy growth, and he tries to scratch it off. "Ouch. It's stuck. What *is* that?"

Veronica can hardly believe Leo didn't see the black stuff himself when he was in the bathroom just now—he obviously didn't check the mirror, because it's hard to miss now that he's taken off his outerwear.

Pulling out his phone, he activates the selfie camera and studies his face. "For cryin' out loud, it's everywhere! That's why I've been itchin' so bad. How did it get on there?" He tries again to peel it off with his nails, and some of it drizzles to the floor, but it's clearly rooted in his skin. "Shit, this isn't dirt," he says, looking closely at his fingertips as he rubs them together. "It's like ... a growth of some kind."

"A growth? You mean like a rash?" Sylvia asks, looking at her own thumb like it's poisonous. Then she stares at Veronica. "It's probably from an STD."

Veronica almost bursts out laughing. Of course Sylvia instinctively thinks it's Veronica's fault. Controlling herself, she shrugs and says with a straight face, "I don't have it."

"There's no STD that does that," Alice says, joining them. She too is looking at her brother with a disgusted look. "But that's a rash for sure. I thought you were just trying to grow a moustache."

Flemming steps into the living room just then, rubbing his huge hands together. "What's the commotion about? You kids already bickering?"

"Leo's caught some nasty skin rash," Alice says, discreetly pulling Molly away. "And we don't know if he's contagious."

"Oh, come on," Leo says. "It's just something I caught from our cat. He must've been—" He breaks into a new coughing fit. It sounds rattly. "Damnit, my throat is all scratchy ..."

Flemming pulls his glasses from his breast pocket and steps closer to his son. Taking his chin with two fat fingers, he turns Leo's head left, then right. "When did it start?"

"Right now, I guess," Leo says, throwing out his arms. "It wasn't here this morning, and Veronica didn't notice anything before now. Did you?"

Veronica shakes her head, again feeling bad for lying. But it's too late to come clean now.

Sylvia has stepped behind her husband, as though using him a human shield, while she peeks at Leo. "Can't he use some of your steroid cream, Flemming?"

"I'm not sure it'll do much good," Flemming mutters. "It's gotta be an allergic reaction for it to appear so quickly. Like hives, or something."

"Hives aren't black and fuzzy like that," Alice says. "Rune had hives once. He bought a watch that had nickel in it. His skin got all red and bumpy. That stuff on Leo looks more like fungus, if you ask me."

"Oh, fuck me," Leo groans, then grins nervously. "Am I gonna end up like a Clicker?"

"A *what*?" Flemming asks.

"He's talking about that stupid show," Alice informs him. "What was it? *The Rest of Us*?"

"*The Last of Us*," Molly corrects her.

Veronica can't help but look at her with surprise. "You watched that show?"

The girl shrugs. "No, but the boys in my class talk about it all the time."

"That's just television," Flemming goes on. "Fungus isn't really that dangerous. I watched a documentary about it. There was one, they called it something like 'asparagus' ... but that was only a problem for people with lung conditions."

"Like my asthma?" Sylvia exclaims, placing her thin hand on her boney chest and pulling farther away from Leo as though he can't be trusted not to lunge forward to try and touch her. "It sure sounds like it's in his airways."

"Let's not jump to any conclusions here," Flemming says. "It's cold season, so could be that the cough isn't even related." He places a meaty palm on his son's forehead. "You're warm. I think you have a mild fever. Grab a glass of water and go lie down. I'll call the doctor."

Veronica has been watching silently. Ever since she noted the black stuff on Leo, she assumed he would experience the same as she did, so she isn't really surprised that he's spiking a fever.

But he seems to be more affected by the strange infection, or whatever it is—at least Veronica never coughed like that.

He'll kick it, just like I did, she thinks to herself, watching Leo shamble off to the bedroom.

But for some reason, she doesn't really believe it.

19

TIM

SOON AS HE STEPS outside, he realizes he doesn't need the jacket he's put on.

The cold air doesn't bother him the least. His body is keeping itself warm with no difficulty. So, he takes it off again and leaves it at the steps.

Buddy—eager to do his business—darts past him and starts sniffing around. Poor guy has been keeping it in all day while Tim was snoozing.

He goes to the truck and checks the bed. Like he suspected, the swan is gone. Left behind are only a few white feathers and piles of dead, grayish moss, some of it already blown away by the wind.

He heads out the driveway to the point where he gets a clear view over the hillside. From up here, he can make out the glow from the city in the dying light of day.

The air is misty. Stringy, white clouds of fog are hovering over the ground. Visibility ought to be low. Yet somehow, he finds he's able to filter out the fog and see the landscape clearly. Staring at the town, his eyesight does that thing again where it suddenly zooms in, just like a camera would. It's eerie. But this time, he's better able to control it.

Holy hell. I've got twenty-twenty vision.

It's like looking through a pair of strong binoculars. He can make out the streets down there, the buildings, even the cars. If he concentrates, he can almost read the street signs.

"Some party trick," he mutters, turning away from the view. "What else can I do?"

Looking down the narrow gravel road, it seems inviting. He hasn't gone for a run since his military days. Anything more strenuous than his daily walk in the forest, and his knees will start to complain.

But he feels like running now. Sprinting, actually.

He begins walking. Faster. His boots feel awkward on his feet. As though he's wearing them for the first time. So, he stops and kicks them off. The dewy ground soaks his socks right away. The cold still doesn't bother him.

He picks up the pace.

Buddy jogs alongside him, his tail wagging as he eyes him excitedly. The dog has never seen Tim run, and he probably thinks he's in a playful mood. Which is true.

"Come on, Buddy," he says, barely out of breath. "Let's see what we can do ..."

He doubles the speed. The wind tugs at his hair, causing his eyes to water. The air seeps in and out of his lungs with ease, his heart beats a little faster, but nothing taxing.

Buddy is giving it his all just to follow along now. Tim feels like he has another couple of gears. It seems risky, though. Sprinting away barefoot on the bumpy road. At this speed, if he trips, he could break a leg or worse.

But somehow, he knows that won't happen. His vision is perfect. His balance like that of a line dancer. His feet automatically find level ground, avoiding holes and bumps, and propel him forward. Faster and faster. Leaving behind Buddy now. The wind howling in his ears.

He stops abruptly, leaving skid marks in the gravel. He breathes evenly. A light sweat has broken out on his forehead. The muscles in his legs are thrumming, begging for more.

He turns to see the cabin almost a mile up road. Buddy comes running to catch up, his tongue lolling.

"You coming?" Tim asks with a grin. "Can't wait around for you all night."

The dog circles him, licks his hand, looking up at him with an expression saying: "I didn't know you could do that!"

Tim gazes towards the trees outlined against the still dimmer sky. Something about the forest is drawing him. The thought of the boulder. Is it still there?

"Yeah," he mutters to the darkness. "It's there."

For some reason, he wants to see it again. Whatever happened to him is because of that strange rock. He needs to take another look at it, wants to know if—

"Gotta be careful."

He spins around at the voice.

No one is there. He holds his breath and scans the surroundings. He's alone on the hillside. Buddy looks at him questioningly.

"You didn't hear that?" Tim asks, chewing his lip. "No, you didn't. It was in my head."

He is used to hearing Anya's voice. She will often chime in with advice or comments on his everyday life. The voice he just heard wasn't hers. It was familiar, though. Someone he knows.

He shakes his head. Whoever the voice belonged to, it's gone now.

Tim decides against going out to the boulder again. Not yet. Instead, he turns and jogs back home.

20

TIM

THE MOMENT HE STEPS back inside the cabin, he once more feels the tingling in the back of his head.

He goes to the living room where he's left the phone. Soon as he enters, sure enough, it begins ringing.

It's not Frank this time. It's a number he hasn't seen before.

He answers, remembering to hold the phone at a good distance from his ear. "Hello?"

"*Tim*?" A woman's voice. Thin. Upset.

"Yeah?"

"This is ... this is Elisabeth Andersen."

"Oh. Right."

The vet's wife. Tim met her a couple of times when dropping by for a cup of coffee or doing some work for Alan. A skinny woman with big, somber eyes.

"I found your number on Alan's phone. Hope you don't mind me calling you at this hour?"

"Not at all. How are you, Lis?"

"*Not so good. I'm calling because ... well, I don't know who else to call, really.*" She utters a brief, nervous laughter.

Tim is standing in the middle of the dark living room, realizing he hasn't turned on the lights. He doesn't need to. "What's on your mind, then, Lis?"

"It's Alan."

"What about him?"

"He ... well, he's been ill."

Tim's heart rate rises slightly. "Sorry to hear that."

"He told me you were sick too?"

"I'm better now."

"Oh, you are? That's a relief."

"How's Alan doing?"

"He, uhm ... he told me he caught it from your dog. The bug, or whatever. He started to feel under the weather last night, and he ... he self-isolated in the guestroom. Said it might be contagious." Lis's voice grows increasingly shaky.

"So, how is he now?"

"Well, you see, the thing is ... I don't know." She obviously fights to keep from crying now. Tim can hear the soft crackling of a paper tissue. *"I checked on him this morning. He was burning up. I almost couldn't get through to him. I wanted to call the doctor, I really did, Tim, but ... you know Alan. He's stubborn. He told me not to call anyone. He didn't want to risk the thing spreading, you know? He didn't even want* ***me*** *in the room. He said the light hurt his eyes. So I let him be. Then ... around ... I don't know, two o'clock, maybe ... I went to check on him again, and ... he was gone."*

Tim frowns. "Gone? You mean ...?"

"No! God, no. Not like that. No, what I mean is, he'd disappeared. He must have wandered off."

"Did you see him leave the room?"

"See, that's the thing. The window was open. He told me to leave it like that, because he was burning up. I think he climbed out, Tim. I called him, but he left behind his cell." Lis begins to sniffle. *"He could be anywhere! He could be wandering around*

town. Maybe he's delirious. Oh, God … I have no way of finding him. And none of the neighbors saw him leave …"

"Have you called the police?"

"I have, but they said they couldn't do anything until he's been missing for forty-eight hours. Can you believe that? They said as long as he'd left voluntarily, they couldn't treat it as a disappearance. That's why I thought of you. I don't know why, I just … hoped you perhaps had an idea as to where he might be? You were the last person he spoke to."

She stops talking, waiting for Tim's reply.

Even over the phone, he can hear her pulse hammering away. He takes a moment to consider. His thought process is much faster than it used to be. As though some resistance has been removed from the neural pathways so that now the electrical impulses are able to pass at light speed. "Well, I'm glad you called me, Lis. I'm not sure where Alan is, but I'd like to try and find him."

A sigh of relief. "*You would? Oh, thank you, Tim!*"

"Sure. Tell me one thing. Did Alan have … was this black, mossy stuff growing on him?"

"*What?*" Horror in her voice. "*God, No! That … I mean, I don't think so. He wouldn't let me turn on the lights, but … I think I would have noticed something like that.*"

"All right."

So Alan hadn't wanted her to see him. Tim expected that. Alan is a proud guy, a private guy, even in his marriage. And Tim felt the same way when he fell ill. Somehow, the mysterious infection felt very personal. Like a secret, almost. Just like with the boulder.

"You at home right now, Lis?"

He asks just to be polite, really. He's already picked up several sounds in the background which told him Lis is in her kitchen. The click from a refrigerator. The creaking from the stool as Lis shifts around on it restlessly. The clinking of ice and spoon in a glass that she apparently stirs round and round as a stress-revealing gesture.

"Yes, I'm home. I know it's late, Tim, and I hate to bother you ..."

"It's fine. Really. I'll be there in fifteen minutes."

Lis thanks him profusely, and they end the call. Tim stands there for a moment, thinking. Buddy is watching him intently.

"You think the same thing happened to Alan?" Tim asks him.

Buddy tilts his head.

"The thing is," he goes on, talking slowly. "It didn't happen to you. Not to the hare, either. You guys came back normal, right? And you had that mossy stuff coming off in droves. I didn't. It just ... went away. And if Alan had shed his, Lis would have found it in the bed." Tim looks out the window. Even in the now thick darkness, he can make out the meadow. "Maybe it only affects humans."

The dog gives a soft whine.

Tim blinks. "I'm just thinking out loud, Buddy. Come on. We gotta go."

They leave the cabin. Just as Tim opens the back door to the truck so Buddy can jump in, that strange, familiar voice comes again.

"Gotta be really careful."

This time, he doesn't look around. The voice is definitely in his head. But it isn't a thought, not exactly. It's more like something from someone else's head. Like a radio signal he picked up on.

And he suddenly knows who's broadcasting.

21

VERONICA

"HEY, NO CHEATING!"

Molly points at Veronica's hand.

"I'm not cheating," she says.

"Yes you are. You flipped the dice."

"I just stopped it from going off the table."

"Yeah, but that caused me to get a two."

"Well, roll it again, then."

"No, it's fine," the girl says. "Whatever. I'm beating you anyway." She moves her knight.

Veronica smiles. She was always good with systems and numbers, and apparently, Molly is the same. Not many preteen girls are into dice chess.

"Veronica?"

She looks up to see Alice standing there. Her sister-in-law has that crease between her eyebrows—the one that appears when she's reprimanding Leo for using foul language around her daughter or Molly forgets herself and laughs a bit too loudly. Right now, however, the wrinkle doesn't seem to be caused by blame or disapproval. Rather, she looks worried.

Veronica immediately knows it's about Leo. She managed to forget about her sick boyfriend for a while, losing herself in the game. "What is it, Alice?"

"Uhm, could you help me out with something?"

Alice never asked her that question before. Veronica glances over at the table. It's already been cleared. The roast was excellent, and dessert was good too. At the far corner of the room, next to the crackling fireplace, sits the Ice Queen in her armchair, rimless glasses at the tip of her nose, hands busy knitting. She doesn't seem to pay them any notice.

"Sure," Veronica says, getting up from the couch.

"What is it, Mom?" Molly asks, clearly sensing her mom's unusual behavior too. "Is Uncle Leo all right?"

Alice darts a quick look in Sylvia's direction. "He's fine, honey."

"No moving anything while I'm away," Veronica tells the girl, sending her the famous two-fingered I'm-watching-you gesture, which makes her grin.

Alice goes to the narrow hallway that separates the living room from the bedrooms. She stops, crosses her arms and rubs her sides, as though to soothe herself. "It's Leo," she says in a low voice. "His fever's worse. Like, it's bad. A hundred and five."

Veronica's heart skips a beat. "Jeez. Did you call the doctor?"

"Dad did, but ..." She gestures towards the window at the end of the hallway. The snowfall is really thick now. All Veronica can see out there is black and white. "There's an on-call doctor at the clinic in Byrum. It's only, like, fifteen minutes from here. But he's snowed in, and the roads are completely blocked all over the island. He said he probably can't make it over here. He was worried he'd get bogged down himself somewhere. Normally, they'd send a helicopter, but that won't work either because of the snow."

"Oh, that's not good ..." Veronica's thoughts are racing. Should she tell? Would it even make a difference? Why is Leo so sick when she wasn't? Will he pull through? Or will Veronica have to live out the rest of her short lifespan knowing she inadvertently killed her boyfriend on her way out? "Did they know what's wrong with him at least?" she asks.

Alice shushes her. "Please, keep it down. We don't want Mom to know. She'll freak out."

"Right. Sorry."

Alice goes on, "Dad got put through to some infectious disease experts or whatever. They did a video call and he showed them Leo's face." She shakes her head grimly. "Said they'd never seen anything like it before. All they could tell us was to try and keep the fever down. Dad already gave him some Ibuprofen, but it didn't do—"

The door to one of the bedrooms opens, and Flemming sticks his head out. "There you are. He's asking for you again."

Veronica assumes it's Alice he's talking to, but Leo's dad is looking at her.

"That's why I asked you to come," Alice explains. "He keeps saying your name."

"Oh." Veronica is very surprised by this. "But why would he ..."

Leo's voice comes through the crack in the door: "'Nica ...?"

"Would you mind?" Flemming asks her earnestly. "I think it might calm him down to hear your voice."

Veronica swallows and manages to squeeze out: "Sure. Yeah, of course."

She steps forward, but Flemming doesn't open the door any farther. "Just a word of warning. He looks ... pretty bad."

"Nica ...?"

Veronica just nods.

Flemming opens the door and lets her in.

22

TIM

LIS AND ALAN LIVE in a quiet, wealthy part of town.

Their house is about six times bigger than Tim's, despite them having no children. They do have a Pomeranian, though. The damned little thing is afraid of everything, so Tim leaves Buddy in the truck.

He's about to ring the bell when he hears quick, light footsteps coming to the door. The lock turns and the door opens. Lis is holding the dog on her arm, and it immediately begins yapping at the sight of Tim.

"Shush, Prince. It's okay. Hi, Tim. Come in, please."

She steps aside so he can enter. As he does, the dog almost leaps from Lis's arm, trying to bite him. He sees it coming and pulls away.

"Prince!" Lis cries out. "What's gotten into you? Bad dog!"

The dog resorts to growling menacingly at him.

"I'm sorry, Tim," Lis says. "He's not usually like this. He's been on edge ever since Alan fell sick. I'll put him in the bedroom. Come in, please."

Tim takes off his shoes—thankful to get rid of them. He only wore them so as to not look weird. They are very uncomfortable, limiting his movements, his ability to grip the ground. Same with the jacket, which he hangs on a fancy coat stand. He notices Alan's jacket there, too.

Following Lis through the house, it strikes Tim as always how vets and bank workers make a very decent living—better than crane operators, at least. The floors are all tile, the walls decorated with fancy art pieces, the ceiling so high you could fit a flagpole in here. The acoustics are a little unnerving. Every sound ricochets around the room.

The dog climbs to Lis's shoulder to scowl back at Tim. It bares its tiny teeth in what is supposed to be an intimidatory snarl. The dog is never very friendly minded towards Tim—it can always smell Buddy on him—but it has never been this hostile. Tim doesn't think it's got much to do with Alan's disappearance.

He can sense something's happened to me. Just like Buddy can.

Lis leads him into the living room, which is more like a ballroom. She turns to send him a quick smile. "Please, help yourself to a drink. I'll be back in a second."

He looks around and sees a bar. He does feel like getting a drink. But not in the usual way. He isn't after the effects of the alcohol; it's the calories which appeal to him now. So, he goes and pours himself a large Vodka-Martini. There are lemons and limes in the freezer, but he doesn't touch those. He downs the whole thing in one go. It burns all the way through his throat and settles in his stomach.

As he puts down the empty glass, Lis comes back without the dog.

"Thank you again for coming, Tim. I really appreciate it."

"Sure."

"Say, didn't you lose some weight?"

He shrugs. "Not on purpose."

"You look taller than I remember, too. Anyway, please, sit."

She gestures to the large leather armchairs facing the terrace. The garden is lit up by projectors showing off the white marble fountain and the well-kept hedges. Even this time of the year, with nothing in bloom, it still looks impressive.

Tim takes a seat, wincing as the leather squeaks loudly under his weight.

Lis sits down opposite him. She wrings her slender hands and looks at him like a student sitting across from a principal. She's wearing black nail polish and tons of rings. She's so skinny that he can make out a couple of ribs through her red blouse. Definitely not Tim's type. Very much the opposite of Anya, who was plump and curvy and soft.

"So," she says, "do you have any idea where Alan could have gone?"

Tim weighs his words. "Not as such, no. But I think I might be able to find him."

"Really?" Hope in her eyes.

"Yeah, I have this newfound ... let's just call it intuition."

A crease appears on her forehead. "I'm not sure I follow?"

"It's hard to explain," he says, feeling like he already said too much. "It's just that, I can ..."

Pick up Alan's thoughts.

"... kind of guess where Alan might be."

Lis looks at me intently. "Is it because of the bug?"

Yes. It made me telepathic.

"I don't know. All I know is, I have a strong feeling I can locate him."

Lis lets out a sigh. "Well, I don't really care how you do it, Tim. If you can get him home, I'd be eternally grateful to you. Can you believe the cops wouldn't help me?"

"I can, actually. One time, at work, this guy went crazy. His wife just left him, and he was depressed. He locked himself in the john with a rifle. Threatened to shoot himself. My boss called the police. They said the guy wasn't doing anything illegal. And that we could call them back in case he shot himself."

Lis covers her mouth with her hand, and Tim immediately regrets telling the story.

"That's terrible," she whispers. "Did the guy ... kill himself?"

"No, he thought better of it. My point is just that, you can't always count on the cops. They usually only show up *after* things have already turned south."

"I guess you're right." She looks away and begins rubbing her palms against her thighs.

"I need to ask you, Lis. Before he left, did Alan ... did he touch you?"

"What do you mean?"

"Did you come into physical contact with him at any point?"

"Oh, you mean if he infected me? No, he was adamant about me not coming into the room, much less touching him. Ever since he came home from seeing Buddy—how is he, by the way? Alan said he pulled through."

"He did," Tim says with a smile. "He's fine and healthy."

"Oh, that's great. I hate the thought of any dog dying."

"Me too. It was touch and go. Alan's a great vet. He cured him."

A curious expression comes on her face. "You know, it's funny. Alan said something about a miracle. He didn't elaborate when I asked. I could tell he didn't feel like talking about it. In fact, he seemed a little ... I don't know, shaken up. He's usually a little absent-minded when he gets home from work, but this was different. What happened with Buddy, exactly?"

Tim shrugs again. "I wouldn't pretend to understand the medical stuff. All I know is, Alan gave him a shot and he got better."

"Huh. Well, I'm glad."

Tim gets up. "Well, time is running. I'd better give it a go. Can I see the bedroom? The one he slept in?"

Lis blinks up at him. "Sure. I mean, I already tidied it up, so there's not much to see."

"Still, it might help."

"Of course. Come with me."

She leads him down the hallway. Stopping by a door on the right, she opens it and gestures for him to go inside.

Tim takes one step into the room and immediately feels it.

It's still in the air. Subtle, but unmistakable. The faint smell of lime.

This is where it happened. This is where he changed.

He turns to look at Lis. "Did you change the sheets?"

"Yes, the sheets have been changed. They were all drenched in sweat."

"No, I mean, did *you* do it? Personally?"

"Oh, no. Our maid did it."

"Where's she now?"

"She's gone home." The look of nervousness returns to Lis's face. "Are you thinking she might have been infected?"

"I don't know. Have *you* felt anything?"

"No, not at all. I feel fine."

"Good. Let me just take a look."

He steps closer to the bed. The air is slightly colder in here, probably because the window has been open all day.

Tim walks around the bed, eyeing it. There's no trace of the moss. Going to the window, he gazes out over the garden from this new angle. Above the tall hedge separating Lis and Alan's garden from the neighbors, he can see the lights of the city reflected against the dark sky. He can smell the grass. Can hear traffic. He filters out the sounds and listens instead for Alan.

He stays there for a full minute. Trying to tune in. There's nothing coming to him.

"Tim?" Lis's voice from the door. "I'm sorry, but ... what are you doing?"

"Give me a minute, Lis," he mutters.

He listens some more. Keeping his mind as open as he can. Searching for any kind of signal from Alan. Still, nothing comes.

He's just about to turn around when—

"This won't work. Not like this. Need to be more careful."

Tim stiffens.

He's still far away. At the other end of town. Down by the industrial area, maybe.

Then he picks up another sound, this one much closer. Boots marching up the steps of the front door.

He turns to look at Lis. "I think someone's—"

He's cut off by the sound of the doorbell chiming.

Lis's eyes grow wide. "That could be him!" She turns and rushes down the hallway.

"No," Tim says to the empty bedroom. "It's the police."

23

VERONICA

HOW IN GOD'S NAME did it come on so fast?

Veronica almost gasps as she looks down at Leo.

Her boyfriend's naked save for his boxers—and those are drenched in sweat. He's not under a duvet or blanket either, despite the fact that the window's wide open. Snow is pouring in and has already formed a dune on the wooden floor. The temperature in the room must be close to zero. At the bedside table is a plate full of untouched roast, a glass of water, and a pill bottle.

Despite the cold, Leo is clearly burning up. Beads of sweat form on his forehead and hairless chest. The skin on his neck is all pink. Almost everywhere else is the black stuff. It's clearly started in the warmer, moister places of his body: the armpits, the groin, the crooks of his knees and elbows, and, most notably, his face and scalp. But it's spread out and is now running in crisscross patterns all over his limbs and torso.

Dear God. He looks like that poor bird.

He smells like the bird, too. That sharp, fruity scent is thick in the room, and had the window not been open, it would probably have been suffocating.

It's clear that Leo can't open his eyes, and Veronica doubts he can hear or smell much, either, the way the black stuff is clogging up his ears and nose. The only way he's able to breathe is through his mouth, and that sounds difficult, too. As she looks closer, she can tell the growth is not only on his lips, but also his gums and tongue. It's probably lining his throat and windpipe all the way down.

"Nica?" he croaks.

"I'm here, Leo," she whispers, glancing at Flemming.

Leo scratches his arm then raises his hand. It's completely covered in the black stuff. He gropes the air, and Veronica takes his hand. The moss is surprisingly soft to the touch. Leo squeezes her hand. "That you, Nica?"

"Yeah," she says, clearing her throat. "It's me. I'm right here."

"Why didn't you tell me?"

Veronica stiffens. "Tell you what?"

"The glove," he wheezes.

Veronica doesn't know what to say. She's suddenly very aware that Flemming is eyeing her from the side.

"He keeps mentioning a glove," her father-in-law says with a shrug. "Any idea what it means?"

Veronica manages to shake her head.

"Hercules," Leo says—at least it sounds like that, but it's hard to tell because he breaks into a weak, rattly cough. When he's able to speak again, he repeats, "Nica?"

"Yes, Leo. I'm still here." She gives his hand a squeeze, and he grips her more firmly.

"Why didn't you tell me?" he asks again.

"I don't ... I don't know, Leo." She almost starts crying.

"Hercules," he says again.

"What about him?" Veronica asks, happy to change the subject. "What about Hercules?"

Leo gives a groan and whips his head from side to side, rubbing the back of his head against the sheet. He's clearly both itching and in pain.

"That's your cat, right?" Flemming asks. "He's mentioned him a couple of times, too." He watches his son thrash on the bed, bites his lip, then says, "You think he could have caught it from the cat?"

"I guess that's possi—"

"*No!*" Leo cries out with a sudden forcefulness Veronica hadn't expected at all. He also sits up, and she can't help but tear free and take a step back. "It wasn't Hercules!" Leo croaks, gnashing his teeth. He manages to open one eye halfway, and it fixes on Veronica. "I thought so, but—*uaargh!*" He doubles over and hugs his belly as though about to puke. "Ow, it hurts so bad ..."

"Lie back down, son," Flemming says, stepping forward. "Relax."

Leo lets his father help him down on his back. He's still moaning. "But the glove," he whispers. "It was yours. You must have known."

"Here, son. Take some more painkillers." Flemming shoves two in Leo's mouth and helps him take a sip of water.

Veronica just stands there, covering her mouth with her hand, shaking all over.

Flemming then turns to look at Veronica. His expression is grave. "I'm sorry. I shouldn't have asked you to come in here. I thought it would make him calmer to have you around."

Veronica takes her hand away and asks, "You think ... you think he's dying?"

Flemming runs a hand over his scalp and shakes his head. "I don't know. This is all happening so fast. I just don't know. I'm calling the doctor again."

As he takes out his phone, Veronica goes to the door, very happy to get out of the room.

Just as she touches the handle, Leo croaks again, "Nica?"

His voice is different now. Deeper. Less shaky.

She turns to look at him, and her heart leaps as she meets that one, staring eye again. It's so white, in the dimness of the bedroom, it looks to Veronica like Leo's iris and pupil are both gone. And to make it worse, his mouth is contorted into something very much like a grin, showing his white teeth surrounded by the black stuff.

"I'm not dying. Not by a long stretch."

There's a long, ominous silence in the bedroom in which only the howling of the wind is heard.

Then Flemming's call goes through, and a woman says, "*North Jutland's emergency doctor's office, how can I help you*?"

"Yes, it's Flemming Brun again," Leo's dad says, clearing his throat. "We spoke three hours ago. I'm calling because there's been no improvement with my son, and we're starting to worry that ..."

Veronica doesn't hear the rest of it. She breaks free from Leo's gaze and quickly leaves the room.

24

TIM

WHEN TIM REACHES THE hall, Lis has already opened the door and is talking to two officers. A man and a woman. The woman is old enough to be Tim's mother. The man is a lot younger.

"We really want to have a word with you," the female cop says.

"Oh, so now you do," Lis snorts. "When I called you earlier, you couldn't even be bothered to come up here."

"We might have news about your husband."

"You do?" Lis's tone of voice changes. "Why didn't you say so? Come in."

The cops enter the house and see Tim standing there.

"Who are you, sir?" the female cop asks. She has gray stains in her sideburns, and her voice is slightly raspy. Her skin is leathery and her eyes piercingly blue.

"I'm a friend of Alan's."

"I called Tim because I didn't know who else to call, and he was kind enough to come down here," Lis says. "Tim was the last person to see Alan before he came home."

"He was?" the female cop gives Tim a thorough look.

"My dog," Tim says. "Alan took a look at him this afternoon."

"Right." The cops exchange a brief look. "We might want to speak to you too, sir."

Tim nods. He doesn't want to stay around, much less be interviewed by cops. All he can think of is going out to find Alan. He has a strong feeling that time is critical.

"You've got somewhere we can talk?" the female cop asks Lis.

"Sure, follow me."

She leads them into the living room. Tim follows along hesitantly. The cops make him feel tense for some reason. Like he's hiding something. Which, of course, he is—the boulder, the moss, the infection. He should have called it in a long time ago. Should have told the cops everything. Should have led the SSI to the boulder. Let them run whatever tests they wanted on him and Buddy. This thing is obviously something very strange and potentially dangerous. Not something he should be keeping a secret.

Still, the thought of spilling everything doesn't feel like the right move. Tim feels strongly that he needs to be the one to deal with this, at least for now. That involving the cops would be like using gasoline to put out a fire.

They have no idea what has happened to Alan. What he's capable of.

Lis offers the cops a drink, which they both decline.

"Have a seat, then."

The female cop sends him another look. "Sir, could you please wait in another room while we have a word with Miss Andersen?"

"Why?" Lis asks guardedly.

"We have rather sensitive information regarding your husband."

"Oh, God. Is he okay?"

"As far as we know, he's fine. But we think you should be the only one to hear about it for now."

Lis looks from Tim to the cops, shaking her head. "Tim is a close friend. He can hear whatever you have to tell me about Alan."

"It's just protocol," the male cop insists—speaking for the first time. His voice is whiny, like that of a teenager. "We prefer to conduct the interviews separately."

"I need to hit the john anyway," Tim says, smiling briefly at Lis. "I'll wait in the hallway."

He crosses the living room, aware that the cops quietly watch him leave. They wait until he reaches the bathroom and closes the door before they start talking.

Tim stands on the other side of the door. Even through the wood, he can easily make out the conversation. To no surprise, the female cop leads the interview.

"Do you know Clara and Johan Birk?"

"No. Who are they?"

"Has your husband ever mentioned their names?"

"No, I don't think so. What's this about? Please, can you just tell me what happened to my husband? Have you found him or not?"

"*We got a report an hour ago,*" the male cop chimes in. "*Your husband broke into a home on Storegade. The next-door neighbor saw him fleeing the scene and ID'd him.*"

"What? That's ridiculous. Why would Alan break in anywhere? We have plenty of money ..."

"He didn't appear to be after their possessions," the female cop explains. "*We're not sure exactly what he wanted, though. He assaulted them both briefly before fleeing the house again.*"

"**Assaulted**?" Lis's voice almost breaks. "*That's nonsense! Alan would never ... I mean, why on earth ...? They must have* *attacked him first. Or maybe he was delirious. I told you about that, earlier, when I called the station, asking you for help. Alan was sick with a fever when he left the house."*

"Yes, about that ... The couple said your husband looked and acted strange. Like he wasn't himself."

"See? That's what I told you! This is exactly why I called you. He's wandering around in some fever haze, and God knows what could happen! He might hurt himself. Get run over or something. You've gotta find him before that happens!"

"We're doing our best to that end. But we need—"

"Are you really? Because it looks to me like you're sitting here talking to me instead of being out there looking for him!"

"We have units searching as we speak. Please rest assured, if Alan's still in town, we'll find him before long."

"What do you mean, 'if he's still in town'? Where else would he be?"

"That's what we wanted to talk to you about. Do you have any guess as to where your husband might have gone?"

"No. If I did, don't you think I would have told you right away?"

"The reason he sought out the Birks could give us a clue as to his motive. Help us figure out where he's going. That's why it's important you tell us if you know anything about your husband's relationship to them. Anything at all. Were they customers of his?"

"I have no idea. Why don't you ask them?"

"We did. They claim to have no relationship to your husband."

"Well, then—"

"Do you think they could have reason to lie? Like, if they owed him money, perhaps?"

"What? No. Wait, are you implying Alan went there to collect some kind of debt? Do you still think he did this on purpose? He's delirious! Aren't you listening? I'm sure he's got no idea what he's doing ..."

Tim decides he's heard enough. He needs to find Alan. Right away. Before the cops do.

Storegade fits with the direction he caught Alan's signal from. It's in the northeast part of town, a ten-minute drive from here.

But he can't exit the bathroom. Not without risking the cops hearing it. They've already made it clear they want to talk to him. There's no chance they will let him go before they've interviewed him.

The bathroom has a window. It's narrow, but just big enough that Tim can squeeze out. As he strides past the mirror, he can't help but catch sight of himself, and what he sees makes him pause for a second.

Lis was right: he *has* lost weight. At least ten pounds. Since yesterday.

He's taller, too. He's always been a big guy, standing a little over six feet four. Now, he's closer to seven feet. Come to think of it, he did notice his hair touching the ceiling of the truck as he drove down here.

His frame is also different. His shoulders sit a bit higher and farther back. His ribcage is more triangular. His arms have grown a few inches longer, as evident by the fact that his shirt sleeves now stop well above his wrists. He looks down to see the same problem with his pants—which also explains why they've begun chafing at the groin.

Guess I'll have to buy myself new clothes.

The thought sparks a memory. Him, picking up Helena from her crib one morning, noticing the onesie being a bit too small. When he suggested they go get a new one for her, Anya told him, "*No, we'll give it two more weeks. Just till her growth spurt is over. Or we'll just have to buy a second time.*"

"You're right, honey," Tim grunts at the mirror. "I'll give it two more weeks. See how big I am after this ... growth spurt is over."

He's about to go to the window, when he notices something else in the mirror. Something about his face. It's subtly different. The shape of his head, too. It hadn't been enough for Lis to notice it, but Tim definitely looks different.

He feels a cold shiver staring at himself. *Who am I? What the hell is happening to me*?

Whatever it is, it's also happening to Alan. And unlike Tim, his friend seems to be reacting to the change in a completely different way. Which is why Tim needs to find him.

Right now.

25

VERONICA

"VERONICA?"

"Huh?" She blinks and finds herself standing in front of a mirror, dressed in her sleeping T-shirt. Next to her is Molly, brushing her teeth.

"Aren't you supposed to turn it on?" the girl asks with a smile.

Veronica realizes she's just been standing there with her electric toothbrush in her mouth. "Oh, right." She clicks the button and it starts rotating.

They brush in silence for half a minute. Veronica's eyes are gritty. It's almost eleven o'clock, and she's exhausted beyond belief. It's been a crazy day. She notices how Molly is eyeing her in the mirror.

"Are you worried about Uncle Leo?" she asks.

"Yeah, a little," Veronica admits.

Of course the girl noticed how absent-minded Veronica was after she went to see Leo. She tried her best to act normal, to engage with the game they were playing, to listen to what Molly told her about her school. But the girl is very perceptive.

And besides, Veronica isn't the only one worried sick. Alice has been pacing back and forth all evening, keeping busy with seemingly pointless tasks. Flemming has been in

Leo's room most of the time. He only came out to use the bathroom or speak briefly with Alice in hushed voices.

The only one seemingly unaffected by Leo's illness is his mother. The Ice Queen kept knitting and listening to music on the radio as though nothing was out of the ordinary. Whether her husband and daughter succeeded in keeping it a secret to her just how sick Leo was, or whether she simply doesn't care, Veronica can't tell. As coldhearted as Sylvia is, she finds it hard to believe a mother wouldn't at least worry when her son falls ill.

Perhaps it's denial. An emotional defense mechanism. Pretend like there's no problem and it might go away. Veronica is no stranger to that strategy herself.

"Don't be," Molly says, trying to cheer her up. "He's already better."

The girl puts away her toothbrush and plugs in her night braces.

"I hope so," Veronica says, spitting in the sink.

"No, he is," Molly insists—her voice a little lispy now because of the braces. "I heard Grandpa say so."

Veronica frowns. "When?"

"Just now. He told my mom that the rash was going away."

Veronica's heart swells with relief. "Really? That's great!" She wipes her mouth in the towel. "Let me just go and get an update."

She rushes down the hallway. From Alice's room she can hear her sister-in-law talk on the phone with her husband. Veronica doesn't want to eavesdrop, but she can tell from Alice's voice she's less uptight. She goes to Leo's bedroom and listens briefly. Only a faint, calm breath. She goes to the living room and finds only Sylvia there. She's put away her knitwear and is watching an old movie with the volume way down. She's got a blanket over her lap and is cupping a mug of tea in her skinny hands. She obviously sees Veronica enter the room, but doesn't look away from the screen.

"I thought you'd gone to bed," Veronica says.

"No, not yet. I can't seem to fall asleep any longer without a big cup of tea. Means I have to get up and pee at least once during the night, but what can you do?" She raises the mug to her thin lips and takes a sip.

"Where's Flemming?" Veronica asks. "Is he with Leo?"

"Flemming's gone to bed."

Veronica frowns. "So ... is no one with Leo?"

"No one needs to be with Leo," Sylvia says in a tone that's annoyingly nonchalant. "He's getting better."

"Oh. So Flemming told you?"

"Flemming doesn't need to tell me anything, dear. I know what's going on." She says that last part in a snide tone.

"Well, that's great," Veronica says. "I'll go check on him."

She's about to leave, when Sylvia goes on, "Whatever you did to my son, I'm not forgiving you. You know that, right?"

Veronica turns back around.

Sylvia still isn't looking at her as she goes on. "Even if he gets better, I'm holding you responsible. And I'm like an elephant ..." She taps her temple with a finger. "I never forget."

Veronica weighs her words carefully. "What makes you think I did this to Leo?"

"Oh, please. He basically said it outright."

Veronica swallows. "It was the fever that made him—"

Sylvia clicks her tongue loudly. "I know you probably didn't do it on purpose, but you gave that infection to him. It's written all over your guilty little face, dear."

Veronica looks at the television, then back at Sylvia. "You know, at least I *feel* guilt."

"No, you don't. You're just sentimental because you're dying."

Veronica freezes. "What … what do you mean? I'm not dying."

"Well, not right now. But soon."

Veronica frowns. "What kinda sick joke are you making?"

"Oh, I'm certainly not joking. Cancer's no joke." She finally turns her head to look at Veronica. "How long did they give you?"

Veronica feels the blood rush from her head as her mind struggles to figure out how Sylvia found out. Veronica didn't tell a living soul. Not even Leo. Only Veronica and her doctor know about her diagnosis, and her medical file is confidential.

"How did you … how did you find out?"

Sylvia takes another sip of tea, making sure to do so very slowly. "It was obvious from the moment you stepped into this house. That irritating, frisky mood of yours. Only morons and terminal patients act like that when they're around people they can't stand. And that tiny puncture wound you've got under your navel? I noticed it when you were stretching. That's from a recent biopsy. Ovarian, I'm guessing?"

Veronica instinctively tugs her T-shirt down a little farther. She feels a flurry of shame and anger. Like Sylvia just exposed her. "You don't … you can't just … you have no right …"

"Oh, get over yourself," Sylvia groans, shifting in the armchair. "We're all going that way. You're nothing special. So … how long did they give you?"

Veronica breathes hard through her nose. "Three to six months."

Sylvia just nods. "And will you be doing chemo? Radiation?"

"Haven't decided yet."

Sylvia shrugs. "Hardly seems worth it for another three months."

"Thanks for offering your opinion."

There's a long spell of silence in the living room, broken only by the last embers sizzling in the fireplace and the howling wind tugging at the roof.

"Don't tell them," Veronica hears herself say.

"Don't tell who?"

"Leo. And Molly."

Sylvia stares at the television, her gaze distant, as though the conversation bores her.

"Please," Veronica says. "Let me be the one to break it to them."

Sylvia sighs. Then she says something completely unexpected. "You know how old I am, dear?"

Veronica blinks. "I'm ... not sure."

"Take a guess."

Confused, Veronica does some quick math. "Leo's twenty-nine, and Alice is four years older. So you must be ... sixty?"

"I'm sixty-eight." She says it like it's something she's very proud of.

Veronica throws out her arms. "What's your point?"

"You know the average lifespan for someone with cystic fibrosis?"

"I don't ... I don't know what that is."

"Well, look it up." Sylvia gets up abruptly, shutting off the television with a grunt of annoyance. As though she really wanted to watch the ending, but now Veronica ruined it for her. "I'm going to bed."

"Wait," Veronica says, as the tiny lady strides past her. "Are you telling me ...? Are you sick, Sylvia?"

Her mother-in-law stops only two feet away from her and looks her dead in the eye. A smile tugging at the corner of her mouth. "Me? Oh, no. I've just got a little asthma." She mockingly clears her throat, then walks on. Remembering something, she stops in the opening to the hallway and turns around. "Oh, and Veronica, dear?" She holds up her palm, as though making a Native American greeting. Even from across the room, Veronica sees thin strips of black running along the creases of her skin. "I'm also holding you responsible for what will happen to the rest of us. Including that poor little Molly whom you're so fond of." She raises one eyebrow. "Goodnight."

Turning, her mother-in-law marches down the hallway, leaving Veronica alone in the silence.

26

TIM

HE RUNS DOWN THE sidewalk barefoot, speeding past houses, crossing streets and turning corners.

The freezing air is pleasant against his skin. Oxygen is being funneled through his system, his heart and muscles work in perfect unison with little exertion.

As he jumped out of the window back at the Andersens', he realized right away he couldn't go to the truck. The engine was loud enough that the cops would hear it from inside the house. And he didn't want them knowing he was leaving.

So, he decided to just run. Turned out to be faster than driving, anyway, since he can take shortcuts through gardens and jump clean over fences and hedges like they were nothing more than speed bumps.

It takes him less than six minutes to reach Storegade. He begins scanning the mailboxes, not needing to slow down to read the names.

He stops abruptly at C & J Birk.

It's an inconspicuous bungalow. There are lights on in some of the windows. A white city car parked in the driveway.

He goes up the path to the front door and rings the bell. Nothing happens right away. That is, nothing anyone with a normal sense of hearing would have picked up.

But Tim hears the television—which is showing a Bruce Willis film—get muted. A man and a woman exchange a few words, asking each other who could be at the door at this hour. The man says he'll go check and tells his partner to stay in the living room. Then footsteps come to the door. Tim can hear the guy hold his breath as he apparently leans closer and peers through the peephole.

Tim makes no effort to hide his giant frame. Instead, he tries for a smile. "My name is Tim Iversen," he says, sensing the guy startle on the other side. "I was hoping I could have a quick word with you."

"*About what*?" the guy asks through the door. "*I don't know you.*"

"I'm a friend of Alan."

"Alan who?"

"The man who was here earlier."

A muffled gasp, and Tim quickly adds: "It's not what you think. I just spoke with the police about the incident you guys had earlier. I figured I might be able to help out. We're trying to find Alan. If you would just let me—"

"So you're working with the police?"

"Yes, you could say that."

Some of the tension goes out of the guy's voice. "*We already told them what happened.*"

"I know. I was just hoping you could … give me a quick recap. It would help me figure out where he's going."

A brief pause. Then the lock snaps, and the door opens. But only five inches. The guy stares out at Tim above the safety chain. “Sorry, man. We’re dead tired. We had gone to bed, actually. Can you come back tomorrow?”

“I could,” Tim says, ignoring the lie. “But I think that would be too late. Alan could be long gone by then.”

“Who is it, Johan?”

A woman’s voice from behind. She comes through the narrow hall, wearing a big sweatshirt which probably belongs to her partner. Tim can tell her mascara has been running.

He can also tell a lot of other things. Like how the woman brings with her a smell that’s discreet but unmistakably citrusy. To a regular nose it would probably smell like part of the woman’s perfume. But Tim recognizes the smell immediately.

As though to drive home his suspicion, the woman reaches up and absent-mindedly runs a finger around the outer rim of her ear. It could be a coincidence or a nervous habit. But it looks very much like her ear is already starting to itch.

“It’s a guy who the police asked to help find the guy,” Johan tells his wife. “He knows him.”

The woman eyes Tim. “Some friend you got there. You know what he wanted from us?”

“Not exactly, no.”

“He tried to rape my wife,” Johan blurts out. “Fucking asshole. He’s lucky I didn’t kill him.”

Tim frowns. “The police didn’t say anything about that.”

“I don’t think that’s what he wanted,” the woman says in a low voice.

“Oh, really?” the guy scoffs. “Then why did he grab you and try to drag you off?”

“He didn’t try to drag me anywhere.” The woman rubs her forearm through the sleeve. Tim observes her closely, trying to make out any of the black stuff around her eyes or mouth. He can't see any. Not yet.

Has she become contagious? Is he already infected too?

Tim hadn't picked up on the smell before the woman came to the door, but that doesn't necessarily mean the guy isn't carrying the spore. Buddy hadn't started to smell before the black stuff became visible.

"What did he do, then?" Tim asks.

The woman looks up at him. "He just ... he grabbed me by the arm, and then ... then he smiled."

"Fucking creep," Johan snarls.

The woman begins to cry softly. "It was ... it was so weird and scary. I've never seen anyone act so ... so strange."

The guy runs his hand through his hair. "Look, are we done here?"

"Please," Tim says, placing a hand on the door as the man starts to close it. "Can I just see it?"

"See what?"

He gestures towards the woman's arm. "Where he grabbed you."

Johan looks at his wife, and she looks at Tim, still weeping. Then, she wipes her nose and shrugs. "Sure, I don't see why not."

The guy—reluctantly—removes the chain and opens the door halfway.

The woman carefully pulls up the sleeve, revealing her thin arm.

A big, dark bruise covers the skin. An obvious imprint of a big hand.

"It's gotten even worse," Johan remarks. "The medic said it might. Nothing's broken, but will you look at that? Who the hell does something like this to a woman? I'm telling you, if I had caught him ..."

Tim isn't interested in what the guy is saying anymore, so he tunes out his voice, and just stares at the woman's arm.

That's not a bruise.

Whether she can't see it yet, or whether she's willfully ignoring it, Tim can't tell. Maybe it's his new, intense vision that allows him to see the tiny flakes that have started to appear around the edges of the mark. Or maybe it's simply because he knows what he's looking at.

Did she infect the medics too? The police? How many people are out there right now, infecting others? How far has this thing spread?

The guy is still talking. The woman gently scratches the mark with her fingernails while staring at Tim, as though waiting to hear his thoughts on the matter. He sees in a flash how the dark spot will grow while the woman sleeps. It will snake its way up her arm, reach her torso, spread out over her entire body. Not to mention the fact that it's almost certainly already inside her. Growing in her lungs, her heart, her brain.

How long she's got? Till morning?

He sends the woman a reassuring smile. And then, surprising himself, he tells her, "I'm sorry for what happened. If it's any consolation, I promise you my friend won't return."

The woman nods once, sniffs, then mutters, "Thank you."

"Okay, look," Johan cuts through. "We're going to bed now. I hope you find the asshole. Seriously, he deserves to ..." The guy stops talking as he notices something and frowns. "What the hell ... Dude, why aren't you wearing any shoes?"

The abrupt shift of attention onto Tim catches him off-guard.

"I … uhm … I was in a hurry," he says stupidly, taking a step back. "Thank you for your time. I'll be out of your hair now."

"Wait." This time, it's the woman who speaks. She steps closer, staring up at Tim's face intently. Her voice is different now. "The other guy, he wasn't wearing any shoes, either. And there's something … something with your eyes …"

Tim suddenly feels very uncomfortable. Lowering his gaze, he takes another step back. But it's too late.

The woman gasps loudly. "Oh, my God …" She pulls back, clasping her mouth with both hands. She stares from Tim to her husband.

"What is it?" the guy asks. "What's wrong?"

"His eyes … they're just like the other guy's!"

Tim spins around and bolts.

27

TIM

TIM KEEPS RUNNING UNTIL he's three blocks over—which doesn't take more than thirty seconds.

He stops on an empty corner to catch his breath. He feels awful. The way the woman had looked at him; the fear in her eyes. Like she was staring at a monster.

He catches his own reflection in a storefront window and steps closer.

He hears the woman's voice, full of shock: "*His eyes ...*"

And he sees with a sinking feeling what scared her so. His irises have faded. That's the best way to describe it.

Tim's steely gray eyes have turned even more piercing because the black parts in the center are almost gone. They aren't static, though. In sync with his pulse, the pupils tune in and out. If he focuses his gaze hard, they become more visible. As he relaxes, they almost disappear.

It gives him a fierce expression. Predatorial, almost.

It's official. I'm a freak now.

Looking at himself makes him uneasy, so instead he keeps moving.

Can't let anyone see me up close.

Except that's too late. The Birks saw him and recognized what's happening to him. They've probably already called the police. Would they be looking for him too now?

What's worse is that whoever comes to their house will undoubtedly catch the infection. Tim isn't sure whether actual physical contact is needed for the spore to jump from one body onto another. Judging by the fact that Alan had grabbed the woman, something suggested that is the case. But it's very likely also airborne—it had certainly attacked the airways of both Tim and Buddy. Surely, every outbreath from the woman is filled with tiny spores. In that case, all it takes is a cough or a sneeze.

There's another, even more frightening question. One Tim hates to even think about.

*Am **I** contagious?*

Whatever Alan did to the woman, he obviously infected her with the strange disease. Tim had suspected that much. But he had hoped Alan hadn't done so on purpose. The way she described it, it sounded very much like that was the case.

"... he grabbed me by the arm, and then ... then he smiled."

Tim becomes keenly aware of his palms as he walks on. Has he touched anyone tonight? What about Lis? He doesn't remember shaking her hand. But he can't be sure.

Forget about that for now. Focus on finding Alan.

Even though the Birks are infected and very likely about to infect others too, that doesn't feel like Tim's primary concern. The Birks can—hopefully—be dealt with later. Once the authorities realize what's happening. For now, the crucial thing is to find Alan and stop him from infecting anyone else.

Tim passes a Red Cross container and stops at a sudden impulse. He opens the lid and looks inside. Plastic bags full of clothes. Rummaging around a little, he checks a couple of them. In the third one, he hits the jackpot.

A pair of ski gloves.

Why anyone would donate ski gloves to a third world country is beyond him ... but it's just what he needs.

He takes them and hurries on, when—

"Damnit! He got me good."

Tim pauses briefly as he hears Alan's voice in his head again. It's much louder now. Which means he's closer. He presses on. Thinking a million thoughts a minute, wondering what he's going to do when he finds Alan. All he has worried about since he got the call from Lis was finding Alan. He hadn't had any time to consider what he'd actually say or do to him once he did.

Since he's so preoccupied, it takes him a second to realize something is wrong with the glove. He can't get it to fit. It's big enough, but something keeps getting stuck.

Stopping, he pulls it off with a grunt of annoyance. Then he sees the problem. It's not the glove.

Next to the base of Tim's little finger sits an extra knuckle. What looks a lot like half a nailless finger is protruding from it.

"Oh, Christ," he mutters.

Holding up his other hand, he sees the same, except this stump is a little longer.

Great. I'm growing extra fingers now ...

Without really wanting to, he attempts to move the stumps. They wiggle willingly, as though they've always been at his service.

Then, suddenly, he feels the tingling at the base of his skull. Automatically, he goes for his pocket, then remembers he's left his phone in the truck with Buddy.

Instead, he hears a woman's voice in his head: "*We have a similar incident, Tom. Breaking and entering. Perp seen fleeing westward on foot.*"

"*Is it our guy?*" another voice asks.

"*Unclear, but sounds like it. Witness spotted him entering an alley. It's close to you. Kobbergade.*"

"*I'll check it out.*"

"*Show caution. We suspect he's delirious.*"

"*Armed?*"

"*Not that we know of. Might be injured. Witness defended himself with a knife.*"

As Tim listens to the conversation, the voices rise and fall slightly in volume and clarity.

It's from the police radio. I'm picking it up like a damn scanner.

He feels dizzy, shakes his head and willfully tries to block out the voices. To his surprise, he succeeds. It feels like turning an antenna away from a signal, and the voices simply fade out.

He looks up to see the street sign mounted on the corner of the building.

It says Kobbergade.

28

TIM

MOVING DOWN THE STREET, he keeps his senses very alert.

Alan is close now. Tim can feel him getting closer with each step. He's sniffing the air for any scents. There are a lot of them. Asphalt, rubber, exhaust, grass, something rotting in a garbage can, even traces of lasagna, fried fish, and other things people had for supper. But he doesn't pick up that characteristic limelike smell. Maybe the breeze is the wrong direction. Maybe Alan just isn't close enough yet. Or maybe ...

Maybe he stopped smelling. I did, and so did Buddy. Once the black stuff goes away, the smell goes too.

Meaning Tim has to rely on other senses if he wants to find Alan. So, he keeps his eyes and ears perched. Whenever a car passes, he makes sure to look away.

As he strides past an alley on the opposite side of the street, he suddenly hears: "*Can't let them take me. Not yet.*"

Alan's thoughts. From inside the alley.

His heart rate rises. He slips across the street and braces himself as he gazes into the dark passage between the buildings. He can make out the wooden fence at the end, a couple of dumpsters, a bike with one wheel missing and other garbage. But he can't see Alan.

He hears him, though. He's breathing fast.

Tim starts walking slowly down the alley. "Alan?"

The breathing stops.

"It's me. Tim."

For a couple of seconds, nothing happens.

Then he hears movement from behind one of the containers, and a head pops up. "Tim? Holy shit ... you were the last person I expected to see!"

His voice is recognizable, though it has become a little deeper and gruffer. It sounds like the words come from farther back in his throat.

Tim steps closer as Alan comes out from behind the container. The vet is clutching his left arm, and he's wrapped something that looks like a ripped-off sleeve around it. The sight of him is pretty damn grotesque. He's still wearing his pajamas, and nothing on his feet. His hair is messy and noticeably thinner than it was just yesterday. Even though he's hunched over, his shoulders rounded, seemingly to protect his injured arm, Tim can tell he's several inches taller.

His features are different, too. Despite him being in shadows, Tim can make out his face pretty clearly. And the sight of it makes his heart sink. Alan's eyes are completely pupilless and seem too big for his face. His mouth is too wide and his lips are gone.

As he comes towards Tim, he moves in a strange, bouncy way, never extending his knees fully. It makes him look like a praying mantis walking upright.

"Good to see ya, pal," he says, a wry smile tugging at his mouth. "How'd you find me?"

The question surprises Tim. He assumed Alan could pick up Tim's thoughts too. Or perhaps that he could even feel his presence from a distance. Apparently not.

"I went to talk to Lis," Tim says. "She was very worried."

"Yeah, I can imagine," Alan says, and he stops and lowers his gaze in something Tim takes to be regret. "You know, I couldn't bring myself to do it to her. Whaddya think of that? Silly, right?"

Tim swallows. "No, I understand."

Alan is still standing next to the container. There is something like fifteen feet between them. A distance they both seem comfortable with.

Alan squints at Tim. "Did you ... did you do it? Did you change her?"

Tim shakes his head.

"Why not?"

"I couldn't. The police came."

He isn't sure where that answer comes from, but it's the right one. The mentioning of the police makes Alan visibly tense.

"Shit. Did they make you out?"

"I don't think so. I got out of there without them noticing."

"Good call, pal. Good call." He looks Tim up and down. "I see you're coming along nicely, too. Gotta say, I expected you to be further advanced than me, what with you catching it first and all. But, hey, looks like I'm winning the race, huh?" He laughs. The sound is so awful, it makes Tim's skin crawl. It sounds like the way Alan would laugh, but more discordant. Like he's laughing into a tin can.

"What happened to your arm?" Tim asks, wanting to shift the focus away from himself.

"This? Oh, it's nothing. The last one got me with a knife, that's all. Cut me pretty deep."

"You'll need medical attention."

"What? Are you crazy? No, look, it's not that bad." He unwraps the cloth to show a gash in his bicep. The skin is stained with dried-up blood. All blood looks black in the darkness, but Tim can tell Alan's blood really is black. "Huh, will you look at that?" the vet says, sounding surprised. "It's already healing up. It happened, like, twenty minutes ago." He sends Tim that mock grin again. "Guess that's another perk, huh?"

"Guess so."

Tim is biding his time, not knowing exactly what to do. Until now, he's been feeling Alan out. He gets the clear sense they aren't at all on the same page about what needs to happen. Which means if Tim wants him to stop, he has to physically force him to do so. And he isn't sure how strong or fast Alan is. He's clearly more transformed than Tim, which could indicate he's also physically superior, despite the fact that Tim still seems to have both the reach and weight advantage.

The only thing clearly in Tim's favor is that Alan thinks he's on his side in this.

"How about the fingers?" Alan asks, dropping the cloth to show Tim his hands. They both have six digits, an extra thumb on each. "Got those yet?"

Tim flashes his hand briefly. "They're coming along."

"They make it easier to grab stuff. How many you got so far? I got four."

It takes Tim a moment to realize Alan isn't talking about fingers anymore, but the number of people he's infected.

Luckily, Tim is spared having to answer, because at that second, they both pick up the sound of a car approaching. Alan dashes behind the container, and Tim slips over to the wall, pressing his back into a doorway.

A few seconds later, a vehicle comes driving by slowly. Red and blue lights flicker across the alley. Then the police car passes.

Alan comes creeping out from hiding and looks at Tim. "We gotta be careful, pal. They're already on to me. We gotta move fast, you know? But unseen. We should spread out, cover different parts of town. That way we're less vulnerable."

"You're right."

"I say we go for the easy ones," Alan continues. "Teens and old folks. Women. People who won't suspect anything and who can't defend themselves. Don't be stupid and take chances like I did with the last guy. He was strong, alert, quick to react."

Hearing Alan utter the word "teens" causes an image of Helena to flash in front of Tim's inner vision. And he suddenly feels burning anger well up into his chest.

Alan apparently considers their meeting to be over, because he's headed for the fence.

"Wait, Alan."

He turns to look back. "Yeah, what?"

"You really think ... this is the right way?"

"Whaddya mean?"

"Going around infecting people. Turning them into ... whatever the hell we are becoming?"

Alan cocks his head. The gesture looks distinctly animal. "You mean you don't know?"

"Don't know what?"

"What we're ... becoming, as you put it."

"No," Tim says honestly. "I don't. Please tell me."

Alan hesitates for a beat. Tim gets the impression he considers whether or not to trust him with the answer. Then, he says in a low voice, "We're becoming so much more, Tim."

Tim is about to say something else, when the door he's been pressing against just a moment ago suddenly opens.

29

TIM

TIM AND ALAN WERE so wrapped up in the conversation that neither of them heard the guy come to the door.

He surprises both of them by suddenly stepping out into the alley, carrying a pair of full garbage bags. He's wearing slippers and a shabby bathrobe. Clearly not expecting to see anyone, the guy jolts as he spots them. "Jesus, you guys nearly gave me a heart attack! What are you even doing standing arou—"

Alan reacts so fast, had Tim not been expecting it, he wouldn't have saved the old guy.

Uttering something between a snarl and a grunt, the vet lunges at the guy like a cheetah taking off after a prey that has unwittingly wandered into its territory. Tim is closer to the door and the old guy standing there, dumbfound—which is another reason he's able to intercept.

He jumps forward and grabs Alan from the side, wrapping both arms around him. They swing halfway around, and Alan bursts free by flailing his arms. He staggers back, glaring at Tim like he has betrayed him in the most callous way.

"What the hell are you doing?" he bellows, no longer keeping his voice down. The words boom like the roar of a grizzly bear, while the dissonant, shrill note in the background also becomes more pronounced, almost making it sound like two people are talking at once.

"Don't do it!" Tim says, holding out both hands. It's all he can think to do. The old guy is behind him, and save for dropping both garbage bags, he hasn't moved a muscle. "Get inside!" Tim shouts over his shoulder without looking back, afraid to take his eyes off of Alan. He knows the door won't hold back Alan if he sets his mind to going after the guy, but at least it will slow him down a bit.

"Why are you protecting him?" Alan roars, spit flying from his huge, lipless mouth. It's only now, with his mouth fully open, that Tim sees how his teeth have turned pointy. They are also whiter, almost shining.

Jesus. He really is a predator ...

"I'm calling the cops," the old guy croaks from behind.

"No!" Tim shouts, turning his head halfway around. "Don't call anyone. Just go back inside, and forget about this. You don't—"

Looking away from Alan for a second is enough for him to make a move. Tim hears him, though, and he's able to jump sideways at the last possible moment, cutting him off again. This time, Alan stops before they collide. He doesn't pull back, though, and they are standing very close now. The vet breathes heavily—not because of physical exertion, but because he's furious. Despite the fact that Tim is several inches taller than him, Alan looks like he is ready to tear him apart limb from limb.

Behind him, Tim hears the door slam, and he feels a temporary surge of relief.

Alan squints at him, hissing, "Are you out of your fucking mind?"

"I was gonna ask you that," Tim retorts, hearing the words before he knows exactly what he's going to say. "What are you thinking, jumping him like that? We can't do it this way! You said so yourself; we need to be careful. If we go around attacking people left and right, they'll catch us."

As he's talking, Alan's expression softens somewhat. He doesn't look convinced, not exactly, but he does look less angry.

"They're already on to you," Tim goes on, glancing out at the street, hinting at the police car from before. "You're pretty much leaving a trail of breadcrumbs, and they're following it, Alan. Keep it up and you'll be caught by daybreak."

This seems to land. The vet blinks, his blank eyes turning pensive. "You could be right," he concedes.

"I am right! And you know it. The cops, they're organized, Alan. We're just two guys on foot. It's a matter of hours before they'll track us down and surround us."

"But we're much stronger and faster than them," Alan says, taking a step forward. He looks up at Tim with an eager expression. Like a dog begging to be taken off his leash.

"Fast enough to dodge a bullet? Strong enough to break out of jail?" Tim shakes his head. "We need to play to our real strengths, Alan."

"And what are those?" the vet demands.

Tim lowers his voice even more and leans closer—despite the fact that Alan's face makes him want to retract. "We know how they think. We know their protocols. *That's* how we'll beat them."

Alan squints again—but this time it's clearly because he likes what he's hearing.

Even as Tim is still talking, his mind is racing to come up with a way to pacify Alan. During their brief scuffle, it had become clear to him just how strong Alan is. He broke free of Tim's bear-hold with little difficulty. He's at least as strong as Tim—which is definitely due to the fact that he's also more transformed, because just yesterday, the middle-aged veterinarian wouldn't have stood a chance against Tim in a wrestling match.

Now, however, he's much more likely to come out on top. So simply grabbing him is out of the picture. If Tim did that, Alan would probably escape to continue his infection-spree and never trust him again. Or worse, Alan might kill him. Those chompers certainly look sharp enough to bite open a jugular.

Tim realizes he's going to need wit and cunning if he's to subdue his friend. He will have to lure him in some sort of a trap.

"You're right," Alan says, nodding emphatically. "You're right, Tim. Thanks for stopping me." He reaches over and slaps Tim's shoulder. "So, how do we do it?"

Tim is about to answer, when they both hear the engine.

"The cops," Alan hisses. "Split up. Meet me in Mammoth Square. An hour from now."

"Wait, Alan—"

It's too late. Alan goes for the fence, and this time, he doesn't stop. Instead, he leaps clean over it and disappears from sight.

30

TIM

BARELY HAS ALAN BOLTED before the police car comes into view again, this time going the opposite way. And this time, it stops just out of sight. Tim can tell because the lights go out, and he hears the doors open.

Tim is just about to follow Alan over the fence, when a better idea occurs to him. He goes to the door the old guy came through. Stepping over the garbage bags, Tim turns the handle and finds it locked—as he suspected. The door looks fairly old, and he can definitely kick it in, but he doesn't want to make that much noise. The cops—he can hear them talking—are still right outside the alley. So, Tim simply grabs the handle with both hands, thinking to himself, *I can't do this. I'm strong, but I'm not **that** strong ...*

Turns out, he is.

Before even putting his full strength into it, the handle gives way with a low snap. It doesn't break off, but something does break inside it, because it turns loose, and the door swings open.

Tim slips inside, and finds himself in some kind of dimly lit, crammed back entryway smelling of mud and leather. There's a narrow stairway leading up and a door leading straight ahead. Listening for a heartbeat, he hears rushed footsteps on the other side of the door, and he crosses the room in three long paces, rips open the door, and intersects the old guy—still wearing the robe, but now also armed with a heavy skillet. He yelps and instinctively swing the frying pan at Tim's head.

Tim plucks the skillet from his hand as easy as if he'd been handing it over voluntarily.

The guy blinks in surprise and staggers back. Looking like he's about to howl out for help, Tim places a finger over his mouth and shushes him.

Obediently, the guy closes his mouth.

"I'm not here to hurt you," Tim says—which seems to remind him that Tim actually protected him in the alley just minutes ago.

"Where's ... where's the other guy?" he asks, glancing at the door.

"He's gone," Tim assures him.

A buzzing sound. Not in his head this time. It's the intercom.

"That's the police," the guy says, his eyes growing bigger. His lips are quivering. "I called them. I know you told me not to, but I did ..."

"That's fine," Tim says. "You can go talk to them in just a second. All I ask is that you deliver a message to them. How's your memory?"

The guy blinks, as though the question takes him by surprise. "Uhm ... fine, I guess."

Tim looks at him briefly, then decides, "No. It's too important. I need to make sure they get the details right. Find a piece of paper and a pen."

The guy needs another second to process what Tim just asked for. When he catches on, he turns around and shuffles back through the hallway. Tim follows him to a tiny kitchen.

Dirty dishes are piled high, along with dozens of empty beer bottles. The air is heavy with bacon grease and booze and coffee grounds.

"Uhm, here, take this," he says, pulling a Christmas card from the fridge door. "You can write on the back."

Tim shoves aside some of the plates and puts the card on the table.

"A pen, a pen," the guy says, patting his chest, then his hips, as though the robe had any pockets, and then he leaves the kitchen. Returning a moment later, he hands Tim a ballpoint pen.

Tim takes it and starts writing.

While entering the apartment and talking to the old resident, a plan has been forming at the back of his mind. It's amazing, really, how he's suddenly able to multitask like this. Anya always gave him a hard time for how he could barely carry on a conversation while pouring water in the coffee machine.

You would have been proud of me, honey.

The guy gives off a gasp that he only halfway manages to stifle with his hand.

Tim looks at him. "What?"

"Nothing," he says, shaking his head. "It's just ... your hands ..."

"Oh," Tim grunts, looking at his extra fingers—which are noticeably longer than last time he checked. "Yeah, I know. I was born that way."

The buzzer sounds again.

"Can I ... can I go answer?" the old guy asks—more nervous now.

"Yes, answer them," Tim says. "But don't let them in yet. Tell them it'll be a minute."

"Oh, okay. Sure." He scuttles down the hallway.

Tim hears him talking over the intercom as he finishes up the note. The guy tells them—just as Tim instructed—that he needs a minute before he can open the door.

When everything Tim needs the cops to know is jotted down on the Christmas card, he gives it a quick read-over.

Name is Tim Iversen.

Carrying a dangerous spore. Unknowingly infected Alan Andersen. He infected Clara and Johan Birk. Whoever they've been in contact with could be infected too. Alan claimed to have infected four people total. Possibly also his wife, Lis Andersen, and his maid. Track them all down and isolate them. Take no chances.

Alan is noncooperative and extremely hostile. I believe I can apprehend him. I will then turn myself over.

He decides to add after his name: "MSgt, ret." Why exactly he feels the need to let them know he's a veteran, he's not sure. They'll no doubt look him up anyway—probably did so already after he ghosted them at Lis's.

He's just about to leave, when he remembers something vital. He quickly adds one more line.

My dog is in my truck, parked outside Alan's house. Take good care of him.

Then, just as he leaves the card and pen on the table, he hears the sound of the front door opening, and two pairs of boots enter the hallway.

"You Gunnar?"

"Yes, I'm the one who called you! One of them is still here! In the kitchen!"

Tim goes to the window, opens it, and jumps out.

When the cops reach the open window and look out, Tim is already half a block away.

31

VERONICA

SHE DECIDES TO CHECK on Leo before she goes to bed.

The first positive sign is that the awful fruity smell has gone. The window is no longer open, and the temperature in the room is almost back to normal.

Leo is lying on his back, covered from his navel down by a blanket. His hands are folded on his chest, and if it wasn't for the fact that he's breathing deeply, he would have looked like a corpse ready for an open casket ceremony. It has finally stopped snowing outside, and a pale, grey moonlight is coming in through the drapes, bathing Leo's pale body in its glow.

Sylvia wasn't lying; he clearly is better. The rash is almost gone. It has completely left his face, and there are only a few stripes left on his arms and torso.

Thank God. He did kick it after all.

Veronica steps over to the bed. "Leo? Sweetie? You awake?"

His breath pauses for a heartbeat, as though he hears her, but he doesn't open his eyes or answer her question. Leo's expression is almost serene; a pleased smile resting on his lips. For some reason, that smile makes her a little uncomfortable.

He's just happy to not be in pain anymore.

She really wants to talk with him. Assure herself that he really is better. On the other hand, she doesn't want to disturb him. He's probably exhausted after having fought off the strange infection, and he needs the rest.

She's about to turn and leave, when she notices something moving on Leo's shoulder. At first glance, she takes it to be a spider, and is about to brush it away, when she looks a little closer. The thing moving is the mossy growth. But it's not going anywhere. Rather, it's disappearing in front of her very eyes. It looks like a time-lapse video of plants sprouting from the ground—only in reverse. The moss is retracting itself back into Leo's skin. Unlike what she saw on herself and the bird, the moss on Leo hasn't turned gray and dull. On the contrary, it looks even more shiny and vibrant now in the ghastly moonlight.

Still, it must be a good sign that it's leaving and that Leo no longer is in pain. At least Veronica does her best to convince herself of that.

Unbidden, the memory of Leo grinning at her pops into her mind. "*I'm not going to die. Not by a long stretch.*"

She looks at his face again, and she gets the weirdest feeling. Her brain tells her she's looking at Leo, the guy she's been dating for a few years and whom she knows pretty well by now. Simultaneously, however, it feels like the person on the bed is a complete stranger. Someone she never met before.

That's just silly. Stop freaking yourself out.

But she can't shake the feeling, and the more she stares at Leo's face, the more unfamiliar he looks. Have his features changed slightly? Is his jaw a bit longer? His mouth half an inch wider? His forehead taller? Or is it all just a play of shadows?

"Veronica?"

The question is softly spoken, yet it makes her jump.

She turns to see the silhouette of Molly peering in from the hallway.

"Is Uncle Leo awake?" the girl whispers.

"No, he's ... he's sleeping," Veronica murmurs, forcing her heart back down her throat.

"Can I come in and see him?"

"I think it's better we let him rest." Veronica manages to smile. She's not sure the girl can see it in the darkness. "Go to bed, Molly. I'll be with you in a jiff."

"Okay." She leaves quietly.

Veronica glances at Leo one last time. And she immediately wishes she hadn't. Because what she sees is all wrong. It's his hands, which are still folded. Leo has soft, stubby fingers with gnawed-down nails. Now, however, his fingers are long enough that the tips reach the wrist of his opposite hand. And his nails are visibly thicker and longer.

God. They look like the hands of Dracula.

Veronica tries hard to find a logical explanation. She's heard that certain diseases can alter the appearance of your hands—like severe arthritis—but certainly not in a matter of hours?

She can't stay in the room any longer. She rushes to the door. Stopping, a sudden impulse makes her take the key from the inside and instead put it in from the outside. As she closes the door, she gets the clear feeling she's just seen Leo for the last time.

And she's right.

32

TIM

HE HAS AN HOUR to figure out how to trick Alan into captivity.

Or rather, fifty-five minutes, because he's already spent the first five minutes in the old guy's apartment, writing the note to the cops. Now he can only hope they take it seriously.

Mammoth Square is on the other side of town—which is probably why Alan chose it. It will take them far away from where the cops are looking for him. Crossing town is a full two-hour walk, but of course for Alan and Tim, it needn't take more than ten minutes.

As Tim is running through the streets, he keeps the pace moderate. Whenever a late dog walker or car passes him by, he slows down to regular jogging speed. He doesn't want to draw any more attention than he has to; he's already pretty conspicuous, jogging with no jacket or shoes in the freezing cold night.

He feels his strength starting to falter somewhat, and he realizes he's ravenous. He needs to eat something if he's to stand any kind of chance taking Alan into custody, so he makes a turn and heads for the McDonalds on Østergade, which he knows is opened around the clock. He's often used the drive-thru on his way back from a late-night drinking spree. Buddy usually got a bag of nuggets, which he ate with great—

"What's happening to me?"

The words come out of nowhere—loud, clear, piercing. It's not Alan, but a woman. There's fear and confusion in her voice. Tim stops dead in his tracks and listens intently. Tries to tune into whatever channel his mind had been on to pick up the woman's thoughts.

Concentrating hard, he's able to hear more from her. What comes through is: "*Oh, God. They have no idea how to stop this!*"

But he can't hold on to the signal, and the words fade after a few seconds.

It's enough, though; he immediately knows what the woman is going through. And he knows that within a few hours, she'll be running around town just like Alan.

It wasn't Clara Birk. It was a voice Tim hasn't heard before. From what he heard, he assumes the woman is in the police's custody. Besides, Clara Birk isn't far enough advanced to be transforming already.

Or is she?

The truth is, Tim has no idea. Alan had surely turned a lot faster than Tim did. Maybe the vet was more susceptible? Or maybe the black stuff is getting better? Maybe it knows the blueprint now, recognizes human DNA and so doesn't need nearly as much time to transform a body.

The thought rings true. Tim has no way of proving it, other than what his gut is telling him. But suddenly, another realization comes to him. The reason why Buddy has survived, but isn't transformed.

The spore might be infecting everything it can get in touch with … but it's only interested in humans.

This also explains the hare, and why both it and Buddy had been resurrected. Buddy had survived a lethal injection, and the hare a broken neck. In both cases, the black stuff had still been very much alive and active in their systems at the time of death.

In his memory, Tim hears Alan's raspy voice: "*Huh, will you look at that? It's already healing up. It happened, like, twenty minutes ago.*"

Just like it healed Alan's stab wound with extraordinary speed, the spore had also regenerated the broken bones and torn spinal nerves in the hare, and repelled the poison from Buddy's system and restarted his heart. It had simply not allowed them to die. The spore had claimed their bodies, because it wanted to find out if they were viable hosts.

But once it realized neither the dog nor the hare was suitable for its purposes, it had simply left them again, leaving the black stuff to wither and drizzle off without initiating the transformation process. This is also why Alan hadn't left any trace of it in his bed—because it could use him, the moss had been integrated into his system.

Now that Tim sees it, it's obvious.

The only question remaining is, why is the transformation going so much slower in him?

"Something's missing ..."

He recalls the words that kept repeating in his mind all throughout the night

And it finally falls into place.

That last, missing piece of the puzzle. Or rather, the missing piece of his brain.

It couldn't take me over because of my condition. It also couldn't leave. It got caught halfway somehow.

Tim just stands there for several seconds, as the realization sinks in properly. The irony almost makes him burst out laughing.

For the first time in his life, he feels lucky to be a freak.

33

TIM

WHEN TIM REACHES MAMMOTH Square exactly twenty minutes later, he finds it all but empty. There are a few cars parked here and there—probably people living in the surrounding neighborhood—but most of the parking lot is empty.

Below ground is the real car park, and that's where Alan told him to meet, so Tim heads for the concrete stairs in the center of the square. Right next to the stairwell is the big bronze statue of a mammoth rearing its head, pointing its trunk at the sky. The statue is lit from below by two large, yellow projectors.

Tim finds the stairwell completely dark. On the wall are embedded lights every six feet or so, but all of them have been bashed in.

Pretty sure I know who did that, Tim thinks, pulling out his phone.

He doesn't know the number to the local police, so he simply dials 1-1-2. As he puts the phone to his ear, he notices the sound of the helicopter has stopped some minutes ago. He imagines soldiers are mobilizing somewhere in town right now.

A woman answers almost right away. "*Emergency dispatch center, how can we help*?"

"Yeah, uhm, my name's Tim Iversen. I'm calling from Hornsted. Please tell the police I'm at Mammoth Square, and that I have the guy they're looking for, Alan Andersen."

A brief pause. "*I'll need a bit more information—*"

"Just tell them. They'll know. Alan Andersen. Make sure they get here ASAP."

He ends the call and shuts off his phone. For now, he won't need it. And the cops will no doubt use it to trace him down if he keeps it on.

Then he starts down the stairs.

His eyes adjust to the dark almost instantly, and despite the fact that the entire basement is pitch-black—save for a faint glow from the city above coming down through the two diagonally placed entry points—he's able to make out everything down there just fine. Not that there's a lot to make out. Besides the concrete pillars, the ventilation pipes running below the ceiling, trash cans and a handful of cars, he sees nothing of interest.

But he *hears* something.

And that's when it finally strikes him: *I haven't heard Alan's thoughts since we separated.*

He doesn't know exactly what that means. Tim clearly hasn't lost the ability to pick up thoughts, because he heard the woman just minutes ago. Maybe Alan figured out how to shut him out. Or maybe ... maybe Alan is no longer thinking. At least not in words Tim can understand.

That last explanation, while leaving him with an empty feeling, seems plausible. And what Tim is about to witness confirms his suspicion.

The sound is coming from the northeast corner of the parking garage—which is farthest from both exits. Straining his vision as he walks across the concrete floor, Tim sees a figure over there. He has his back turned, but Tim recognizes what is left of the checkered pajamas pants. The shirt is mostly gone. Alan's skin, which is visible in multiple places, has turned dark-gray, even black in places, and it looks hard and leatherlike. Almost like a lizard's.

If Tim didn't know any better, he would have thought Alan was puking. He's hunched over, head ducked, leaning against the wall with one hand, and the noises he makes are wet and guttural. Tim also hears things drip to the floor, and something that can only be described as scrunching. Almost like someone chewing messily, except punctured by the occasional, sharp snap, like a branch breaking.

Alan isn't puking. The stuff on the floor isn't coming out of him. It's going in.

What gives it away is the thing on the floor.

It isn't really a person anymore.

Save for a pair of shoes and a severed hand still wearing a wedding ring, not much gives away the fact that the bloody pile had been a middle-aged man.

As Tim watches in horror, striding still closer, Alan reaches down to grab a row of ribs with flesh still clinging to them. He uses his foot to stomp down on the spine, stopping the entire carcass from lifting from the floor. As he tugs harder, most of the ribs come free with a juicy sound very similar to when you break a thigh off a roast turkey. Then, with the gusto of a kid eating barbecue ribs, Alan digs in, producing growls and groans of pleasure.

At this point, Tim hesitates and almost turns around. Not so much because he fears for his life—but mostly because what he sees makes him doubt he can still communicate with his friend, much less reason with him.

Tim glances down at his own hands, and sees that the second pair of thumbs hasn't grown since the last time he checked.

I'm no longer transforming.

A surge of relief. He's not exactly thrilled walking around in this half-alien body, but he still much prefers it to what Alan has become. If Tim turns out to be permanently stuck at this stage of the process, he'll still consider himself blessed.

Looking back over at his friend chowing down the human remains, he can't help but feel a deep stab of sympathy.

I'm really sorry about this, Alan. I should have never called you.

He's about to step forward, when Alan senses him and spins around.

It's all Tim can do not to gasp.

34

VERONICA

THAT NIGHT, VERONICA HAS a terrible nightmare.

She dreams of black moss growing out her eyes and her mouth, suffocating her, filling her skull and making her unable to move or speak or think.

She also dreams of werewolves. Huge, manlike beasts who roam the snowy darkness outside of the cabin. And at some point, she even hears one of them howling. The sound is so full of pain, so piercing, that it wakes her up. Lifting her head from her pillow, she sees Molly staring at her from the other bed. The girl's eyes are wide and terrified.

"Did you hear that?" she breathes. She points at the window with her eyes, then looks back at Veronica. "There was a scream."

Veronica's mind is still shrouded in the images from the nightmare, and she can't discern whether she's really awake or not.

"I think it was just the wind," she hears herself say.

"No, the wind is gone," Molly insists. "Listen."

Veronica listens, and she realizes the roaring swoosh she's hearing is actually her own pulse thrumming behind her eardrums. Molly's right; the wind has died down completely. The night is absolutely quiet. The glowing digits on the alarm clock read 4:21.

And then comes another scream. Not as loud, and with less force behind it. It sounds less like someone in pain and more like someone dying.

Molly gasps and hugs her blanket tighter. "See? I told you …"

"It was an animal," Veronica says, trying to sound like she's not affected. "A deer or something. They can scream pretty loudly when they want to."

"I think it sounded more like a person," Molly insists.

"No, it was a deer. Don't worry about it, sweetie. Try and go back to sleep."

Veronica lies back down, feeling her heart pound in her chest. She's confused and exhausted, and she's almost drifted off again, when Molly says, "I can't sleep, Veronica. I really need to pee."

Veronica forces her eyes open again. "Okay, well … go pee then."

Molly—sitting up in her bed now—glances across the room. "I don't … I don't dare go out there alone."

Veronica sighs. "Fine, I'll go with you."

"I'm really sorry, it's just that …"

"It's fine, really. Come on."

Veronica pulls the duvet off and gets out of bed. Her limbs feel like someone poured sand into them. Molly grabs her hand, and Veronica leads her to the door. Opening it, she shivers as a cold draft meets her. Clearly, the fire in the fireplace is no longer going.

Passing her in-laws' bedroom, she can hear Flemming snoring in there. She opens the door to the bathroom, reaches in and turns on the light. "There," she says, squinting at Molly. "You want me to wait out here?"

"Yes, please," the girl says, slipping into the bathroom. She gently closes the door.

Veronica leans against the wall and yawns.

Another cold breeze snakes around her bare legs, giving her goose bumps.

Is there a window open somewhere?

She walks down the hallway and stops by Leo's door. She can immediately tell the cold is coming from the crack under his door. She's about to open it, when she remembers that she locked it and brought the key to her room. Instead, she leans closer and listens. No sounds.

"Leo?" she whispers. "Are you awake?"

No answer.

She checks that the door really is locked. It is. Meaning that no one else has been in the room since Veronica.

Leo must have opened the window himself. Did his fever come back?

She doesn't think so. And she doesn't get to ponder it any further, because she hears the toilet flush, and she goes back to the bathroom door. Molly comes out, and they go back to bed.

Just as Veronica lies her head down on her pillow, Molly asks, "Can I sleep with you?"

Surprised, Veronica looks at the girl sitting at the edge of her own bed. "You mean you wanna sleep in my bed?"

"Uh-huh. I'm sorry, I know it's silly. It's just ..." She glances at the window. "That scream. I'm still a little scared."

"Sure, why not?" Veronica says, scooching closer to the wall. "I guess we can both fit in here."

Molly brings her duvet and climb in next to Veronica. They lie close but not touching. The girl sighs deeply, and within a minute, Veronica can tell she's sleeping. Watching the back of Molly's head, Veronica can't help but smile. Despite herself, she feels less anxious too, sharing the bed with someone.

Just as she drifts off, she hears something.

It's a series of rhythmical, plaintive squeaks. It grows louder, pauses for a few seconds, then resumes and fades away.

Veronica hoists herself up onto her elbow. Once again, she can't tell if it was something from her dream or something real.

But she could have sworn she heard footsteps in the snow just outside the window.

35

TIM

ALAN—OR WHAT USED TO be Alan—is a gruesome sight.

His skull is completely hairless, and the shape of it is all wrong. His face looks almost like it has shrunk, his features squeezed together in the center. His eyes bear very little resemblance to the guy Tim used to know. For one thing, the pupils are gone, and so are the irises, leaving the eyes blank and ghostlike.

In a flash, Tim sees those green faces again. The ones he saw on the night that he died. They had shiny orange eyes. He was halfway expecting Alan to look like that. But he doesn't. Not at all. Apparently, those strange faces were just some random images Tim's dying mind conjured up.

Alan's nose is flat and long, his cheekbones very wide, which gives him a reptilelike look. His mouth is halfway open, revealing that his jaw has grown along with his face, and now looks wide enough to swallow a soccer ball if he opened wide. Between the dangling threads of skin and flesh, Tim can make out razor-sharp, ragged teeth.

All in all, there's very little left of his friend in that gruesome face.

And yet ...

Yet he recognizes Alan.

The creature in front of him doesn't look completely foreign. It looks exactly like what it is: something that has taken over Alan's system and transformed him in to something else. But the original blueprint is still there. Alan's features haven't been erased; they have simply been merged. Either because the transformation isn't completed or because the end goal of the nasty process was never to eradicate Alan. Rather, the spore—that is, whatever intelligence operated in its alien DNA—seems to have built upon what was already there.

As Alan shifts his weight and takes a step towards Tim, this becomes even more evident. As strange and un-human-like his movements are, Tim detects an echo of how Alan used to walk in them. And as Alan starts toward him, the one thing that makes him stand his ground is the fact that he recognizes Alan's way of walking in those alien limbs.

"Alan," he says. "Good to see you, pal."

It takes all the guts Tim can muster to make the words sound conversational; as though he had simply happened upon his old friend in the grocery store. And it seems like he pulls it off. Because Alan stops and cocks his head.

For a long moment, he just looks at Tim. His six-fingered hands open and close—Tim notices thick, curved nails at the end of them. Fresh blood still drips from his mouth.

He's about to ask Alan if he recognizes him, when Alan speaks suddenly.

"Tim?"

The word sounds like it comes from very far away. Like something he had to pull from the recesses of his memory bank. His voice is distorted. Rattling and whiny at the same time. It's like if a crocodile had learned to speak.

"Yeah, it's me," Tim says casually, helping Alan's memory along. "Sorry it took me a little longer."

"Thought you gone." Alan blinks—he still has eyelids, but they come up from below now. "Trouble?"

"Nah, I was careful. Just had to stop and eat. I see you got the same idea." He nods at the carcass.

Alan doesn't take his eyes off of him like Tim had hoped. Instead, he smiles. At least that's what it looks like. One side of his mouth pulls up way too far, almost reaching his eye.

Jesus Christ. That kisser's big enough to swallow me whole.

It isn't—but it could definitely span across Tim's arm, or even his leg, and he dreads the thought of how it would feel to have all those teeth sink into his flesh.

"So much food," Alan growls. "Everywhere."

"Yeah, I know," Tim agrees. "Too bad we can't eat 'em all, or there'd be no one left to join the party."

As though this reminds him of something, Alan gives Tim a once-over. "You not change?"

Tim shrugs. "Guess I'm a late bloomer."

He's very aware of his back pocket. Approaching the parking basement, he checked it several times. Now, he really wants to do so again, but he can't. He just has to trust the thing hasn't slipped out while he walked. If it did, he's done for. Plain as that. Being this close to Alan, Tim no longer holds any illusions he can take him down in a fight. Not without some kind of weapon.

Can't use it while we're staring each other down like this. Need to get him to lower his guard. Turn his side, or at least look away for a second.

Tim feels pretty sure he can close the distance between them fast enough to surprise Alan. All he needs is one little opening.

"Look, we need to make a plan," he says, hoping to shift the focus away from himself.

Alan wipes his mouth on what's left of his sleeve, and Tim can swear that for a split second, his hand goes to his chest where his packet of smokes used to sit, as though he feels the urge for an after-lunch cigarette. It's not a conscious gesture, more like a habit. But it's definitely there.

"Yes," Alan snarls. "Plan." He blinks and looks at Tim like he expects him to go on.

Tim has no idea what's going to come out of his mouth before he starts talking. "They taught us in the military that strategy flows from objective. So, what's the objective, Alan?"

Alan lowers his chin slightly as he whispers a single word. "Spread."

"Yeah. Spread it to as many as we can. But for what?"

Alan tilts his head again in that questioning way.

"Why are we doing it?" Tim asks. "What's the endgame?"

Alan stares at him for the longest time. Tim isn't sure if he's thinking or trying to read his mind. Then, finally, Alan says, "Annihilation."

Tim nods, ignoring the shiver that runs down his back. "Every human being on the planet. Right?"

"Right."

"But if we do that, what will be left for us to eat?"

The question clearly confounds him. For the first time, his eyes leave Tim briefly and go to the bloody mess by his feet.

Tim takes the chance to step a little closer. He makes sure to do so as casually as he can. Pretending like he wants to make sure no one is listening, he lowers his voice. "We can't very well eat each other, can we? And I don't know about you, but I'm not going back to turkey sandwiches. I want fresh meat." He can tell he has Alan's full attention now. Evidently, food is a subject he cares about, and Tim feels the moment coming. "So I say we make sure to let some of them live. Consider it livestock. The ones that can't run away or fight back. The fatties. The juicy ones."

Alan has literally started drooling now, and he licks his mouth with a thin, ash-colored tongue to keep it from dripping. "Yes," he hisses. "Juicy."

"Exactly," Tim tells him, taking one more step forward. "The more meat, the better. We could even—" He abruptly stops talking and looks to both sides. He's aware of how risky it is, being this close to Alan and taking his eyes off of him. Alan could basically lean forward, take a swing and cut open his throat with his claws. But he doesn't. He stares at Tim intently.

"What?" he whispers.

Tim places a finger over his lips—an old magician's trick: casually show your hand empty just before you load it with something. There was a guy in Tim's unit—he forgot his name, but they called him Copperfield—who used to entertain them with party tricks, and Tim learned a few techniques from him, which he in turn used to make Helena laugh when she was little. Pulling coins from her ears, making cards spill out his mouth, stuff like that.

"Did you hear that?" he asks Alan, lowering his hand as he turns sideways just enough to hide the fact that his hand keeps going all the way to his back pocket.

Alan just shakes his head, his blank eyes boring into Tim's. His nostrils are flaring, and Tim can see his pulse drumming away at his temples, making the black skin bounce up and down.

"I think they're coming," Tim goes on. "But how in the world did they ...? Wait, is that a camera?"

He fixes his eyes at a point above Alan's head. There's nothing there, except the naked concrete wall. But Alan buys the bluff.

He whips his head around.

As he does, Tim pulls out the syringe, leans forward and plunges it into Alan's neck.

36

TIM

ALAN GIVES A ROAR and reflexively lashes out at Tim even before having turned his head back around.

Tim is sort of ready for it. At least he knew he had to get the hell away from Alan the second he emptied the syringe into his neck. Letting go of it, he reels back while at the same time blocking the incoming punch.

He should've just ducked. But he's a tall guy. Ducking was never a good defense for him.

He successfully shields the blow, but Alan's claws tear right through his sleeve, his skin, and into the flesh on his lower arm. He feels the tendons snap as those razor-like nails slice through them. Had it not been for the bone, they would've likely severed his entire arm right below the elbow. Instead, they only leave a huge, gaping gash, from where the blood immediately starts pouring.

Tim staggers backwards, clutching the wound. Alan spins around to glare at him, confusion and rage taking over his face. The syringe is still protruding from his neck. Whether he doesn't feel it or he doesn't care, Tim can't tell. Either way, his attention is completely fixed on Tim and nothing else.

Alan bends his knees, spreads out his arms, and for a moment it looks like he's backing off. Then Tim realizes he's coiling up before he takes off in a leap, coming right at Tim. Tim throws himself to the side, narrowly avoiding another deadly slash from Alan's claws as they whizz by within a few inches from his head.

He rolls around on the concrete, feeling a stab of pain from his wounded arm, but he ignores it and jumps back up. The second he turns around, Alan comes charging at him again. Tim has nothing to defend himself with. He didn't bring anything, because he was sure Alan would have made him out right away and either killed him or fled. Just bringing the syringe had felt like a huge risk, but one he had to take. He hadn't considered the fact that the tranquilizer wouldn't work.

Alan swings at Tim wildly several times, and Tim has no other choice but to dodge and back up. He isn't going to risk getting cut open further by blocking any more of Alan's haymakers, so he tries to simply flee.

Except he can't. Alan is faster. He effectively has Tim cornered, and he moves to the side every time Tim tries to make a run for it, cutting him off. Tim steps in the blood from the carcass and slips, knocking his back against the concrete wall.

Alan seizes the chance and launches into an all-out assault.

Tim's one last option is to fight.

He hasn't used his combat skills for almost two decades, save for one occasion in a bar when a drunk guy picked a fight with him and Tim twisted his arm around until he yielded—but other than that, Tim hasn't fought anybody. When you're six feet four, most people are wise enough to steer clear.

Yet it turns out his hand-to-hand fighting abilities are still there. In fact, combined with his newfound superhuman speed, they feel fresher and more potent than ever.

He blocks Alan's next three blows, while carefully avoiding the claws. He ducks, swerves, and then lands an uppercut hard enough to make Alan stagger backwards.

That's the moment they both realize Tim actually stands a chance. Judging by Alan's momentarily rattled expression, he's as surprised by this as Tim. He barely has time to take it in, however, before Alan comes at him again

Tim is ready. Using his own speed against him, he doesn't try to jump out of the way, as Alan clearly expected. Instead, he turns sideways, grabs him around the waist and throws him over his hip, slamming him into the wall.

Alan drops to the floor with a grunt of pain and surprise. As he quickly gets back up to his feet, Tim takes a couple of steps back. They have switched places now, and Tim is no longer cornered. He could bolt. But something keeps him back. Maybe it's stupid pride. Maybe he wants to prove to himself he can beat Alan's ass. Either way, Alan doesn't hesitate. He gives off a roar loud enough to make Tim's ears ring, and then he flies at him yet again.

Now that Tim isn't on the defense, he's winning. It's not so much that he has overestimated Alan's speed and strength—rather, he's underestimated his own.

He dodges, slips or blocks everything Alan throws at him. And he moves constantly and counters it all with well-placed kicks and punches. Wanting to avoid getting his hands close to Alan's mouth, Tim focuses on the body instead. Every time he lands an inside kick to his knee, Alan groans and wobbles, and every time Tim's fist or knee digs into his gut, he croaks and gasps for breath.

Soon, he starts panting and doubling over, protecting his organs. His will to fight falters too, and that's when Tim starts aiming higher. Using his shins and elbows, he connects three or four times with Alan's skull, and suddenly, he collapses.

Tim is so focused on fighting, it takes him a couple of seconds to realize Alan is down.

Curled up into a fetal position, he coughs and rasps. Blood seeps from his mouth, and a few teeth clatter out onto the floor. It looks like he slipped into unconsciousness, or at least a state of complete exhaustion, and it's clear he isn't getting back up.

Holy hell ... I beat him ...

While Tim would love to take full credit for bringing Alan down, he can't. The tranquilizer from Alan's own clinic has clearly kicked in after all and subdued him. Tim had no idea how much of the drug would be needed to pacify a person, much less an alien-hybrid, so he just filled the syringe completely. Turns out, it was about the right dose. He simply hadn't factored in the delay before the stuff would work.

He looks at his wounded arm. It's bleeding, but not as badly as he feared. He can move his thumb, but not the other fingers. Ripping off his already torn sleeve, he wraps it around his arm and tightens it. He will have to deal properly with it later.

Because of the intensity of the fight, it's only now Tim notices the engines idling above. They've wisely come with no sirens, and as he turns around, he sees cops coming down both exits.

37

TIM

TIM WAS HOPING TO see a large group of special units in full riot gear with automatic weapons and protective masks.

But the cops approaching through the parking basement are clearly just locals. And there are only six of them. He recognizes the silver-haired woman and her younger male colleague. All aiming their guns at him, the cops spread out into a fan shape, blocking his exit routes.

Raising his hands, Tim intends to send a signal of surrender. But he's not sure the sight of his extra thumbs does anything but cause more tension in the cops. Several of them start shouting for him to get on the ground.

"Okay, all right," he tells them, getting to his knees. "Take it easy now. It's all right."

He's instructed to get all the way down and to interlace his fingers behind the back of his head.

"Okay, but before I do that, let me just—"

"Get down! Get down right now!"

"I just need you to understa—"

"Get on the ground! Face down!"

"You can't—"

"This is your last warning! Get down, or we will be forced to open fire!"

Tim isn't sure what he'd expected from law enforcement, but he thought they'd at least let him get a word in. That they might even get to work together to bring in those infected folks still at large. But evidently, these guys are here only to apprehend and arrest him along with Alan.

They are still shouting at him, and the closest of them has a pair of handcuffs.

Normally, Tim considers himself a pretty laid-back guy. He rarely gets angry or loses his cool. He simply doesn't see the point. Anya and he hardly ever argued, and he doesn't often rise to the challenge when his boss gives him a hard time.

But when the cops keep screaming at him, he loses his patience.

Sucking in air, he roars out, "***Listen to me***!"

It's the first time since his transformation started that he really utilizes the full scope of his newer, bigger lungs and deeper voice. The effect is pretty impressive. It feels kinda like he's shouting into a microphone connected to a couple of very big speakers, and the acoustics in the basement only amplify it.

The cops certainly feel it too, because they all jolt, and some of them even take a few steps back.

"I will cooperate fully," Tim goes on, lowering his voice to regular volume. "But you need to listen. First off, none of you are coming near me or Alan without proper protection. I'm talking hazmat suits, masks, the whole shebang. This thing is most definitely transferred via touch, and I suspect it might also be airborne. You two are already too close."

He gestures at the pair of cops who'd moved within twenty feet of him. They exchange a quick look, then withdraw.

"Second," Tim continues. "Those handcuffs? They're not gonna do it, fellas. Believe me, he's gonna pop 'em like a rubber band." He's not completely sure whether that's true or not; whether Alan really can break the handcuffs—especially not in his drugged-induced semi-coma—but he needs to make sure they get the point. "Send for something stronger. Chains, a cage, whatever you've got. And get the basement sealed off if it isn't already." Alan gives off a groan, and Tim looks back. "Better get a move on. I think he's waking up."

The woman—apparently the lead officer—calls out to the others to stand firm. Then she steps back a little and says something into a radio. She probably thinks Tim doesn't hear it, but of course he does. The cop relays what Tim just told them, and she asks for respiratory equipment and even calls in a sweat box, but it's still obvious from her voice that she doesn't fully trust much of what Tim said.

Then the cop steps forward and addresses Tim. "Iversen."

"Yeah, that's me. At least some of me." That last part he mutters under his breath.

"We can talk briefly, but you need to understand that if the person behind you gets up, I have no choice but to open fire."

"I understand," Tim tells him, glancing back at Alan, who is still out.

"Ulla Lundbeck," the cop goes on. "Police Inspector."

"Glad to see you again," Tim tells her with no sarcasm. "Though I was hoping to see the military or the SIU."

"You called in to have us come pick up Alan Andersen," Lundbeck continues, ignoring his remark. "Is that correct?"

"Sure is. That's him right there. Not the poor prick he was eating; I don't know who that was."

The cops don't outright say anything at this, but some of them groan, and others shift restlessly. They've already spotted the bloody, bony mess behind Tim, but apparently it's only now they realize it's human remains.

"Andersen killed him?" Lundbeck asks. To her credit, her voice doesn't falter.

"Yeah. He was long dead when I arrived."

There's a moment in which none of them speak. Tim feels them all eyeing him closely, and it dawns on him there's no way for him to prove he hadn't been chomping away at the tartar buffet behind him alongside Alan. Or at the very least he could have had something to do with the murder.

"Look," he says. "I know I'm freaking you guys out. But I'm not like Alan. He's … fully transformed. Evidently, he considers humans nothing more than snacks now. I hate to sell him out like this, because he was my friend, but it's true. And it's also true that I'm not on his side. If I was, why would I risk my life pacifying him and calling you guys? Ever since I started finding out about what's happening, I've been trying to stop it, and—"

"What the hell are you?"

It's the younger cop that speaks. It sounds like he forgot himself and just blurted out the question.

"Hansen," Lundbeck snaps at him. "Keep your damn mouth shut."

Hansen glances at his senior. "But he lied to us, Chief. He's one of them."

Lundbeck points a finger at him. "One more word out of you, and you're gone."

Hansen looks back at Tim, breathing audibly through his mouth, but he says nothing.

At that moment, another voice comes into Tim's head. It's not the woman; it's much deeper. A man, already close to fully transformed by the sound of it. It's not so much his raspy voice as what he says that convinces Tim of this.

"God Almighty ... I've never felt so ***powerful!****"*

His tone is one of awe, of lust and exhilaration. It gives Tim the chills. Whoever this guy is, unlike the woman, he's way past the point of trepidation. He's embracing his new self with gusto.

Lundbeck asks Tim something, and he snaps out of it.

"Huh?"

"I said, do you know what this is? The infection?"

"I have no idea," Tim says bluntly. "I saw some strange rock drop from the sky, and I was stupid enough to go near it. That's where it came from."

Another moment of silence and heavy breathing.

"But I know what it's doing," Tim goes on. "It's turning people into predators. And this thing, whatever it is ... it's clever. It's fast as hell. And I'm pretty sure it's learning." He looks right into Lundbeck's pale eyes. "You need to take this very seriously."

"Trust me, we're on it. We already apprehended—"

"I know about Clara Birk, but there are at least two more out there. Another woman and a man."

Lundbeck frowns at this. "Did you infect them?"

"No, I only infected Alan. Or rather, my dog did. Is he safe? I told you to take care of him."

Lundbeck apparently doesn't hear the question. "So Alan infected all the others?"

"Yeah. And like I said, two of them are still at large. I can help you find them."

"Do you know where they are?"

"No, but I can track them down."

Lundbeck shrugs. "How?"

"Well, you're not gonna believe this," Tim says. "But I can hear their thoughts."

38

TIM

LUNDBECK TELLS TIM TO stay exactly where he is, reminding him—quite unnecessarily—that half a dozen guns are aimed at him.

Tim tells her he isn't going anywhere, as long as she promises to get Alan restrained ASAP.

The cop nods, then steps back and leaves the basement with brisk paces.

Tim can hear more engines idling out there now. Boots running, hushed voices. Sounds like they called in every cop in town. He can also hear them pulling shut metal grids to secure both exits. There are several radio and phone signals going on. Tim picks up fragments, but he willfully shuts them out, because it's like listening in on a radio where someone is turning the dial back and forth ceaselessly.

Instead, he listens for more voices from the infected. He's hoping to catch something that will allow him to guess where they were, so he can go and find them. But none of them come through right now.

Tim glances back at Alan. He's starting to stir a bit and looks like he could be coming out of his coma soon. Tim was hoping he would stay out for at least twenty minutes. But he also knows Alan's system immediately began to counteract the effect of the drug, expel it from his system and bring him back to consciousness as soon as possible.

Tim discreetly checks on his arm. The wound seems to have closed up. At least he can tell it isn't bleeding anymore. He still can't move most of his fingers, and his palm is prickling as though it's sleeping. Alan clearly cut through everything in there. Tim can only hope that—

Suddenly, he picks up a certain signal. It seems to come through quite on its own. As though his subconscious knows it's important. He recognized one of the voices right away: Lundbeck, on the phone with an older guy.

"Think we can trust him?"

"Honestly, Balle, I don't know. Hard to get a read on him."

"But willing to help us?"

"Says so, yeah."

"Could just be that we've got him pinned down."

"What I was thinking."

"*Damnit! Whole thing's making me queasy.*" A short pause. Tim fears he has lost the signal. Then, Balle goes on: "*The Xylazine there yet?*"

"Just arrived."

"Sedate him and bring him in. If he's genuinely willing to help us, he can do so from isolation."

Tim's pulse is rising. He stands absolutely still, betraying nothing to the cops in front of him. He's never heard the voice of the older cop, but he recognized the name. Johannes Balle, the regional director of police.

Lundbeck goes on: "*Sure he'll still cooperate if we bring him in like that?*"

"A risk I'm willing to take."

"I don't know, Balle. That guy he took down, Andersen ... you should see him. Looks like something out of a nightmare."

"If Iversen could deal with him single-handedly, so can we."

"But he claims to be able to track them down. Says he can—"

"This isn't a damn Batman movie, Lundbeck. Letting some mutant vigilante run wild, that's just not happening."

"Might be willing to work within some boundaries."

"So you'll keep him on a leash, will you? How long till he transforms completely and starts attacking you and the men? You told me what Andersen did to Person Unknown. I'm not running that risk, Lundbeck. Pacify them both. I need you by the park. We just had another report. Get moving."

The signal is cut.

Tim blinks and comes to. The cops are still eyeing him closely. There is no way he can make for a clean getaway. As fast as Tim is, if he takes one step, they'll open fire, and at least one of them will get a shot in.

Need to wait for an opening.

It dawns on him then just how naïve he's been in regards to the cops. Of course they wouldn't trust him. How could they? He's not even human any longer. Tim is furious with himself for making so blatant a mistake.

Lundbeck returns a minute later, now wearing a mask with an air filter. She strides to the front of the group of cops. Stopping, she places both hands on her hips, probably to seem nonthreatening. Her weapon is in the holster, and as far as Tim can tell, she isn't carrying a tranquilizer gun.

She's not the one who'll be doing the shooting, Tim thinks, seeing a group of four cops enter via the opposite entrance, all of them wearing protective masks.

"Here's what's going to happen," Lundbeck says, speaking loudly, clearly wanting to draw Tim's attention to her.

And Tim does listen to her, but he keeps a firm eye on the four soldiers as well. They move quickly, and two of them have automatic rifles. They are also carrying a heavy-looking cage between them. The other two have rifles too, but funny looking ones. It's most definitely dart guns.

"We're going to play this safe," Lundbeck tells him. "First, we'll bring Andersen into isolation. We'll take no chances."

Perfect cover, Tim thinks to himself, looking at Lundbeck. *They pretend it's safety measures. That the tranq is meant for Alan if he wakes up.*

Out loud, Tim asks: "Then what?"

"Then we'll track down the others. We're already closing in on one of them."

"And if more pop up?"

Lundbeck draws a breath through the mask. "We could use your help on that. If you could tell us what you know, that would be a big help. You'd be our informant, if you like."

"Sure," Tim says calmly, nodding towards the soldiers who put down the cage off to the side. "But will I be doing it from inside that?"

Lundbeck doesn't flinch. "Of course not. But the best place for you to be right now is at our command center. You'll be temporarily instated as ..."

This is the point where Tim stops listening. Still staring right at Lundbeck, he's only aware of his periphery. On each side, things are happening. On his left, they open the cage. The dart gun operators have discreetly spread out through the group of cops. One of them has moved all the way over to Tim's right. This is where Hansen is.

"... so we'll bring you there now." Lundbeck is still talking. Tim is still pretending to listen.

As the dart gun operator on the far right passes by Hansen, the cop makes his second mistake that night—one he'll live to regret.

Obviously sensing something is going down, he glances sideways at the dart gun operator.

It's the moment Tim was waiting for. A brief lapse in attention.

He explodes off his feet and closes the distance to Hansen in less than a second.

Three of the soldiers fire, but all of them miss. Tim feels the projectiles zipping by, hears them burrow into the wall.

Just before he reaches Hansen, the cop turns his head to look at him. An expression of shock comes over his eyes, and he fires his gun out of reflex. But Tim is already within reach, and as Hansen presses the trigger, Tim slaps the gun sideways. Then he grabs him, swings him around and wraps his arms around him, catching him in a perfect chokehold.

He then backs away, using Hansen as a shield.

The cops shout and almost break formation.

"Hold, hold!" Lundbeck cries, waving both arms. "No one shoots!"

No one does. But they all look like they really want to.

"Tim," Lundbeck says, holding up her hands, palms facing down. "Please, don't hurt him!"

Hansen is wriggling to get free. But Tim is way stronger, and he only needs one arm to keep the chokehold, so he uses the other to pin Hansen's arms to his body. Then he lifts him clean off the ground. Hansen croaks and squirms, but remains helplessly trapped.

"Please!" Lundbeck cries, ripping off the mask. "Let him go, Tim! Or I'll have no choice but to have them shoot you!"

Tim knows she won't do that. Not as long as Hansen is alive. Because it would no doubt mean killing him, too. And no matter the threat, the police would never execute one of their own.

"I can break your neck with very little trouble," Tim says in Hansen's ear. "You know that, right? You feel it. Tell them."

Tim releases his grip just enough for Hansen to suck in a mouthful of air. "Help me! He'll break my ne—"

"No, that's not what I said," Tim interrupts him, squeezing his windpipe shut again. "I said, *I can*. But I won't. Not if your comrades just step back a couple yards. That's all I'm asking." Raising his voice slightly, Tim says to the cops, "Do it now, and we'll all get out of this basement alive."

The cops hesitate, keeping their guns aimed at him.

"There's no way I'm giving that order, Tim," Lundbeck says, sounding almost overbearing. "You know that. Please, put yourself in my shoes. You understand you're not walking out of here."

"You're right, I'm not," Tim says, edging sideways. He only needs a few more steps now. He's pretty sure none of them have guessed his plan. They move along with him, though without coming any closer. But they clearly want to cut him off from the entrance, which they seem to think is what he's going for.

"We have a dozen men at each exit," Lundbeck says. "As fast as you are, Tim, you're not getting through."

She's right. Even as they're speaking, the folks outside have caught on to what's happening. Tim can hear them clamber to reinforce the gate.

As far as the cops are concerned, Tim is trapped in a giant concrete tomb with only two ways out, and they have both exits securely covered.

There is a third way, though. One they don't consider an option because, well ... they are still only humans.

Taking a few more steps sideways, Tim reaches the spot he's going for.

"That's it, Tim," Lundbeck says, raising her voice. "No more leeway. If you take one more step, I'm having them shoot you."

She looks and sounds like she really means it. Tim figures she's referring to the dart gun operators. Accidentally shooting Hansen with one of the tranqs wouldn't be as bad as killing him.

"Get Alan into that cage," Tim tells her. "He's waking up."

And he really is. No one is looking at Alan right now, and one of his arms has started twitching.

"Get him in the cage!" Lundbeck cries. "And give him more sedative!"

The attention shifts briefly from Tim. Again he uses the opportunity.

Releasing Hansen, he pushes him hard forward. At the same time, he crouches down, very much like he saw Alan do, and then he leaps straight up into the air.

The air duct is suspended a full fifteen feet overhead, but Tim reaches it with enough force to burst through the grid with his head and arms. He latches on and pulls himself up. Not wasting any time, he crawls immediately to the left. Ten yards from where he is, the duct ends in another grid, which is where it exits the basement. He hears the cops shouting below, shots are ringing out, bullets pierce the metal behind him.

Tim moves forward as fast as the enclosed space allows him to, and as he reached the second grid, he throws himself into it shoulder first. It doesn't give way on the first try, because some kind of machinery is behind it, so Tim gives another hard thrust, and he goes through, but gets caught halfway. He finds himself with his torso sticking out of a huge AC box at the far corner of Mammoth Square, staring at the street in front of him, with the busted remains of the AC box scattered around him. His legs are still inside the duct, and as he pulls them along, he feels a sharp pain in his shin.

He grunts and rolls out onto the pavement. Getting to his feet, he glances back to see that Lundbeck didn't exaggerate; there probably are close to two dozen cops crowding the square, along with several vehicles, floodlights and barriers. Most of the activity is centered around the exits, however, and Tim is far away from them, meaning no one is close enough to notice him as he darts down the street as fast as his wounded leg allows him to.

He disappears into the nearest alleyway.

39

VERONICA

"MOLLY? ... *MOLLY*! ... Oh, God, she's gone too!"

Veronica is pulled from a deep, dreamless sleep by a shrill voice she recognizes as Alice's.

Opening her eyes, she sees the room dimly lit by a white daylight coming in from the window. Alice—who's pacing the room—has yanked the drapes aside.

"What's going on?" Veronica croaks, sitting up. Next to her, Molly stirs too.

"Leo and Molly are both gone!" Alice cries out, spinning around to stare at Veronica. "They're nowhere in the cabin, and—" She cuts herself off as she sees her daughter peering out from the blanket. "Molly! Oh, thank God! I thought you—what are you doing in Veronica's bed?"

Alice comes over, arms outstretched, intending to grab her daughter. At the last second, Veronica notices it.

"Wait ... wait, no, *stop*!" she shouts. "Don't touch her!"

Alice reluctantly hesitates and stares at Veronica. "Why?"

"Your hands," Veronica says, sitting up. "You got what Leo had."

Alice turns her hands over and stares at her palms, her eyes widening even further. "Oh, Christ!" she moans. "Not me, too ..."

Veronica can tell Alice still really wants to hug her daughter, but to her credit, she takes a step back instead. Looking closer at her, Veronica can also make out the black stuff around one of Alice's eyes.

Molly is waking up properly now, and she starts breathing fast, looking from her mom to Veronica. "What's ... what's happening? Are you sick, too, Mom?"

Alice just stands there with her hands in front of her chest as though holding two invisible cups, staring at them and shaking her head. "Oh, Jeez. I thought I was careful ..."

"What was that you said?" Veronica asks. "About Leo being gone? Alice?"

Her sister-in-law blinks and looks at her. "Huh?"

"Leo? Where is he?"

"He, uhm ... he left during the night."

"What? Why would he do that?"

"No idea."

"Well, did he say where he went? Did he at least leave a note?"

"No, nothing. We tried calling him, but he left his phone."

Veronica tries to get up, but Molly clamps onto her arm. "No, please don't go, Veronica!"

"Let go of her!" Alice cries out. "Don't touch her, Molly!"

For an awkward moment, Veronica thinks Alice is being jealous.

Then Alice adds, "You shouldn't even be that close to each other. She could be infected, too." She sends Veronica a distrustful look.

"It's okay. I already had it," Veronica blurts out.

Both Alice and Molly stare at her.

"You did?" Molly asks, nonplussed. "Then why aren't you sick?"

"I kicked it," Veronica shrugs, deciding that she might as well come clean. "See?" She shows her palms. "Nothing. The hands are one of the first places it appears, at least it did on me. And it grew around my eyes, too. But as you can see, it's gone now."

Alice leans closer to investigate Veronica's hands and face. Veronica lets her, confident she won't find any trace of the black stuff. Apparently satisfied, Alice instead touches her own eyelid. "Do I …?"

"Yeah," Veronica tells her. "Left one."

Alice touches the other eye, and, feeling the growth, she groans again, sounding like she's close to tears. "I've been feeling itchy ever since I woke up, but I thought … I thought it was just my mind playing tricks on me …"

"Oh, Mom," Molly says, and she actually does start crying.

"It's okay," Veronica assures them both. "I beat it, so you can beat it too, Alice. And if Leo really left the house, that must mean he's better, too."

Alice scoffs. "It's not what you think …"

Veronica frowns. "What do you mean? I thought you said he drove off?"

"No, I said he left. I didn't say how." Alice keeps running her finger over her eyelid as she breathes through her nose.

"Well," Veronica says, gently releasing Molly's grip and getting to her feet. "How did he leave, then?"

Alice shrugs. "He climbed out the window and just walked off. Didn't even bother to put on his clothes."

Veronica frowns, and glances at the window. It's caked with snow, and the flakes are still coming down. "But … it's freezing out there."

"I know," Alice whispers, her lower lip quivering. "And the nearest neighbor is, like, five miles away."

A moment of grim silence in the room.

"Do you ... do you think Uncle Leo ...?"

Before Veronica or Alice can answer, a much deeper voice says, "I'm sure he's fine."

Veronica turns to see Flemming standing in the doorway. She notices the eyeliner-like rims below his eyes right away. Even from across the room, she can tell he's farther advanced than Alice. It's running along the lines on his forehead too, and hanging from his earlobes like black diamonds earrings. It's also growing inside his moustache, making it appear darker than it actually is.

"Grandpa!" Molly exclaims. Her short-lived glee turns sour. "Oh ... you've got it, too."

"I do," he says grimly, staying where he is. "Only you and Grandma seem to have dodged it. Let's try and keep it that way, shall we?" He sends Alice a significant look, and to Veronica's surprise, she obediently slinks farther away from the bed. Veronica has never seen her sister-in-law take directions from anyone other than her mother, but apparently, the seriousness of the situation makes her compliant.

"Is Sylvia not infected?" Veronica asks—hoping the surprise isn't too evident in her tone.

"No, she slept in the spare bedroom, and I think that saved her," Flemming says. "She's still in there. You guys should stay in here, too. Isolate yourselves."

Did Sylvia kick it? Or is she hiding the fact that she's infected?

Veronica decides not to inquire further into her mother-in-law. Whatever reason she has for lying to her husband, Veronica doesn't really care right now.

"I don't need to be isolated," she tells Flemming. "I already had it, and I'm fine."

Flemming raises his eyebrows. "Really? When did you get it?"

"On the ferry over here," Veronica lies. "By the time we reached the cabin, it was gone again. I didn't get nearly as sick as Leo."

"That's encouraging," Flemming says, scratching his forehead. "Knowing that we might all be fine. What's less encouraging is that you brought it here and infected everyone." He says that last sentence in a very dark tone, glaring at Veronica.

She throws out her arms. "I had no idea what it was. By the time I even noticed it, Leo was already infected. But I thought, since it didn't make me sick or anything, that it was just a weird kinda rash or something. How was I supposed to know it was more serious?" As she hears herself talking, she sees the bird in her mind's eye, sees the glove overgrown with the mossy stuff.

I should've known. I should've stayed home. Should've even stayed away from Leo.

Flemming sighs and plucks at his ear. "Well, let's not play the blame game. Nothing useful will come from that."

"Did you call the doctor again?" Alice asks, rubbing her arms as though she's freezing despite how warm the bedroom is. "I mean, it's hardly snowing anymore, and the wind has settled. Can't they come over now?"

Flemming nods. "They'll send over a helicopter as soon as they can get some special equipment they need in order to land in the snow. The police are coming, too."

"The police?" Veronica asks.

"Yes. My son is missing, in case you forgot."

Veronica glances at the window again. It's still coming down, but less so now. "I'll go out and look for him," she says, getting up from the bed.

"What?" Alice exclaims. "Are you out of your mind? It's below zero out there. You'll get lost."

"I agree," Flemming says. "You'll never find him anyway. You'd be much more useful to us here in the cabin, especially if we're gonna fall as ill as Leo was."

"Have you at least tried calling the neighbors?" Veronica asks, pulling on her clothes. "He might have made it over there."

Flemming coughs into his fist. "I don't have their numbers. And I doubt very much he made it that far. He didn't even bother to bring his clothes."

Veronica pauses. "He left without his jacket?"

"Without his jacket, shoes, shirt or pants. As far as I can tell, all his clothes are still here. He wandered off in his boxers and his T-shirt."

"Jesus," Alice groans.

"Well, I'm still going out to have a look," Veronica says. "I'll bring my phone. I'll use the GPS. Make sure I can find my way back." She strides towards the door, but Flemming doesn't move.

"Look, I didn't wanna say this outright," he says, lowering his voice, glancing over at Molly. "But there's a very high probability that Leo … didn't make it. That he collapsed somewhere and … well, froze to death."

"Oh, God," Alice says, and Molly starts weeping.

"And if that's the case," Flemming goes on, staring intently at Veronica, "then you'll never find him, because he'll be buried under three feet of snow."

Veronica looks at Flemming while searching her own heart. Then she shakes her head. "Like you said, I brought this upon us. I'll never forgive myself if I don't at least try to find Leo. Maybe he found shelter somewhere. Maybe it's not too late to bring him home."

Flemming breathes through his nose—Veronica can hear his nostrils are clogged. "And what if something happens to you?"

"Don't worry about me. I'm used to running in snow and freezing weather. Besides, I'll take the snow scooter. It's got a full tank, right?"

40

TIM

TIM SITS UP WITH a jolt.

The first thing he notices is the smell of laundry. He's lying on a concrete floor in a strange room. The lights are off, but a pale beam of sunshine is coming down from a window sitting high up. He's in a basement. A washing room. All around him are wrappers and packaging from all kinds of food.

His memory gradually returns. He found the window open and squeezed through. There's a fridge next to the washer, and Tim ate basically everything in it before falling asleep.

How long was I out?

He checks on his arm. The wound is all but gone; left is only a discreet scar that's hard to even see. He moves his fingers and find them cooperative. He also has his sense of touch back. Tendons, muscles, nerves, everything has clearly been restored to perfection.

Considering what he's been through, Tim feels surprisingly good. No soreness as he's used to—even despite the fact that he slept on the floor. In fact, he feels like—

"They're not checking passports, are they?"

Tim stiffens as the voice enters his head.

As brief as the message is, he picks up on several things about it.

Firstly, it's a woman. Fairly young.

Second, her tone is anxious. Tense. Secretive. Like someone afraid to be found out.

Third, there's a slight accent. Spanish, maybe.

And lastly, she's far away. Tim can tell the signal crossed a far bigger distance to reach him than any of the others so far.

She's not in town anymore, that's for sure ...

Not only has the woman skipped town before the cops found her—she probably got out before they started looking—it also seems she's about to travel somewhere even farther away.

Aalborg is twenty-five miles away. The airport is located just northeast of the city. It's the closest airport.

Of course, she could also be in Frederikshavn or Hirtshals. Those towns are both around thirty minutes away, and both of them have seaports with passenger ferries coming in and going out basically around the clock. They mostly take tourists back and forth between Denmark and the neighboring countries Norway, Sweden, and England.

There's also a third possibility. Depending on how long ago she was infected, the woman could have gotten in her car and driven to the German border. That's a good three hours away, but it's not at all impossible.

Either way, it's bad news.

If the woman really is in Aalborg Airport about to board a plane, that could spell disaster. Once in the air, she could infect everyone. And wherever they land, that's where the real trouble begins. The thought of a Boeing 747 crammed full of half-aliens touching down in Heathrow, Amsterdam, or Charles de Gaulle, airports that are all surrounded by millions of people living in close proximity ... that would be impossible to stop, and would almost certainly mean game over for mankind.

Same goes for a ferry, which could carry several thousand people. If the half-aliens aren't afraid of the ice-cold water in the North Sea, they could even jump ship and simply swim to land. Meaning they could spread all over most of Scandinavia within days.

If the woman is headed through security, will she be made out? That would still be bad, because security probably can't apprehend her, and she would likely escape from the scene. But it wouldn't be as bad as her boarding the plane or ship.

Assuming she's at the airport, and she does manage to get on the plane ... how much time does Tim have to get there? Even with his newfound speed and endurance, he probably can't sprint all the way to Aalborg from here. Even if he could, it would take him at least an hour. She could be airborne by then.

Contacting the cops seems like a better option, at least in terms of reaching the airport and seaports in time. If he gets in contact with Lundbeck, maybe he can persuade her to send someone to all three places.

Tim pulls out his phone and turns it back on.

Outside the window, he can't really hear any traffic, which must mean the cops placed a curfew. He can't hear any sounds or voices from upstairs; the house seems to be empty, just like he found it.

As soon as his phone starts up, several voicemails check in. Three of them are from a number he doesn't recognize, but there's also one from Helena.

Frowning, he plays it. It's very brief.

"Dad? It's me. Can you please call me as soon as you get this?"

That's it. Her voice was tense, as though straining to hold back emotions.

Tim stares at his phone for a few seconds. Then he calls up his daughter. She answers it almost right away.

"Dad?"

It's most definitely her. He can tell even before he hears her voice. Her breathing is shaky.

"Hey, honey. Didn't expect to hear from you today. What's up?"

She never calls him, and there is no way she doesn't know what's going on—of course the cops contacted her in the hopes that she knew where he was. Still, Tim decides not to say anything.

She doesn't answer right away. "*Dad. Could you please …? Look, there was a woman. A police officer. She, uhm … she told me … something happened to you*?"

Tim closes his eyes. "Yeah, I guess that's true."

"Is it … is it some kind of illness?"

"Guess you could call it that." He quickly adds: "But I feel fine. I'm not sick. In fact, I'm—" He cuts myself off. "Don't worry about me, honey. Okay?"

"*Jesus, Dad*." She's on the verge of tears, which he really wasn't expecting. He hasn't heard her cry since Anya died, and he certainly never thought she would shed a tear for him of all people in the world. "*They say it's some unknown infection, and that it … that it* ***changes*** *people*."

"Yeah," he says, grinding his teeth at the thought of Lundbeck talking to his daughter, scaring her half to death. "Too bad it's not a change for the better, huh?"

His attempt at lightening the mood doesn't work.

"They say you infected Alan Andersen … and that he infected a bunch of other people …"

"I didn't mean for that to happen," he tells her. "I didn't know what was going on. It was Buddy. He caught the thing, and I had to take him to Alan. But he's fine now. Buddy, I mean."

Helena sniffs, and says with no trace of irony, "*I'm glad.*"

Tim knows she still feels affectionate towards Buddy. They were best pals when he was still a pup. On those rare occasions Helena and Tim have met since the passing of her mother, she seemed happier to meet Buddy than her father. She's the one who named him after she saw him playing with one of Tim's empty Budweiser cans one day.

"So it's just … humans it affects?"

"Yeah."

There's a pause. He hears a voice whisper something in the background, instructing Helena to ask him something. Tim isn't surprised—he already heard noises from at least one other person.

"*So, Dad, listen …*" She takes a deep breath. "*Are you sure you should be on your own right now?*"

"I'm fine, honey. Really."

"Yeah, but … I don't like the thought of you running around like a … like a fugitive. You're sick, Dad. You need medical attention."

"There's no doctor that can cure this," he tells her, seeing in a flash Anya lying in the hospital bed.

"*Don't say that, Dad,*" she pleads, and then—as though reading his mind—she says, "*Just because they couldn't save Mom doesn't mean they can't help you.*"

Tim swallows. "This is very different, honey. Believe me."

The person—a guy—says something again.

"Is that Dennis there with you?" Tim asks her, a shade of annoyance creeping into his voice.

"*Uhm, yeah*," she says, sounding a bit embarrassed. "*He's worried about you too.*"

"That's nice. Tell him I'm fine."

"*You keep saying that, but they told me ... Dad, I can't believe this ... it all feels like a horrible dream ...*" She's about to cry for real now, and it somehow triggers a parental instinct in him that he hasn't used for years. It's like he suddenly channels his late wife.

"Sweetie, I'll be honest with you. I don't look like I used to. My body has ... altered a bit. But listen to my voice. Hear what I'm telling you. I'm still right here. I'm still me, okay? That old, grumpy, half-brained excuse for a man you call your dad—that's him talking."

"Don't talk about yourself like that, Dad."

"I'm just joking. But you believe me, right? You can tell I haven't changed—as a person, I mean." He's surprised to hear the words and find how true they ring. It's at that moment he's finally able to believe fully that he won't transform any further. That whatever humanity he's possessed before the spore entered his system has dug in and isn't going anywhere.

Helena takes a shaky breath. "*You sound like yourself, yes, but ... they said it could take hours, maybe even days ...*"

"Not for me. I'm done." He didn't mean to state it so bluntly, so he adds, "I'm not like the other infected people, I mean. The infection can't take me over completely. It would have done so by now."

Dennis speaks again, but then Helena says, "*Look, just let me talk to my dad, okay*?"

Tim could have kissed her.

He hears Dennis mutter something, then shuffle out of the room and close the door behind him.

"Dennis is gone now, Dad."

"I know. I'm sure he's just trying to help." Tim has to push out those last words.

"Where are you, Dad?"

"I'm still in Hornsted."

"Yeah, but where exactly?"

For the first time, it strikes him that his daughter might not be calling just to make sure he's OK.

"Let me ask you something, sweetie. Did the officer tell you to call me?" He doesn't sound upset or suspicious, because he isn't. He is a bit disappointed, though.

"She did," Helena admits—and he's glad she comes clean without any lies. *"She wanted me to ask you to come help them. She said something about stuff that only you could do."*

Tim bites his lip. "I don't think it's a good idea for me to go there, honey. The cops want me in custody. This whole thing with them talking to you ... it could all be a ploy." He doesn't want to say it out loud, but he also doesn't want to lie to her.

"Why don't you want to help, Dad?"

"I do. I just ... I can't do much good if I'm in jail."

"But it's dangerous for you to be out there. I don't want you to get hurt."

"Don't wo—"

"Please don't tell me not to worry. I ***am*** *worried, Dad!"* She suddenly sounds outright angry with him. *"Don't you get it? You're all I've got left. I can't ... I can't bear the thought of losing you too ..."* The anger turns to tears. *"Please go to the cops, Dad. Help them. Then when it's over, they can work on a cure for you.*

Please, I know you don't trust the authorities or me or anyone, but please just do this for me, I'm begging you ..."

She keeps crying softly while waiting for his answer.

He has no idea what to say. He's never heard her talk to him like this. He knows without a shadow of a doubt that this isn't the cops talking through his daughter. She isn't trying to manipulate him to turn himself in. She is genuinely worried about him. Because she—incredibly—still loves him.

"You got one thing completely wrong, sweetie," he finally tells her. "I do trust you." Then, before he can change his mind, he gives her a promise. "I'll go talk to Alan."

41

FELIX

"FUCK!"

Felix smacks his phone onto his thigh.

"Language, please," Pia hisses, looking away from her nails in order to send him a stern look. "There are other people around."

Felix glances out over the lounge. Pia's right, of course. The benches are occupied with other travelers. But they're either staring at their phones, sipping coffee or nodding off.

"None of them heard me anyway," Felix grumbles. "Stupid game. I keep running out of ammo."

"Are you still playing that ridiculous zombie game?" Pia moans, shaking her head in that annoying overbearing fashion.

Yeah, like your hobbies are any less stupid.

Besides applying makeup for hours, all Felix has ever seen her do is practice on the pole his dad installed in the basement. Seriously, who in their right mind wants to become a professional pole dancer? She says it's nothing sexual, but Felix has a hard time believing that. Why would she do it just in her underwear, turn down the lights and put on the soundtrack from *Dirty Dancing*?

Of course, Pia is young enough that she could probably make a career for herself. At 24, she's only ten years older than Felix, and he can't help but view her more like an annoying big sister than his new stepmom.

"It's aliens," he mutters, plugging in his earbuds.

"Wha'?" Pia asks, already busy filing away at her nails again.

"I said, it's an alien invasion game," Felix says loudly, causing Pia to shush him again.

"Will you keep it down? You're making a scene."

A fat guy with a tiny laptop who barely managed to squeeze his ass between the armrests glances over at them but doesn't say anything.

"I don't care what you're playing, just please act normal when we get there, okay? The last thing I need is for you to mess this up. It's a huge chance for me to network, you know? Finally meet someone who actually matters in the business."

"The business," Felix scoffs. "Is that what they call it?"

"It is," Pia says, ignoring his sarcasm. "And it's a tough one. I need to make the right first impression."

Felix eyes her as she works away at her nails. She could potentially be pretty if she wasn't covered in layers of cosmetics, and if she hadn't bleached the shit out of her hair. Also, she's very young to have gotten breast implants. Felix can't fathom what his dad sees in her. She's pretty much the opposite of Felix's mom. Which—come to think of it—might just be exactly what attracted his dad to Pia. Ever since Felix's mom got admitted the first time, their marriage had been a struggle.

"I don't even know why I had to come," Felix yawns. "Honestly, I think I prefer school over this shit."

"Language," Pia snaps again. "And this is much more important than school. Your dad agreed. This is *culture*. You can't learn that from teachers—you need to experience it." Pia pulls a brochure from her bag, flips it open and points at a name in the corner. "See that? That's the guy I'm hoping to meet. He's the founder of the entire show."

Felix looks at the pictures of ice skaters and singers dressed as princesses and fairies. He never heard of the winter festival before Pia mentioned it, and he would've never dreamed of going if his dad hadn't made him.

"It'll do you good, son. You're staring into that phone all day long. Pia's right, you need to see some real people doing real stuff."

"But, Dad, why can't ***you*** *go?"*

"I told you, I can't get off work."

"But—"

"Besides, it'll be a great chance for you and Pia to connect a little."

The last thing Felix wants—besides watching grown people in costumes sing Disney songs all night—is to connect with Pia. In fact, he wishes she'd never come into their lives. If there had been any chance of his parents working things out, that chance surely died when Pia moved in.

Felix pauses the game to check Messenger. No new texts from Mom. She probably isn't awake yet. The one from last night reads: *Getting drowsy. Will try to get some sleep. Love you with all my heart.*

Felix had texted her back: *Love you too, Mom.*

The thought of her lying in a room somewhere, drugged up, with people checking in on her every hour, it's enough to make his heart wrench. She's not even allowed to use her phone after dinner, but she's been clever enough to bring two, and they lock up the decoy every night. Felix likes to think he would have thought of the same trick if he'd been in her place. After all, they're very much alike, his mother and him. That's what his dad always tells him. Also—

His train of thought is interrupted as a black-haired woman bumps into the fat guy's leg with her rolling suitcase. The guy does little to retract his legs, instead just sending her a cross look. The woman does an awkward dojo bow and pulls away from the man, almost as though she's afraid he'll get up and punch her. She has her back to Felix, so he can't see her face.

"I'm really sorry, sir," she says, bowing again. Her voice is a bit scratchy. As if she has a sore throat. She also has an accent of some kind. South American, maybe.

"No harm done," the man grunts, looking back down at his screen.

The woman quickly scurries on down the row, and as she does, Felix gets a glimpse of her face. She's wearing a COVID mask and thick glasses. The lenses are fogged because of her breath seeping out the top of the mask, which explains why she didn't see the guy's leg.

She hurries to the far end of the row and sits down. Felix can't help but watch her. She seems restless, uneasy. Her glasses are still fogged, but she doesn't do anything to wipe them clean. Instead, she just sits and fiddles with the suitcase zipper. She also keeps looking discreetly around, as though waiting for someone.

When her eyes fall on Felix, he quickly looks down at his phone. After a few seconds or so, he glances back over at the woman. She's scratching her hair, and as she lowers her hand again, she looks at it, freezes for a moment, then gets up and goes to the restroom. She looks like she's straining not to run.

Felix can't help it, he's too curious, so he gets up from his seat.

"Where are you going?" Pia quips immediately.

"Just stretching my legs," he tells her.

"Okay, but stay where I can see you. We'll be boarding any minute now."

Felix ignores her and strolls down the row of seats, pretending like he's just casually killing time. As he reaches the woman's seat, he sees a nest of auburn hair. It looks like a dog sat here and scratched itself, except the hairs are too long.

He saunters back to his seat. As he sits down, the woman comes back. She's walking slightly more casual now, but still seems in a rush. Apparently, she didn't need a pee. Instead, she's pulled her hair up into a ragged bun that's held in place by several pins and bands.

Pia notices Felix looking at the woman and elbows him in the side. "Stop staring, will you? That's rude."

"She's losing her hair," he whispers.

"Who?"

"The woman with the mask."

Pia follows his gaze. "Oh. Poor thing. She's probably going through chemo."

"Yeah, probably."

"All the more reason you shouldn't be gawking at her."

Pia returns to her nails, and Felix pretends to resume the alien game. But he darts a look at the woman every few minutes.

He can't help it.

42

TIM

TIM ENDS THE CALL and sits there and looks at the phone for a long moment. His heart is pounding, but for once it isn't due to fear or adrenaline. It's another emotion swirling around his chest, one he hasn't felt for years.

Then he checks one of the other voicemails, and sure enough, it's Lundbeck, asking him to contact her. Tim calls her up.

The inspector answers right away. Her tone is unmistakably hopeful. "*Iversen. Glad you ca—*"

"Listen, and listen carefully. The woman you're searching for, she's at an airport or a seaport, and she's about to board a plane or a ferry. Either that, or she's driving into Germany."

He gives the cop three seconds for the info to sink in. Lundbeck doesn't say anything, but Tim can hear her breathing turn stiff.

"I don't have a name or a location on her," Tim goes on. "In theory, she could be anywhere in Jutland. Since I can still hear her thoughts, that means she's probably not far enough turned that she can't slip through border control. At least she's gonna try."

Another brief pause.

"*Fuck!*" Lundbeck spits. Tim is surprised to hear such an emotional outburst from the woman who's so far seemed very composed. Of course, he gets it; she's been awake for several hours now, and the scope of the situation must be clearer to her now. "*This is bad, Iversen. Really fucking bad.*"

"I know. You need to shut down everything if you haven't already. Ground all planes, cancel all ships, close the border. Send out as many cops as you can, but make sure they take proper pre—"

"*Hold on, hold on.*" Tim can hear Lundbeck walk, and the noise in the background tunes out somewhat. Once she speaks again, her voice is low. "*Who do you think you're talking to here? The prime minister? I can't just 'shut down' the entire bloody country because you tell me to.*"

Tim is stunned. "I thought you wanted my help? Well, this is me helping. I'm telling you, the woman you're looking for is about to leave Denmark."

"*And I believe you.*" Lundbeck lowers her voice still further until it's barely more than a hiss. "*But after that stunt you pulled in the parking basement, I seem to be the only one.*"

"I can't ... I can't believe this." Tim rubs his forehead. He thought Lundbeck was reaching out on behalf of the authorities, but it sounds more like she's asking him for a personal favor. "Are you telling me you can't do anything?"

"*Look, I risk my job just talking to you here.*" Another short pause. Tim gets the impression Lundbeck discreetly checks around to see if anyone is within earshot. "*But I'm running out of time. This thing ... I've seen what it does. We've caught seventeen infected people by now, four of them officers of the law who were getting themselves in harm's way. Colleagues of mine. But this last woman ... we have two separate witnesses who saw her, but she's hiding somewhere, and we can't find her.*" She pauses, then goes on in a slightly calmer tone, "*I can say we have a lead. Get them to check the passenger lists for the nearest airports and seaports. See if a woman from Hornsted is meant to be on one of the planes or ships leaving within the hour. That should narrow it down."*

"But it won't be fast enough."

"I know. If I push it, I can maybe send a group to one of the locations. Which one is more likely in your opinion?"

Tim's gut tells him Aalborg, but he doesn't answer the question. "No," he says instead. "This isn't the right way to do it. Sending a batch of cops to sniff around. She'll spot them a mile away and disappear again ... if she's not already on a plane or a ferry."

Lundbeck groans. "*You're probably right.*" He can hear her gnawing at the inside her cheek. "*How about this then? You come and talk to Andersen.*"

Tim scoffs. "Alan? But he's no longer ... I mean ..."

"*Andersen must know who the woman is,*" Lundbeck goes on. "*The timeline fits; it could only have been him who infected her. So if he can just give us a name, we can narrow things down by a lot. We can find her within minutes ...*"

"Listen, Ulla, even if I could understand him, I really don't think Alan would be in the mood to talk to me."

"*But that's the thing,*" she exclaims. "*We have his wife here, Elisabeth. She got him to calm down. I believe he recognizes her, Iversen, and he's talking to her, but she can't understand him. So maybe if you come, he'll recognize you too, and he'll talk to you.*" The desperate hope in her voice makes Tim feel bad for her.

He takes a deep breath, then asks, "Where you keeping Alan?"

"At the detention facility at St Knut's Boulevard. I just arrived here myself."

"I know where it is," Tim says, getting to his feet and going to the window. "I'm less than two miles out. Let Alan know I'm coming."

"*Where are you*?" Lundbeck asks. "*Gimme a location, and I'll send someone to pick you up.*"

"Don't bother," Tim says. "I'll be there in three minutes."

"All right," Lundbeck says. "*Thanks, Iversen.*" Tim is about to hang up, when she adds: "*Oh, and one more thing. Come to the back of the building.*"

43

VERONICA

IT'S NOT AS COLD as she feared. In fact, it seems to be thawing slightly.

Before pulling the scooter from the garage, Veronica checks all around the cabin. Just as Flemming predicted, there are no prints from Leo. She also searches the garage and all three cars, hoping to find him huddled up on the backseat of one of them. No such luck.

So, she drives off.

The snow scooter leaves deep tracks but moves well enough. The sporadic flakes still coming down melt away on the helmet's visor.

Initially, she follows the road, but not only does it quickly become difficult to see where the road even is, it also makes more sense—according to the GPS on her phone—to simply head for the nearest neighbor in a straight line. It means driving over fields and hills, passing patches of trees and bushes, and at one point she even has to drive across a fence which is almost buried under the snow. Still, she shaves maybe twenty minutes off the trip.

Had she been more confident riding the scooter, she could have gone faster. But she only tried it once before, and the last thing she wants is to tip over and get stranded out here in the middle of nowhere. So, she drives slowly, checking for hidden obstacles.

As she drives, her mind wanders. She can't help but ruminate about what she's seen and heard.

Leo's hands.

The scream from outside the cabin.

Had it been him? Or someone else? What has the mysterious infection done to her boyfriend? Is he still alive? And if so, is he aware of what he's doing?

Coming around a low dune of snow, Veronica notices another fence protruding from the snow—this one looks electrical. And sure enough, on the other side is a large shed and in front of it a group of cows looking at her. She almost overlooked them; they're milky white and blend in with the snowy landscape. They've trampled the snow and eaten away at two large bales of hay. There's an old bathtub serving as a drinking trough, and the cows have managed to break up the ice to get to the water.

Veronica notices something and stops the scooter. The cattle just keep eyeing her as she pulls off the helmet. What caught her eye is something on one of the cows. A striking, dark pattern on her face. Veronica gets off the scooter and sinks to knee-level. She makes her way closer to the cattle. They're clearly used to people and don't get nervous. She looks closer at the one with the dark pattern, and she finds exactly what she feared. It's not a natural coloring of the animal's fur; it's the black stuff growing on her.

He came by here, Veronica realizes with a sinking feeling. She can't help but look around. Except for the cattle, she's completely alone. No visible footprints in the snow, either.

"Leo came this way," she mutters to the cows. "And he infected you. Why would he do that?"

The cow with the black stuff just looks back at her.

For some reason, Veronica doesn't feel like sticking around. She goes back to the snow scooter, climbs on it and takes off.

44

FELIX

THEY'RE JUST ABOUT TO get on the plane when Felix's phone vibrates.

He's been keeping an eye on the woman with the mask. Every few minutes, she'll get up and pace around the lounge, then sit back down. As though eager to get going. And when they finally make the call over the speakers for them to board, she jumps up and rushes to the gate.

Felix takes out his phone and sees his mom's name. He's very surprised to get a call from her, much less at this hour. She should be at breakfast.

"Come on," Pia urges him, hoisting up her handbag. "That's us. Put that phone away now."

Felix ignores her and answers the call. "Mom?"

"I'm so glad to hear your voice, sweetie."

His mother is talking very low, and Felix can barely hear her. All around him, people are bustling, getting up from their seats, yawning and stretching, so he sticks a finger in his ear. "Can you speak up a little, Mom?"

"*I'm so sorry*," she says, and he can hear her being on the verge of tears. "*I messed up big time.*"

A fist tightens in his gut. "What happened, Mom?"

"They found my phone. They wanted to take it away. I lost my temper. I slapped the woman."

"Oh, shit," Felix mutters, rubbing his forehead. He knows all too well what getting physical with the staff means. "Well, I'm sure they understand you only did it because—"

"*It gets worse*," she says, breaking into a brief, hysterical laughter. "*I'm in the bathroom. I jammed the door with my toothbrush. I'm so sorry, Felix. It's all my fault. I messed up*."

Straining his hearing, Felix picks up knocking and voices calling his mom's name.

"Are you coming? Who are you talking to?"

Felix turns to see Pia waving at him impatiently. The other passengers have formed a queue by the gate, and the first ones are starting to trickle through security. The woman with the mask has already boarded.

"*I just wanted you to know how sorry I am*," Mom goes on in his ear. "*It'll probably be a while before we talk again. But I'll call you as soon as I get the chance, okay?*"

"Mom, listen—"

"Is that your mother?" Pia frowns. "I thought she wasn't allowed to call you?" She comes closer, and Felix steps farther away. "You need to call her back later, Felix," she says, using her strict trying-to-be-a-mother-voice. "You hear me? We'll miss the plane." She reaches out for him, and Felix slaps away her hand.

"Get off me!"

He surprises both Pia and himself. For a moment they just stare at each other, Felix with the phone pressed to his chest.

There's that famous Haiberg temper, a voice in his head says.

Pia points at him with one of her newly done nails. "Don't you ever do that again."

"Then don't touch me," Felix retorts. "Just gimme a freaking second, will you?" He turns his back and puts the phone to his ear. "Mom? You still there?"

She is, but she's no longer holding the phone. Judging by the noises, she put it down somewhere. Felix can hear her talking to at least two men who are telling her firmly to come with them. Unlike Felix, his mom doesn't have the option of refusing.

"*I love you, Felix!*" she says loud enough for him to hear.

"*Phone's in the sink,*" one of the men says. A moment later, it's picked up.

Felix can hear his mother being escorted away. He can't tell whether whoever is holding the phone is listening or not.

"Please don't lock her up again," Felix says. He holds his breath, waiting for an answer. None comes, but he's pretty sure the person heard him. "Please," he goes on. "She didn't mean to hurt anyone. She just gets a little—"

The call is ended.

Felix swallows and slips his phone back into his pocket.

He turns around, expecting to see Pia there. But she's gone to join the queue, standing with her arms crossed, pretending not to give a damn whether Felix comes with her or not.

And for a moment, Felix seriously considers not going. It wouldn't be too late. He could simply turn and walk back out of the airport. Call an Uber and have it drive him home. Or better yet, to the psychiatric hospital. The only thing on his mind at that moment is to go see his mom. But the logical part of his brain knows he won't be allowed to.

The first time she was admitted to the secure facility, it took them three weeks to clear him for visitation—and only because his dad came too. This time, he doubts very much he can talk his father into joining him.

"*Your mother is doing this to herself, son,*" he told Felix the last time they spoke about it—"it," of course, being Toby.

"She's the only one who can fix herself, and she won't do it. Trust me; I've known her for twenty years."

It wasn't his words, not really. He didn't use to speak like this. Not before he met Pia.

Still, the last thing Felix wants is to get on that plane and go to Copenhagen. But if he doesn't, not only will Pia freak out, his dad will also be upset with him, and that'll only further lower Felix's chances of seeing his mother again any time soon.

Felix doesn't agree with his dad. Not completely, anyway. His mother might be responsible for her own life, but not for her demons. She's doing her best, but sometimes, they get the better of her. Like they just did this morning.

"Fuck," he hisses, rubbing his brow, fighting himself. Go or stay? Go or stay?

Paradoxically, what makes him decide is the woman's suitcase.

It's still sitting next to her seat.

She forgot it.

Felix looks over at queue. The woman is at the front of the queue, about to board. Pia is sending him a sour look, raising her thin eyebrows as though to say, "You coming or what?"

Felix goes to the suitcase. He tells himself he wants to make sure the woman gets it, but really, it's more curiosity that draws him. It's not very big. When he picks it up, he pauses. It's light. Too light. As though it's empty.

Felix is just about to unzip it, when he sees the woman come towards him. He jolts and instinctively holds out the suitcase while feeling the heat rush to his cheeks.

"Uhm, you forgot this," he mutters guiltily. "I wanted to bring it to you ..."

"Thank you," the woman says in that low, hoarse voice as she yanks the suitcase from him. He doesn't have time to read her eyes behind the foggy glasses before she turns around and walks back to the front of the queue. He's left with a whiff of the woman's perfume; it's a sour, fruity scent, almost like lemon juice.

Felix forgets all about his mom for a moment.

All he can think of is, why would anybody bring an empty suitcase on a trip?

45

TIM

ALREADY FROM A DISTANCE, Tim can tell the detention facility is clearly being used for something outside of regular protocol.

For one thing, half a dozen service vehicles are parked outside, some of them still with the flashers going, and the lights are on in every window. For another, two armed cops wearing respiratory gear are standing by the entrance. If they are trying to not draw attention, they are doing a poor job of it.

A horde of curious onlookers have gathered at a safe distance across the street. Probably no reporters yet; they just look like civilians who've noticed the commotion as they brought Alan in and decided to go take a peek. Tim can hear them mutter to each other.

He makes sure not to come close enough that anyone notices him. Jogging around to the back of the building, he finds a large parking lot empty save for an idling helicopter with two soldiers standing next to it. Lundbeck is by an open door, talking on her phone. She's wearing a protective suit, and it's only her gray hair that gives her away. As soon as she spots him, she ends the call and waves him closer.

"Thanks for coming. He's right in here."

Tim follows her into a corridor, leaving the door open.

She gives Tim a quick look over the shoulder. "I hate to ask, but ... sure you're not contagious?"

"Positive," Tim tells her. "Would have infected a whole lotta folks by now if I were."

"Good. Don't take it personally."

"I'm not."

Tim has never been inside the facility, but it looks pretty much like any old municipal office. Cream-colored walls, linoleum floors. It isn't exactly setting the scene for what is happening. Still, he can feel it in the atmosphere. And there are a whole lotta folks rushing back and forth. Mostly police officers, but also what he takes to be forensic scientists—it's not easy to tell with everyone dressed in safety outfits. None of them pay much attention to Tim.

"We're running every possible test we can think of," Lundbeck tells him, as though reading his mind. "The doctors set up a temporary lab in the east wing."

"They found out anything yet?"

"They're almost sure it's not airborne, but that's about all we know. They're saying it's a mutation, but they've never seen anything like it. 'Nigrumycosis' is the name they've given it." She sends him another glance. "This thing really came from outer space?"

"Pretty sure it did."

Lundbeck buzzes them through a door, they turn down another hallway, this one quieter, and Tim sees Lis sitting on a chair, hugging herself. She looks very tired and even through the mask it's obvious she's been crying a lot. Next to her are two armed cops.

Tim isn't sure why the three of them are hanging around in the middle of the hallway—not until he comes close enough to see through the tiny, square window of the nearest door.

He expected something like the scene from *The Silence of the Lambs*. He's not looking into a creepy basement, however, just a regular, windowless holding cell. Inside it is Alan. He isn't tied to a stretcher, and he isn't wearing a muzzle. He is wearing an ankle chain, though, and it's secured to the bed which is bolted to the floor. It looks strong enough that Alan probably won't be able to rip free, and the door seems pretty sturdy, too. Still, Tim doesn't feel good about the setup.

"This is just temporary," Lundbeck tells him, once again guessing his thoughts. "They're moving him to a proper secure facility as soon as they can get it ready." Both guards react when they recognize Tim, and but Lundbeck raises her hand and tells them, "It's okay, he's supposed to be here."

They stand down, even though Tim notices she didn't say on whose authority he's here.

"You sure he can't get out of here if he sets his mind to it?" Tim asks quietly.

Alan sits on the floor, slumping against the bedpost, his head lolling from side to side, like a bus passenger fighting not to nod off.

"We're keeping him just barely awake," Lundbeck assures him. "Before they got the dose right, he did that." The cop gestures to the lower part of the door. It's only now Tim notices the bulge in the metal. "Damn near broke through."

"Tim?" Lis's voice, weak and distorted by the mask. She looks up at him. "God, it's you ..."

"More or less," he tells her. "How are you holding up?"

The skinny woman gets to her feet and strides to him with surprising speed. He can tell from her eyes she isn't going to hug him. Reaching up, she flings him a stinging slap across the cheek.

"*You* did this," Lis hisses up at him, baring her tiny teeth. "*You* did this to him ..."

She slaps him again, hard enough that she loses her balance. Tim catches her and helps her back to the chair as she bursts into tears.

"I'm really sorry, Lis. I know I fucked up."

"I'm never forgiving you," she weeps, her boney shoulders bopping.

"Me neither," he mutters. "I'm here to try and fix it. I know it probably won't do Alan much good, but maybe I can stop others from catching it."

"You do what you want," Lis sighs, bowing her head.

Tim swallows, then goes to the door. He expects one of the guards to unlock it. They both just stare at him, so he looks back at Lundbeck. "I'm not going in there?"

"We can't open it. He can hear you, though."

Tim has to hunch over to look through the window. "Alan?"

He can tell his voice is being carried into the cell through hidden speakers. Alan rolls his head to the side, as though he hears the words, but can't pin down where they come from. His eyes go to the ceiling, then back down to the floor.

"He's off his rocker," Tim frowns. "He's not gonna talk like this."

"We can wake him up a bit more," Lundbeck says, pulling out her phone. She calls up someone and tells them, "Yeah, I need him able to talk. Right now. Thanks."

Within thirty seconds, a short, heavyset guy with thick glasses under his mask comes hurrying down the hallway. He fumbles open some kind of kit, dropping the plastic wrappings on the floor. He's wearing gloves, which doesn't make it easier, but he manages to fill a syringe with a clear liquid, then injects it into what looks like a dart. He hands it ceremoniously to one of the guards, who takes a gun from his belt.

Lis groans at the sight of the weapon. She clearly knows what is going to happen.

So that's how they're keeping him tranquil, Tim thinks. *Shooting a dart in his ass every fifteen minutes.*

Whatever they're about to administer now obviously isn't a tranquilizer. More likely adrenaline.

He steps aside to let the guard insert the gun into a small hatch in the door, probably meant to exchange meal trays. The guard crouches down, takes aim and fires.

Alan gives a grunt as the dart burrows into his shoulder. He reaches up a six-fingered hand that doesn't really look human anymore and brushes it off absentmindedly. Tim counts at least five other ampules on the floor already.

The guard steps aside, and Tim takes his place by the window. "Alan?" he tries again.

His friend is clearly already feeling the effects of whatever cocktail was in the dart. He's breathing faster, his ribcage going like an accordion, his nostrils flaring. His shoulders are rolling, and his legs are twitching. He sits up a little straighter, and then, for the first time, he looks Tim dead in the eye. Tim can tell right away he recognizes him. The dark skin on his forehead contracts into a row of furrows, his eyes narrow, and his unnaturally wide mouth opens in what could be a grin.

Alan then utters a string of noises. It sounds like gravel being shaken inside a tin can, mixed with a dolphin screech.

"You know who I am, don't you?" Tim asks.

Alan's jaw bobs, but no sounds come out at first. Then a low, short squeal. He breathes it out, and Tim isn't even sure it's a word.

"Can you nod or shake your head?" he asks.

Alan repeats the rattling noises. He sounds agitated. As though Tim had said something to insult him.

"Look, I'm really sorry," he tells him. "Had I known, I would have never involved you, Alan."

Alan doesn't answer. He appears to lose interest, because he looks down and starts examining his surroundings. He finds the chain and yanks it hard, testing the strength of the bedpost.

Tim hears Lundbeck tell the guard, "Get another tranq dart ready."

"Alan," Tim says louder, tapping the glass with his finger. "I need you to talk to me. Can you do that?"

Alan looks up at him, sends him that weird grin again, and then he gets to his feet. He sways a little, almost keels over, but then finds his balance. They've apparently tried to clothe him, because pieces of fabric still cling to his legs. Most of it he's torn off and thrown into the corner. Tim doesn't exactly care to see Alan's full body like this—it reminds him all to vividly of what he himself almost turned into—but he also can't help but stare.

Alan is a weird sight to say the least. Lean, almost scrawny. Alien, yet human. The most heartbreaking thing is that Tim still—even at this final stage of the transformation—recognizes Alan in there. Tiny clues give him away. Something about his posture. The way he moves his head. And his left knee is turned slightly outwards. Tim recalls him having surgery on that knee after a skiing accident ten years ago.

You have to have known Alan beforehand to notice these things, though. Tim can only imagine how bad Lis must feel looking at him; she no doubt sees even more of her husband in the grotesque figure in the holding cell.

Alan splutters another string of sounds. This one is a little different.

"That's it, right?" Lundbeck asks. To Tim's surprise, she looks at Lis. "That's the same sentence he's been saying over and over, isn't it?"

Lis gives an almost imperceptible nod.

Tim stares at Alan as he repeats the noises twice. He looks right at Tim as he does it. Tim listens, tries really hard to understand. To pick out some kind of word that holds any meaning to him.

"We have no idea what he's saying, but we're working on it," Lundbeck says. "A tech team is in the next room, listening, and they're trying to find patterns, trying to translate—"

"Shut up," Tim says, not taking his eyes off Alan. "Say it again, pal. Slower if you can."

Alan does his grin again, and it gives Tim the chills. He can't tell if Alan is simply amused by the guessing game, or if the smile has more sinister undertones. Then he starts talking again, repeating the same sentence over and over in a chanting sort of way.

Tim closes his eyes and shuts out everything else.

At first, it's merely noise. Then, gradually, as the sounds keep flowing through Tim's mind, they start to reverberate. It feels like waking up to someone talking on the radio. At first, your brain doesn't recognize the words, but as you wake up a bit more, the sounds suddenly start to make sense.

The language Alan now speaks is so different from any Tim has ever heard. Normally, a word is a sound that corresponds to a thing, or idea, or person, or whatever. This isn't the case with what Alan is uttering. Rather, the sounds are like emotional outbursts. It isn't enough that Tim *hears* it; he has to interpret the meaning from *the way* Alan is speaking. It's much more an intuitive sensing than a linguistic task—which is why Tim realizes for a fact the codebreakers next door will never get anything out of it.

He keeps listening, keeps filtering away variations that don't feel right, until finally, it clicks into place.

Tim opens his eyes, and Alan must see understanding dawn on his face, because he stops talking.

Tim feels an icy chill come over his entire body, and he trembles slightly despite himself. He becomes aware that both guards, Lundbeck, Lis, even the short doctor, are all staring fixedly at him.

"You got it?" Lundbeck whispers.

Tim gives a single nod. "Yeah, I got it. He's saying, 'You cannot stop it; you will all perish.'"

46

FELIX

"SO, WHAT DID YOUR mother want?"

The question pulls Felix from his gloomy thoughts. He thought Pia was sleeping. She's sitting with her eyes shut and her head leaned back. On the table in front of her is a half-eaten vegan sandwich she brought from home.

Felix was reading on his phone about compulsory treatment.

"Nothing," he mutters, turning the screen discreetly so Pia can't see it—not that she's looking; she still hasn't opened her eyes. "Just ... wanted to say hi."

"Not really like her to be casually chatting."

Of course Pia doesn't buy it. She must have noticed how flustered Felix got when talking to his mom, and now she wants to snoop.

Felix ignores the remark and looks out the window. They're over the sea, and they seem to have reached cruising altitude. Which means they'll start to descend again soon; it's only a 45-minute flight.

Since they boarded the plane, his mind has been going back to worrying about his mom. He hates the thought of her being restrained. They might even drug her. According to the law, if "it is essential for the recovery of a very disturbed patient's condition, the doctor may decide that the patient must be forcibly given a sedative." So basically, it depends on how much of a fight his mom put up when they came to take her away. Felix really hopes she was able to keep herself calm.

"You know, it's really not fair of her to put this on you."

Felix looks at Pia. She's finally looking back at him, and for once, he sees a trace of real empathy on her face.

"She's not putting anything on me," he says. "She's sick."

"Yes, and you're her son. She shouldn't burden you with her problems."

Felix snorts. "So, what? She's just supposed to sit alone in her room all day and not have anybody to talk to? I'm all she's got, you know. After you—" Felix cuts himself off. "After Dad stopped talking to her."

Pia sighs, and, to Felix's dismay, puts her hand on his. "Your father and I are trying to move on. To create a better life for all three of us. I get why you're torn, but I really think you should place your trust in us. There's no future with her, Felix. My aunt, she worked as a psychiatric nurse, and she told me how these people, they never get better. The best they can hope for is to run out the clock without too much pain, but at the end of the day, they're not able to have meaningful relationships. They're simply too messed up. And if their loved ones aren't careful, they'll drag them down with them. I'm sorry, but it's the truth."

Pia stops talking, gaging Felix for a reaction.

He stares at her, hardly believing what he just heard. The way she said it, it sounded almost kind. Felix feels a boiling anger begin to simmer in his gut.

"Your aunt really said that?" he asks evenly.

"Uh-huh. Was a nurse all her life."

"Well, it's no wonder the system is so fucked up. With psychos like her working there."

Pia takes her hand away with a look of surprise and insult. Before she can say anything, Felix goes on.

"I mean, what kind of pessimistic bullshit is that? No hope? No future? Like they're just black holes and not people." He leans closer and bares his front teeth. "Fuck your aunt and every other nurse in that system. My mom is gonna be fine. Oh, and by the way, I'm not torn. Not at all. I'm never trusting you, Pia. If you were on fire, I wouldn't piss on you."

Pia's face contorts into an angry mask, and she looks like she's about to scream at him. For a second, it seems like she might even slap him. Felix hopes she does. And if her nails could cut his cheek open a little, that would be even better. He couldn't wait to show his dad. If there's one thing that might overrule his irrational crush on Pia, it would be her hurting Felix. As infatuated as he is with her, Felix still trusts his father not to tolerate any kind of violence.

But to his complete surprise, Pia's expression deflates, and she instead tears up. "You're such a mean person," she sniffs. "I don't know why I even try." She puts in her earplugs, folds her arms over her breasts and turns away.

Despite himself, Felix feels bad. He was probably too harsh, cursing at her like that. But he's stressed out. He feels very emotionally raw after talking with his mom, and Pia just had to stick her nose in his business.

Screw her. She got what she deserved.

Yet he can't fully convince himself. Pia's an asshole for sure, but his mother once told him, "Be kind to those you meet, because everyone is fighting a battle." It was a quote by a Greek philosopher, and Felix figures it probably applies even to Pia.

He sighs. "Look, Pia ..."

Pia doesn't hear him. And Felix never gets to finish his sentence.

Because at that moment, the woman with the mask gets up from her seat. She's four or five rows ahead of Felix, on the other side, so he has clear view of her. She adjusts her clothes, turns around and strides right past Felix. She's once again walking in that brisk-but-trying-not-to-look-rushed manner. As she passes, he sniffs for that citrusy smell again. But it's gone now. He can only smell sweat from the woman.

He leans out into the aisle and looks back. The woman slips into the lavatory.

Felix sits there, feeling his heart beat a little too fast without him really knowing why. He counts the minutes, glancing back now and then.

Finally, the woman comes back out. She has once again fixed her hair, which looks to Felix like it's even thinner and messier now. He quickly pulls back his head as the woman comes up the aisle. She passes him again, and this time, he smells something metallic.

Felix watches the woman sit back down. She briefly places her hand on armrest, and Felix sees a trace of what can only be blood smeared across the back of her hand. Then she retracts the hand and it disappears from his view.

She's bleeding too. Boy, she really must be sick.

Felix feels a stab of sympathy for the woman. He also can't help but be curious. He gets up and goes to the restroom. As soon as he steps inside and closes the door, he can smell blood and sweat. There are no visible traces of blood, neither in the sink nor the toilet. Felix crouches down and checks the floor, not really sure what he's looking for. Maybe a drop of blood. What he spots under the sink is something else entirely. Two white molars.

Jesus, Felix thinks, feeling his gut drop. *Does chemo do this to a person? Isn't that more like heavy radiation poisoning*?

He flushes the toilet and exits the lavatory. Walking back to his seat, his legs are slightly shaky. Something about the woman is unnerving him. The seat belt signs come on just as Felix sits back down.

Like on cue, the woman suddenly gets up and reaches for the overhead compartment. She fumbles with the lock, manages to get the hatch open and starts rummaging around the luggage, when a stewardess approaches her with a smile. "Excuse me, we're about to begin the descent, so if you could just take a seat and put on your belt, please."

The woman mutters something, closes the hatch and sits back down.

The stewardess looks a little closer at the woman, and her smile falters. "Are you feeling all right? You look a little pale."

Felix can't see the woman, and he can't hear what she answers, but it apparently reassures the stewardess enough that she continues down the aisle, putting the smile back on as she checks the passengers' belts.

Felix gestures discreetly at the stewardess, and she stops. "Yes?"

"You know what's wrong with her?" he says in a very low voice.

"Excuse me?" She leans closer in order to hear him.

"The woman with the mask," Felix whispers. "Do you think what she's got could be contagious?"

Understanding dawns on the stewardess's face, and that annoying smile returns. "She's been thoughtful enough to wear a mask, so I'm sure there's no risk."

"But I saw—"

"Please fasten your seat belt."

"Okay, but let me just tell you what ..."

Clearly not wanting to discuss another passenger's health issues any further, the stewardess pretends the conversation is over and walks on.

As she's out of view, Felix sees the masked woman lean out, turn her head around and dart a look at the stewardess. The way she does it makes Felix's gut tighten up. It looks like her neck is able to move farther around than should be possible for a human. What's worse, she tilts her head slightly forward so that she can look over the rim of the glasses, and for the first time, Felix sees her eyes clearly. It's only for a flash, but it's enough.

Both her pupils and irises are completely gone. It's not that her eyes are cloudy like a blind person's—they're completely blank.

Shit. This is not an illness. Something's seriously wrong with her.

The woman gets back up and goes for the overhead compartment again. Her movements are more rushed now, almost hectic. As though she's desperate to get whatever she's looking for.

Does she have a bomb?

The thought sends a cold rush of fear down the back and front of Felix's torso, and he instinctively gets to his feet just as the woman pulls out her pink suitcase. He's about to approach her, not really sure what he intends to do, when another stewardess comes from the front of the plane.

"I'm sorry, but you need to sit back down. Please leave the luggage in the overhead compartment. You too," she says, seeing Felix. "Take your seats, please. We're about to—"

"Get away from me!" the woman with the mask shrieks as the stewardess goes to take the suitcase from her. She holds it up, facing the stewardess, as she goes on. "This is a bomb! If anyone comes close, I'll set it off!"

The stewardess backs away, covering her mouth, her eyes huge. A lot of the passengers cry out, some even get to their feet.

"Stay where you are!" the woman screams, her voice breaking as she spins around to make sure no one's coming close. "Stay back, or we'll all die!"

As she turns all the way around, she simultaneously rips off the mask and her glasses with one hand, and Felix realizes what he already suspected on a subconscious level: that they were both only disguises. The sight of the woman's face immediately reveals why she covered it. Her jaw is visibly too big, her mouth too wide, her nose flat and animallike. As she speaks, Felix sees pointy, razor-sharp teeth. Her blazing, blank eyes sweep over the passengers, causing screams of horror.

"Oh, fuck ... she's a monster," Felix breathes, not realizing he's talking out loud.

The woman doesn't hear him because of a lot of other people shouting and rummaging. Some are getting into the aisle and scrambling to the back. The stewardesses are trying to guide them back to their seats.

In the turmoil, Felix spots a big guy—clearly someone who works out—coming at the woman from behind. He apparently sat close by, and he makes a dash for her. He's much taller than the woman, and she has lowered the suitcase just enough that the guy can wrap his muscular arms around her and pin her in place.

"*Get it!*" he roars out. "*Someone get it away from her!*"

Another man—older and not as physically strong, but still bigger than the woman—gets up and lunges for the suitcase.

It looks like no match; between them, the men must outweigh the woman by close to 300 pounds. The other passengers utter cries of encouragement, and for a few seconds, Felix actually thinks the guys will neutralize the freak woman and the situation will end well.

Then she starts fighting back.

She opens her huge mouth and buries her teeth in the guy's bicep. Ripping off a big chunk of muscle, he screams and has no choice but let her go. The other guy is still trying to get the suitcase, but with her arms free again, the woman rips it from him, and—holding it under one arm like a football—she grabs the guy's jaw and cranes his head back, producing a sickening crunch. He goes limb and collapses in the aisle. The passengers scream as the woman rounds on the first guy who's clutching his bleeding arm. He tries to get away, but the woman lunges for him like a predator.

Felix sees it all in glimpses as fleeing passengers keep obstructing his view. He can also only hear the guy's death cries in broken intervals through all the other noises. And he's thankful for it. Because from what he can tell, she basically rips him apart until he looks like a dummy someone ran over with a lawnmower.

He does catch one clear image from the uneven fight: the woman biting off one of the guy's hands and swallowing it whole, bones and all.

Then she suddenly jumps up, still clutching the now bloodstained suitcase under her arm. The woman herself is also covered in blood, especially her face, neck, and what's left of her hair.

"*Everybody get back to your seats!*" she screams, her voice screechy and crackling. "*Anyone who doesn't comply will end up like these two!*"

Felix feels a hand grab his arm and tug at him. Pia is looking at him with huge, terrified eyes. She mouths the words, "Sit down."

Felix does so. He moves like in a dream. He sees most of the other passengers sit back down, too. A guy is hiding under the seats and another guy has to pull him out and force him to take a seat. A woman has fainted in the aisle, and two men hoist her up.

The monster woman just stands in the middle and watches everything.

After a few minutes, everyone is seated—except for the two dead vigilantes. Most have fallen quiet, with a few still crying or pleading.

"I will be back in thirty seconds," the woman says loudly. "Nobody move a muscle."

She turns and strides to the front of the plane.

Felix stretches his neck to see what she's doing. The stewardesses have taken their seats next to the door to the cockpit, and he can hear one of them talk to the woman as she rushes by them. It sounds like, "Please, I have a son."

The woman ignores her and kicks the door to the cockpit so hard, her foot punches right through. A few cries of surprise from the passengers. It takes the woman another couple of blows to break down the door and force her way into the cockpit. Felix can't see her for a moment. As she's out of sight, someone says, "No, please, sit back down!"

Felix looks back to see a young man who's gotten to his feet. He's leaning out into the aisle, as though he's considering making a run for it. Then his expression changes as the woman comes back out from the cockpit and looks out over the rows of seats.

"*Listen!*" she shrieks—giving them a couple of seconds to quiet down. Her blank eyes scan the faces, her upper lip quivers. She's clearly on edge and won't hesitate to kill anyone else at the slightest sign of resistance. "You all stay seated, and you get to live," she goes on. "Anyone gets up or fights back, and I will set off the bomb and kill all of you." She lets the message sink in before continuing. "No one else needs to die. I've instructed the pilot to land the plane as planned. Don't fight me, and you will get back down safe and sound."

A murmur goes through the crowd. People exchange looks. Felix sees worry on their faces, but also signs of hope.

"She won't crash the plane," Pia whispers, her voice breaking. "If we just ... if we just do as she says, we'll be okay."

Felix doubts it. He very much wants it to be true, but he can't bring himself to believe a word the woman is saying. For one thing, he doesn't believe she has a bomb. That's just a convenient lie to keep people compliant.

"What does she want?" he whispers back, not taking his eyes off the woman. "It doesn't make sense to hijack a plane and then just have it land again."

"It doesn't matter," Pia hisses. "She's insane. We just have to play along until we're safe on the ground."

Felix leans sideways again as the woman begins moving. She goes to the stewardesses and reaches out her free hand. The women recoil, but the woman doesn't seem to want to hurt them. She simply grabs their hands, as though greeting them. Then she moves on to the passengers in the first row. Felix can't see what she's doing, but the way she moves from one to the other, pausing only briefly in front of each person, it looks like she's shaking their hands, too. He can see one of the stewardesses look at her hand with an expression of surprise and confusion. From what Felix can see, her hand looks okay; the woman didn't seem to scratch her or break anything. She simply—weirdly—shook her hand.

What the hell's going on?

Felix watches as the woman moves on to the next row, reaching over to shake the hands of every passenger. His pulse is already high, but now it skyrockets. He can't put his finger on it, but something about what the woman is doing is utterly terrifying to him.

He sees in a flash the woman in the airport, scratching her head and losing a patch of hair. Now, as she's making her way through the plane, she's all but bald.

She's mutating. She was probably a regular person before something caused her to start changing ...

As though drawn by something, his eyes go to the floor. The two dead guys are still lying there. The guy who got his neck broken is facing Felix, his eyes shut but his mouth open. On his chin and along his jawline, exactly where the woman grabbed him, is a clear, dark mark from her unnaturally long hand.

And it finally hits home for Felix what the woman is doing. Why she never intended to blow up the plane. Why she doesn't even have a bomb.

She's doing to all of them what happened to her.

She's spreading whatever horrible disease is transforming her into a flesh-eating monster.

And she's only three rows away from Felix now.

47

TIM

THE MOOD IN THE hallway doesn't exactly improve after Tim manages to decipher Alan's ominous message.

Lis breaks into tears again.

Lundbeck is the first to talk. Clearing her throat, she says to Tim, "Ask him about the woman. We still need a name."

"The woman, Alan," Tim says, not expecting much of an answer. "The one who's still out there. You know who she is?"

Alan seems to have lost interest in speaking to them. Instead, he starts testing the strength of the chain again. The harder he tugs, the more it looks like the bolts keeping the bedpost fixed to the floor might give way.

"Alan," Tim says louder, tapping the window. "Please, pal. We need your help."

Alan just glances over his shoulder at him—the way he turns his neck reminds Tim of an owl—and makes that single, low squeal again, then goes back to pulling the chain. He gives off a groan as he puts his full effort into it. The chain groans too, and the floor starts cracking around the post.

"That's it," Lundbeck says. "He's going back under. Move aside, Iversen. Hit him, Torben."

"Wait," Lis says suddenly, stepping in front of Tim. "Let me talk to him while he's still coherent." She takes off the mask and adjusts her hair.

Lundbeck is about to protest, but apparently thinks better of it.

"Alan? Darling? It's me."

The voice of his wife causes Alan to stop what he's doing. He drops the chain and comes as close to the door as he can. As Alan looks at Lis through the window, Tim for the first time sees Alan in those big, blank eyes, if only for a flash.

"Please, sweetheart. Help us. Help *me*. Tell me who the woman is. Just tell me."

Alan veers his head—not as a gesture of denial, but more like frustration. He spits out a quick tirade of almost angry sounds.

Lis mutters, "What did he say, Tim?"

Tim shakes his head slowly. "I think he's fighting himself."

Lis lowers her voice. "I want you to know I love you, Alan. With all my heart. I don't care what's happened to you. I will love you till I die."

Alan turns his face away and utters a string of what can best be described as raw emotion transmitted via sound. Tim can swear he hears sorrow in it.

"Alan, please," Lis goes on, her voice breaking. "Give them anything that can help them find her in time. We can't let innocent people suffer. Think of all our friends, Alan. Think of your nephew."

Alan flings out his arms and roars so loudly, Lis gasps for breath, and Lundbeck instinctively grabs her shoulders to pull her back. Lis regains her bearings and pulls free.

Alan now starts shouting his message from before, repeating it over and over. Into his rant he mixes that distinct low screech whenever his eyes fall on Tim, and Tim starts to get the feeling Alan is calling him some kind of name. He can't translate it, but judging by his tone, it isn't exactly a pleasantry.

Stepping even closer to the door, Lis pleads with Alan through the glass. "I know you know, darling. I know you can help us. Please! We need to find her. Where is she? What's her name?"

Alan keeps shouting for a few more seconds. Then he falls quiet. He's breathing heavy, and he just stares from Lis to Tim and back again. And then Tim sees whatever shred of human is still in him come forward for a split-second. He utters a single word. Tim doesn't immediately get it, because unlike everything else Alan has said so far, this word is very simple and has only one meaning. It's a name.

Then Alan completely loses it. He spins around, grabs the chain and tries to chew through it, breaking his teeth. When that doesn't work, he resumes pulling it frantically, like a rabid dog that has been tied down. He bellows and screeches and spits.

"I'm sorry," Lis says to Lundbeck, turning away with a pained expression.

"That's okay," she tells her. "You tried. Hit him, Torben. Before he tears loose."

Tim is pushed aside as the doctor sweeps in from the side with the dart gun. This time, Alan sees it coming, and he roars out in rage and jumps to the side like an overgrown grasshopper. The chain still holds, but the pull is so violent, the entire bedpost breaks off. Alan doesn't get time to enjoy his freedom, though, because the doctor hits him in the back with a dart.

Even as Alan is still on his feet, Lundbeck starts giving orders. "Get the chain fixed. Put two on him. And make sure he doesn't wake back up again." She rounds on Tim, her eyes grim inside the visor. "Thanks for trying, Tim. You can leave."

"Ulla?" Tim says.

She was about to turn away, but now she hesitates. "Yeah?"

"I got it," he says, feeling his heart beat fast.

Lundbeck eyes him intently. "You did?"

"He said 'Felicia.'"

Lundbeck frowns. "Felicia?"

Lis gasps. "That's our maid's name. Felicia Acosta."

Lundbeck looks perplexed. "But we cleared her. We checked her right after our first talk, and she was allowed to—"

"It's her," Tim cuts her off. "I noticed an accent in her voice when I heard her in my head."

Lundbeck's eyes jump from Tim to Lis and back again. "That's good enough for me." She pulls out her phone and makes a call. "Suspect's name is Felicia Acosta. She's no longer in town, I repeat, suspect has left Hornsted. We need to ..."

Lundbeck keeps talking, but Tim doesn't listen. He turns to Alan who's still struggling, even though the sedative is clearly setting in. He has dropped to his knees and can't seem to get back up. Yet he spins around and throws himself at the door with a loud crash, causing the hinges to rattle. For a brief second, Alan's eyes fix on Tim, and he utters another brief sound. Another name. Then he slides down the door with a groan and passes out.

Tim is suddenly frozen in place. Everything around him slows down to a crawl. He can hear his own heartbeat.

"What?" Lundbeck barks into the phone. "Are you positive? ... God, that's *excellent* work, Mick! ... Where's she headed? Don't tell me it's an international flight ..."

Lundbeck listens, and so does Tim. The guy on the other end says, "*Copenhagen. Scheduled to land again in half an hour.*"

"Can we stop it?" Lundbeck asks. "Can we contact the pilot and get him to keep them in the air?"

The guy on the phone says something about giving it a try, and Lundbeck ends the call. Turning to Tim, she says, "My guy already went through the passenger list. She's on her way to—"

"I heard. You need to get me to Copenhagen."

Lundbeck shakes her head. "We've got this now, Iversen. Our people in Copenhagen will be ready if and when the plane lands. Thank you for—"

Tim grabs her collar and lifts her clean off the ground, pulling her close enough that his breath fogs the glass of her mask. "I'm not asking."

The guards come to grab him, but Lundbeck tells them again to stand down. "Let go of me, Tim," she says in as calm a tone as she can muster.

He reluctantly releases his grip. Lundbeck sinks back down onto the floor, adjusts her suit, then looks up at him. "What's gotten into you? What's wrong?"

"I need to be there when that plane lands. In case they can't prevent it from landing."

"That's a hundred twenty miles, Iversen. There's no way we're doing that in thirty minutes."

"That helicopter outside. If we leave now, it should be doable."

"We'll have dozens of people ready. They're already mobilizing. Trust me, we're finally taking this seriously, Tim. Even if she's infected the entire damn plane, we will handle it."

Tim breathes hard through his nose. "You don't get it. I need to be there."

"But why?"

Tim glances towards the cell. "Alan gave me a second name."

Lundbeck frowns. "What name was that?"

He can barely get the name across his lips. "Helena."

48

FELIX

FELIX'S MIND IS REELING. He's watching the woman make her way closer, one handshake at a time. She moves with grim determination. Clearly not doing it to greet anyone, but simply to get the job done.

Some of the passengers are hesitant to take her hand—understandably so—but the woman needs only bare her teeth in a snarl to remind them of the alternative, and so everyone eventually complies, and she makes sure to skip no one. The ones whom she's already touched are looking from their hands to each other with perplexed looks, some of them even muttering to each other, relief in their voices, as though thinking "Was that it? Was that all she wanted?"

Felix knows better. He knows it's no regular handshake he's about to receive.

He looks at the seat in front of him. Save for some brochures and a puke bag, there's nothing he can use. On the table in front of Pia is a juice box and the sandwich. An idea jumps into his head, and Felix grabs the sandwich.

"What are you doing?" Pia whispers. "How can you eat now?"

Felix isn't hungry. He rips the cellophane off and drops the sandwich back onto the table. The woman is at the row in front of them now, and Felix can hear the man sitting there ask her, "What ... what do you want?"

"Gimme your hand," she tells him. "Let me shake it."

Felix bends over and fumbles with the cellophane. It's a little greasy from the nasty chickpea mayo that Pia uses, and it keeps crumbling up so he has to try and straighten it out.

I won't make it. There's not enough time.

And there really is only a matter of seconds before the woman will reach Felix's seat.

Luckily, though, the guy in front asks, "What? Why?"

"Just do it." Her tone offers no room for resistance, but to Felix's surprise, the man still doesn't comply.

"I'd just ... I'd just like to know why you would want to—hey!"

Felix is so busy working with the cellophane, he doesn't see what the woman does, but he feels the seat in front rock a little, hears some scuffling, and it seems like the woman simply reaches over and grabs the guy's hand.

It buys Felix five more seconds. Which is just enough to get the cellophane in place and smooth it over so that it's almost not visible.

Just as he leans back and places his hand in his lap, casually covering it with the other, the woman steps into view.

He looks up at her, and his heart sinks. She's a terrifying sight up close. Not only because of the blood smeared all over her—Felix is also pretty sure she's transformed even more in just the few minutes that have gone by since she took over the plane. Her face is longer, her mouth wider, her eyes closer to each other. She also seems taller, and her arms a couple of inches longer. She looks less human now, more monstrous.

She leans over Felix to offer Pia her hand. Felix looks at the hand. The fingers are long and boney. The nails thick like claws.

"Gimme your hand," she hisses at Pia.

Pia visibly needs to force herself to raise her arm. As soon as she does, the woman snatches it, squeezes it briefly, then let go and moves her hand in front of Felix.

"Now you."

Felix looks up at her. Those blank, white eyes bore into his. He lifts both hands, making sure only to reveal his right hand at the last possible moment. Without looking at it, the woman grabs it, gives it a quick squeeze, and then she turns her attention to other side of the aisle.

Felix places his hand back down into his lap and rests the other one on top of it. He stares at the seat in front of him, feeling his pulse hammer away inside his ears.

Did it work?

His hand is buzzing, but that could simply be from the woman's grip.

"What did you do?" Pia whispers in his ear as the woman moves on down the plane. "What's that you put on your hand? Let me see."

Felix wants to show her. He wants to check for himself. But he suddenly can't move. So, Pia, impatiently, takes him by the sleeve and raises his hand to look at it. She frowns at the sight of the cellophane.

"I think ... I think it worked," Felix hears himself mutter. The clear plastic is still in place, unbroken, and it's covering his entire palm, the back of his hand, and all five fingers.

Feeling a tiny hope, he regains control over his motor system and is able to peel the improvised glove off and drop it to the floor. He studies his hand. Save for some greasy traces of vegan mayo, he sees nothing else.

"Why would you ...?" Pia shakes her head. "You didn't want her to touch your skin. How come? Do you think she ...?" The last question dies on her lips as she raises her own hand and looks at it.

Across her palm, the skin is already darkening. It's not much, not nearly as dark as the dead guy's jaw. But it's clearly there.

Felix looks ahead and sees some of the other passengers with aisle seats study their hands. Dark bruises are showing up everywhere.

Felix checks his own hand again. Still nothing but fair skin.

Pia is rummaging through her purse. Taking out the hand sanitizer gel, she empties the entire bottle onto her palm, then slathers it all over her hands and rubs them thoroughly.

That won't work, Felix thinks to himself, inhaling the sharp smell of the gel. *Whatever this is ... alcohol won't kill it.*

"Everyone, please fasten your seat belts. We're about to land."

The message comes over the speakers, and it's only now Felix realizes they've been descending for the past ten minutes. Looking out the window, he sees Copenhagen coming closer fast.

"*We will land as planned at Kastrup*," the pilot goes on. His voice is strained, even though he's trying to sound calm. "*We should all remain calm, and everything will be fine.*"

Felix clicks his seat belt shut, just as the woman comes striding past him. "The pilot is right!" she says loudly. "As long as you all stay seated, nothing bad will happen." She stops to turn around and show the suitcase to everyone. "But if any of you get up or tell anybody about what happened here, this bomb will go off. Make no mistake, it'll kill everyone onboard even after we land. And I'll be watching from the back."

She sends a menacing look out over the passengers, and an anxious murmur goes through the plane.

Then the woman rushes back down through the aisle. Felix turns his head to see where she's going. Passing the lavatory, she disappears through a door marked STAFF ONLY.

"It's not coming off," Pia says, still rubbing her hand. "What is this?"

Felix doesn't say anything. For one thing, Pia hasn't connected the dots yet, and for another, he can't know for sure that his theory is right, so there's no reason to worry her.

Outside the window, the runway comes into view. As they touch down, Felix checks his hand again.

Still clean. The dark mark should be visible by now.

I did it. I saved myself. He feels a short-lived rush of relief as he looks around at the other passengers. *Now I just need to get out of here before the rest of these people become contagious* ...

49

VERONICA

IT'S HALF PAST THREE when she finally reaches the neighbor's house.

The sun is setting, and the heavy cloud layer means it's already dark.

The house is a proper year-round home, not just a cabin like her in-laws'. The lights are only on in one room. The driveway has not been cleared of snow, and the car that's parked below the pent roof has clearly not been driving anywhere today.

Veronica parks the scooter in front of the house, turns off the lights and kills the engine. The tank is half empty, which means she should be able to make it back home again; she probably needn't have brought the extra gas, but better safe than sorry.

Taking off the helmet, she listens.

The wind has finally settled, and the early evening is completely quiet. The temperature has gone back down below the freezing point, and her breath is visible as white puffs of smoke.

Veronica gets off the scooter and feels her phone vibrate. It's a text from Molly.

Did you reach the neighbor yet? Did you find Leo?

Obviously, the girl is concerned, both for Veronica and her uncle, and she sends her a quick text back to reassure her: *I just got here. I'll call you soon. Don't worry, sweetie.*

She puts the phone back into her pocket and takes out the flashlight instead. Lighting her way, she goes up the driveway. As she does, she sees what must be footprints. It's a little hard to tell, because more snow has come down after someone walked here, but she's pretty sure at least one person has either left or come to the house on foot.

Leo?

Veronica's heart begins beating faster. For some odd reason, she suddenly wishes she had a weapon. A gun. A knife. A can of Mace. Anything to ward off someone who might try to hurt her.

Who would do that? What are you scared of?

The answer is obvious, though she really doesn't care for it.

She approaches the front door, and, to her surprise, she finds it open. Her first thought is that the residents saw her coming and opened the door to greet her. But no one's there, and the door has clearly been open for quite a while. Snow has blown into the entrance hall, forming a knee-high dune on the floor that's only halfway melted.

Veronica peeks inside. The lights are off, but she's pretty sure the hall is empty. A sign on the door says "Jytte & Asbjørn Thomsen." Sounds like an elderly couple. And the coats, shoes, and old-fashioned decorations on the wall all seem to confirm it. She can make out the door to the living room. That too is ajar.

"Hello?" Veronica croaks. "Is anybody home?"

No answer.

She debates with herself about what to do next. Her guess is that no one is home. Had they been, they wouldn't have left the front door open like this.

But judging by the way they left the house, something bad could have happened in there. An emergency.

If that's the case, then the next question becomes, why would the old couple leave their home on foot? And apparently without bothering to put on shoes or jackets, either.

The answer that's presenting itself isn't pleasant, but it makes sense. If Leo had come by here and infected the old couple, and if they'd ended up in a similar state to the one he's in, then it's very plausible they too could have wandered off into the cold.

So, if the house is very likely empty, Veronica asks herself, *then why am I afraid to go in there*?

She gathers her courage, reminds herself that Leo is sick, that it's her fault and that she's here to help him. Then, just as she's about to step into the house, there comes a noise from the backyard.

She spins around and points the flashlight in the direction. She can't see anything but a snow-covered lawn and some bushes and a couple of leafless apple trees.

What was that?

It sounded almost like a floorboard creaking. Except wetter. Like someone taking a step in the snow. Was someone lurking just around the corner?

"Hello?" Veronica calls out, a little louder this time. "Who's there?" Then, when no answer comes, she asks, "Is it you, Leo?"

Still, no reply.

Must have been the snow, she thinks, forcing her heart back down from her throat. *It's re-freezing. That's why it made the noise.*

Still not fully convinced, Veronica suddenly feels less inclined to stick around outside the house, and so she steps over the snow to enter the hall.

50

TIM

TIM CALLS UP HELENA for the third time. It goes to her voicemail again. He doesn't bother leaving her another message, but simply ends the call.

"Damnit," he mutters.

Lundbeck probably can't hear him over the noise from the rotors, but she's watching him. "Still no luck?" she asks—Tim can hear her just fine; his ears automatically filter out anything but her voice.

Tim shakes his head. "I don't get why she would turn off her phone. It makes no sense."

Lundbeck hands him a set of headphones. He puts them on and turns on the radio.

"I'm sure she's fine," Lundbeck says, her voice coming through tiny speakers inside the headset.

"I hope so," Tim mutters. "Any word from your guy?"

Lundbeck checks her phone, then shakes her head.

Tim looks out at the horizon. They are headed due east, and the sun is hanging above the water, poking its thin, steely grey rays through the cloud cover. Zealand is visible up ahead. They are over halfway. Less than ten minutes out. Luckily, the wind is the right direction. They just might make it.

"I've got a daughter too, you know."

Tim looks at Lundbeck. "You do?"

"Yeah. But we haven't spoken for years." She shrugs with a tired smile. "Mothers and daughters, you know."

"It can happen for fathers and daughters too," Tim grunts.

Lundbeck eyes him for moment. "I called her earlier. Just before you showed up. I told her to get the hell away from here. Get on a plane to Australia. Wait this thing out." She sneers. "The first time she hears my voice for so long, and I'm telling her to buzz off. Of course she didn't believe me."

"You were trying to protect her," Tim says, surprising himself.

Lundbeck turns her head and looks out the window. She's not a pretty woman, at least not in Tim's eyes. But her inner qualities are shining through, and he can't help but feel a certain attraction to her—which is another surprise; Tim hasn't thought that way of a woman since Anya died.

In another life, maybe, Tim thinks to himself. Then, a more rational thought: *Nah, wouldn't work. We're too similar.*

Tim is a cold person, and so, clearly, is Lundbeck. Anya was warm. Not cuddly, not even particularly soft, but warm. Her heart was open, and that was why she could pry Tim's heart open just enough for him to let her in.

As though confirming his thoughts, Lundbeck looks at him again and says, "You were in the army too, right?"

He nods.

"Me too. Stationed once, never got to see any action. Then I figured I'd rather work at the problems at home. Never thought I'd end up in a case like this ... and now ... assuming the world won't come to an end, I'm at the very least out of a job."

"For telling your daughter about what's going on?"

She raises one eyebrow. "And for trafficking you across the country without permission."

"Oh. Right. Well, if it's any consolation, you're doing the right thing."

"For you or for the rest of the world?"

Tim doesn't answer.

The helicopter is over land now, racing across the countryside, the capital now within sight.

Then, Lundbeck asks, "Why would Andersen mention your daughter's name?"

Tim shakes his head. "I keep telling myself it could just have been random, but ... I don't know."

The truth is, he does know. It was a warning. Alan mentioned Helena to let Tim know that something bad is going to happen. Why it involves his daughter, Tim has no idea.

But he doesn't believe it's a coincidence the plane is headed for Copenhagen.

If anything has already happened to her ...

He takes out his phone and calls her again. Still no answer. As he puts his phone away, Lundbeck takes out hers and reads a text.

"It's my guy," she tells Tim. "Your daughter wasn't home. No signs of a break-in or fighting."

"Okay," Tim says, feeling somewhat reassured. "So she left voluntarily. Maybe she's just gone shopping."

"You called the place she works, right?"

"I did. It's her day off."

"University?"

"They haven't seen her today, either."

"Perhaps try and—" Lundbeck's phone starts ringing. She answers the call, moves the headphones and presses the phone against her ear. "Yeah? ... All right ... Okay, thanks ...

No, I'm headed there now ... That's none of your business ..." She ends the call and looks at Tim. "They haven't been able to contact the pilot. He sent out a secret distress signal five minutes ago, indicating that the plane's been hijacked. It's about to land at Kastrup."

Tim's breathing speeds up. He looks out the front window. "Is that it?"

They are still a couple of miles out from the airport. He can just make out a white airliner flying very low and going lower still.

"*I think so*," the pilot says, checking his screens. "*Yeah, must be. They're landing now*."

Tim sees the plane touch down and immediately slow down. On the ground, he can make out several vehicles. It isn't hard; they are running their flashers like damn Christmas trees.

So much for the element of surprise. She certainly knows we're waiting for her.

"Get me down," Tim tells the pilot. "As close as you can."

"*I can only get you to the next runway over*."

"That's fine. Hurry up." Tim is already getting to his feet. He pulls off the headset and turns to the door. He opens it, and the icy wind roars into his face.

"*Jesus, Iversen, what are you doing*?" Lundbeck cries out.

"*Too early*!" the pilot shouts. "*Close it again*!"

"*Just get me down*!" Tim bellows back. "*Now*!"

And he does. The helicopter descends abruptly, and Tim has to grab the handles in the ceiling so as to not fall. He feels the pressure drop as they rapidly come closer to the ground. The pilot deftly slows the descent, and when they are about three stories up, Tim jumps out.

Flying through the air, faster and faster, he prepares himself for the pain.

He barely feels the impact, though. He lands on his feet, rolls over once, and is immediately able to jump up and run towards the plane, which has now come to a full stop about two hundred yards away. Tim runs with everything he's got.

Soldiers have surrounded the plane, driving their jeeps in front of it so it can't take off again, and someone with a megaphone is shouting for the pilot to make sure no one leaves the plane.

Tim is coming up from the rear. As he reaches the perimeter the soldiers have put up, he makes a decision. He isn't going to waste time asking the commander's permission to go in and find the woman; he knows he won't get it.

So, instead of slowing down, he simply keeps going, sprinting in between the vehicles, zipping through armed soldiers.

Some of them cry out for him to stop. Tim enters the circle and heads for the plane, and the guy with the megaphone stops shouting at the pilot. Instead, he addresses his men. "*Do not open fire! I repeat, do not fire!*"

Tim heads for the emergency door, the one just over the wing. In one huge leap, he jumps onto the wing and grabs the handle.

Ripping the door open, he bursts into the airplane.

51

VERONICA

IT'S ONLY SLIGHTLY WARMER inside. She goes to the door to the living room and peeks inside. What she sees makes the muscles in her legs and arms tense up. Something dramatic clearly took place in the living room. Chairs are knocked over, the floor is littered with stuff, and one of the windows is cracked. She can even see—

A noise from behind.

Veronica screams and whirls around, raising the flashlight to use as a club.

No one's there, at least not within striking distance, so she turns the flashlight over and sees a pair of glowing yellow eyes staring at her from the chest by the wall. A black cat is perched there, its tail whipping back and forth.

"Jesus Christ," Veronica breathes. "You were there the whole time, weren't you? You little jerk."

The cat meows once, then raises one of its paws and begins licking it.

Veronica turns back to the living room. If anybody really is in the house, they no doubt heard her, so there's no real reason to be quiet. Yet she still steps carefully onto the parquet floor. She reaches out for the switch and turns on the ceiling lamp.

The light is comforting, but it also reveals in greater detail the chaos that went down in here.

Looking down, Veronica sees what can only be blood on the floor. Not a lot, but definitely more than a nosebleed.

I should leave. Call the cops and let them handle this.

But the thought of Leo makes her press on. This feels like her responsibility. If there's even the slightest chance that Leo can still be helped, it'll surely be too late by the time the police reach the island.

She goes into the kitchen, turns on the light, and then she regrets dearly that she entered the house.

The kitchen is even more of a mess. Everything has been torn from the counter. Blood has sprayed onto the cupboards. And on the floor, splayed out on his back, is an old guy. At least Veronica assumes so. There are very few telltale signs left. A tuft of curly, white chest hair. One slipper. And a set of dentures. The latter is lying on the floor right next to the head of the guy. It looks like a car drove over his skull. It's squashed like a watermelon, the brain matter visible, and any facial features are completely erased. The guy's chest has been ripped open like a book, and most of his insides have been removed. Huge chunks of flesh are also gone from his arms and legs. There are lots of visible bite marks. What makes the whole thing so much worse is the sweet, metallic smell of blood and guts.

Veronica turns away, bends over, and throws up onto the floor. Her stomach keeps retching until it's completely empty. She spits into the pile and, not wanting to look at the guy again, she staggers back into the living room.

The cat comes waltzing across the floor, not a care in the world. Veronica barely notices. She fumbles to get her phone out, as a single thought keeps repeating.

He ate him. He ***ate*** *him.*

The bite marks gave it away that the old guy had not just been murdered and mutilated, but that someone had feasted away at him. And not only are there no predators around here big enough to eat an entire person—there had been barefooted prints in the blood all around the guy.

This can't be Leo. It can't have been him who did it.

But it must be. Who else?

She finally gets her phone out and dials 1-1-2.

Just as it begins ringing, she hears a sound from the next room over.

Veronica freezes in place. Disconnecting the call, she stares at the closed door at the end of the room.

Someone's in there. And it's not the cat, because he's now sitting on the dining table, licking his paw.

Veronica is about to turn and leave, when her boot hits something hard. Looking down, she sees a Browning sports shotgun. Her father, when he was alive, had been an avid hunter, and since he never had a boy, he forced Veronica to join him on a couple of hunts, hoping the hobby would rub off on her. It hadn't. But Veronica had learned how to load and fire a shotgun.

She picks it up and checks the chambers. Both are loaded. Looks like buckshot. She notices a little blood on the comb. Apparently, the old guy got his weapon ready and tried to defend himself when his murderer entered the house. As far as Veronica can tell, while he managed to load the gun, he didn't get a chance to fire it.

Another sound from the door.

Veronica leaves the flashlight on the table and shoulders the shotgun. Aiming the barrel at the door, she approaches it slowly. Being armed with a loaded weapon, she feels not only safer, but also a bit more confident. She can taste puke, and her stomach is still churning, but she forces herself to breathe through her nose and keep walking.

Whoever is in there, I need to know.

52

TIM

TIM IS NOT SURE what he expected. Probably for the woman to attack him the moment he entered the plane.

No one comes at him.

Instead, he stares around at the passengers who are mostly still seated, except for two guys who lie in the aisle, clearly dead—one has a broken neck, the other is reduced to a bloody pile of limbs. Everyone else has turned their heads to look at Tim, fear emanating from the faces.

"Oh, God! It's another one!" a woman cries.

"It's okay," Tim shouts, holding up his hands. "I'm here to help! Where is the woman?"

A long moment of silence—except for something beeping from the back. Tim's eyes and ears scan everything within the airplane. He can't see the woman anywhere. She doesn't appear to be hiding, either, because all it took to blow her cover was one nervous look in the direction of her hiding place from one of the passengers. But they all just stare at Tim, as though he's the danger.

"Where is she?" he asks, a little louder.

"Please don't hurt us," an elderly woman bursts out.

"I'm not going to," Tim says. "I just need to know where she is."

"We ... we're not supposed to tell," a teenage boy says. "She told us to stay seated, and she said she'd blow up the plane if we—"

His mother slaps her hand over his mouth and shushes him hard. As she does so, Tim notices a clear, dark bruise on her skin. Looking around, he notices similar spots on a lot of hands.

She infected every last one of them.

He shakes his head and says in a calmer tone, as he looks around at the passengers, "Don't worry. There's no bomb. I assure you. She wouldn't blow up the plane. She was bluffing. Now, tell me where she is. Tell me please, before she gets away."

Another moment of silence, briefer this time.

Then the teenager stands up and points. "She went to the back!"

"Felix, no! Sit down!"

Tim immediately runs down the aisle. He rips open the door to the tiny toilet. Empty. There's a door leading to the back area where only the crew is allowed. Tim looks at a middle-aged business-looking guy sitting in the last seat and points at the door. The man's eyes are big, and his moustache quivers as he nods.

Tim takes a breath and bursts through the door.

Once more, he expects to be faced with the woman coming at him teeth and claws.

Once more, he's wrong.

It's some sort of combined rest and kitchen area. The incessant beeping grows louder. The place definitely isn't meant for people Tim's size; he has to duck and walk sideways to squeeze through. He comes to a narrow door marked with several signs. *CARGO AREA — No entrance! Warning: Pressurization! Danger! Do not open!*

Someone clearly ignored the warnings, because the door has been kicked open and is unable to close properly anymore. Above it is a red lamp blinking, and it's here the irritating beeping comes from.

Tim sticks his head through and squints at the darkness. His eyes immediately adjust and allow him to see a pile of bags and suitcases. There's a strip of daylight at the other end, and he can make out the inside of what seems to be a hatch—probably the one they load the luggage through.

Did she ...? No, the soldiers would've stopped her.

He can hear the jeeps idling outside, but no one has shouted or fired a shot since he went into the plane. Had the woman jumped out, they would have reacted.

Still, Tim is certain she's come this way, so he climbs over the suitcases and reaches the hatch. In front of it is a nylon net meant to keep the bags from tumbling around. It's been torn. He fumbles with the hatch and opens it.

He stares out at the soldiers still surrounding the airplane. He's on the other side of the plane now.

Almost immediately, someone spots him, raises their gun, and within seconds, the soldiers are all shouting at Tim.

Where is she? Where the hell ***is*** *she?*

"Listen to me!" he roars out, causing the soldiers to fall quiet. "Everyone on this plane is infected. Let no one leave. You hear me? No one leaves!"

The soldier with the megaphone calls out, "*Copy that, Iversen. What about the woman*?"

It's only then Tim realizes that of course the commander has been briefed by Lundbeck about who he is. She might even have told him not to interfere, which would explain why they didn't shoot Tim down when he came running. He sends her a quiet thank you in his thoughts.

"The woman is still at large," Tim shouts. "I don't think she's on the plane anymore!"

"*Impossible*!" the soldiers retorts. "*No one's left the plane since it touched down*!"

"No, I know," Tim mutters. He turns over and climbs up on top of the plane. Standing up, he stares down the runway the plane just landed on.

Because the area is so flat, and thanks to his new vision, he sees her.

Almost two miles out. At the outskirts of the airfield. Running for the fence. Headed for the city.

"Oh, Jesus Christ," Tim breathes, as it finally hits home that the woman used the exact same technique he did when he left the helicopter. "She jumped out before they landed ..."

53

FELIX

"YOU HAVE TO LISTEN to me ... I'm not infected!"

The soldier has ignored him so far, but now he finally pauses to send Felix a look through the visor in his hazmat helmet before he continues escorting him across the runway. "Save it for the doctors, kid."

"Here, see! Look at my hand. There's no mark!"

"Look, I'm sorry," the soldier tells him, his voice distorted through the mask. "I'm just following orders. You'll have to come along."

"No, you don't get it," Felix says, pulling the other way—but the soldier is too strong and simply drags him along. "If you put me in there with the others, they'll infect me."

The soldier isn't listening. In front of them are six large ambulances, which look more like busses. Also on the runway are dozens of military and police vehicles, along with hundreds of soldiers. Not all of them are dressed in full hazmat suits like the ones escorting the passengers from the plane—those who aren't are staying at the periphery of the scene, standing with their weapons, watching the infected people being loaded into the ambulances with grim looks on their faces.

We're like cattle being led to the slaughter.

Felix glances back to see Pia a few paces behind him. And behind her are more passengers. Every single one firmly gripped by a soldier. Most of the passengers aren't even wearing their jackets, despite the freezing cold morning weather. As soon as the soldiers entered, people clamored to get off the plane, and in the chaos of the evacuation, Felix seems to be one of the only ones who thought of bringing his outerwear.

The moment Felix saw the huge, half-transformed guy come into the airplane, he knew for a fact that his theory was right: That this thing is contagious and that everyone on the plane would turn into monsters just like the woman.

And yet he immediately sensed that the tall guy was different. He couldn't put his finger on it, but even before he spoke, Felix knew he hadn't come to attack anyone. So when he asked where the woman was, Felix told him. After the big guy left, it took the soldiers only a few minutes to board the plane. They instructed people to follow along in an orderly fashion and told them they would be taken to the hospital for immediate treatment.

And now, Felix is about to be loaded onto a bus that's already crammed with people.

I can't get on that thing. I need to find a way to escape.

But it looks like an impossible task. Even if he tore free and made a run for it, there are soldiers all around him, and he'd be tackled—or worse, gunned down—within seconds.

The soldier stops by the door to the bus. Another soldier—a female, also fully dressed in hazmat gear—is holding a tablet. She points with a touch pen at Felix. "Full name?"

"Look, like I told him, I'm not infected." Felix shows both his freezing hands, turning them over. "See? No marks. I made sure she didn't—"

"I just need your name," the woman tells him. "You can give further details upon arrival to the hospital."

"No, please, *please* listen," Felix says, putting his hands together in a prayer gesture. "I am not infected. But I will be if I get onto that bus. I'm perfectly happy to go get checked out by doctors, but please don't put me in with the rest of them."

The woman glances sideways. For a second, Felix takes it to mean she's considering his request. Then she asks: "More suits? We don't need any more. Just put 'em there."

There's a pile of hand luggage left on the ground—apparently, the passengers aren't allowed to bring them to the hospital. Another soldier has come with a bunch of clear plastic bags. In them are what appears to be blue hazmat suits like the ones the soldiers are wearing.

The soldier puts them on the luggage, then walks away.

"I'd like to help you," the woman says, addressing Felix. "But we don't have time, and we can't offer you separate transport. Please give me your name so we can move things along."

"No," he says, feeling his heart pound away in his throat. "No, I'm not gonna give you my name until you promise I won't be put in there with the others."

"Listen," the male soldier growls, tightening the grip on Felix's arm. "I'm not sure you get the severity of this situation. You're not in a position to—"

"Just tell them what they need to know, Felix!"

He looks back to see Pia waiting there with her own escort, sending him a pleading look. She's pale and shivers.

"Felix Haiberg?" the female cop asks. Then, answering her own questions, "There's only one Felix on the passenger list. You can get on now."

The male soldier urges Felix forward. Just as he's about to step onto the bus, Felix instead rips free and jumps sideways. The soldier shouts for him to stop. Felix doesn't; he goes for the pile of luggage and grabs one of the hazmat suits. Turning around, he holds it up like a shield. "Let me put this on! That's all I ask ..."

The soldier comes for him with anger in his eyes, but the woman stops him with her hand. "Let him. He already touched it." She looks at Felix and raises her eyebrows. "You've got ten seconds."

Felix rips the plastic open with his teeth and puts on the suit as fast as he can. It has a hoodie but no helmet. Instead, there's a fabric mask very much like the one the woman wore to disguise herself. It'll have to do, so Felix puts it on.

Hopefully, this thing is only transferred via skin contact. He has a feeling it might. Why else would the woman bother going through the entire plane to touch everyone? At least with the suit on, no one will accidentally touch him.

He thanks the female soldier and steps up into the bus.

Just as he does, someone screams from behind. Felix and the soldiers all turn their heads. A woman who was waiting in line is clutching her hand, staring at it. Even from over here, Felix can see her skin is all darkened and her fingers are longer.

Jeez, it comes on fast ...

The woman begins moving away from the line, and soldiers quickly move in from the sides to stop her. As they grab her, she begins struggling.

Felix becomes aware that everyone is watching the fight. And he sees his opportunity. Stepping back down onto the pavement, he gets down onto his stomach and scooches under the bus. He places himself directly at the center and looks in every direction. He sees a lot of boots, but no one crouches down to look in at him. Because no one noticed him.

After a few seconds, the woman is subdued, and the soldiers continue ushering people onto the bus, as though nothing happened. Clearly, they assume Felix got on the bus.

I did it. I got away.

But he's not scot-free yet. There's still a big risk they'll catch him again. As soon as the bus drives away, he'll be exposed. He needs to be ready for whatever happens.

So, Felix lies there on the frozen asphalt. Breathing evenly. Watching. Waiting.

54

VERONICA

SHE REACHES THE DOOR and listens.

Another noise. It sounds like something thumping on the floor.

Veronica doesn't knock or call out. She simply rips open the door and steps back.

The room is the only one with the lights on. Had Veronica thought to go to the window to check before she entered the house, she would have never gone inside.

It's a bathroom. In the tub is the wife of the old guy. She's naked, lying face-down, and she's not as badly wounded as her husband, although she's also clearly been eaten away at. The assailant—probably full from his first meal—has limited himself to a few chunks of the woman's back, shoulders and thighs. Obviously enough for her to bleed out.

But there's a big difference.

The black stuff. It was nowhere to be seen on the guy, but on the woman, it's growing in healthy patches all over—especially in her wounds. The smell in the bathroom isn't nearly as nauseating as in the kitchen—Veronica can still smell the blood, but the lemony scent is even stronger.

The woman's leg jerks and produces the thumping sound as the knee knocks against the inside of the tub.

God ... is she alive or dead?

Keeping the shotgun aimed at the woman's torso, Veronica steps into the bathroom. She peripherally notices more bloody footprints on the tile floor. Coming closer to the woman's head, she peeks over the edge of the tub. Her face is turned to the side, her mouth open, eyes closed. She certainly looks dead. The color has completely drained from her face, tiny blue veins visible on her forehead. There's no water in the tub, but there probably was when the woman was attacked—the plug has been yanked out during the fighting. Veronica surmises that the woman was in the bath when her husband got attacked.

"Hello?" she asks. "Can you hear me?"

Another jerk of the leg.

Then the muscles in the woman's face start twitching.

Jesus Christ ... I don't ... I don't know what to do here ... Do I perform CPR? Is she already dead?

In the next instance, it becomes abundantly clear to Veronica what needs to be done.

Because the woman suddenly twists her neck and opens her eyes to look up at her. Her eyes are completely blank, and as the woman opens her mouth, Veronica can tell it's way too wide, and her teeth are way too sharp. The woman hisses and attempts to leap up from the bathtub. It's probably only the damage done to her back that stops her from lunging at Veronica. Instead, she lands clumsily over the edge of the bathtub. Reaching out her thin arms, she claws away at the air with fingers way too long—just like Leo's.

Veronica takes one step back and fires the shotgun.

The sound wipes out her hearing immediately. The top of the woman's head is peeled back like the lid on a can. Blood and brain are splattered over the wall. She slumps back down into the tub and stays still.

Veronica, her head vibrating from the shot, stumbles back into the living room.

She notices a movement from a windowsill. The cat is sitting there, glaring at her, clearly annoyed by the loud noise she produced. Then it looks out the window, and Veronica can tell its eyes fix on something.

For some reason, she feels drawn to find out what it is. So, she goes over there. But she can't see anything out in the darkness—her eyes clearly aren't as good as the cat's. She goes to turn off the light, then returns to the window, almost tripping over a chair.

This time, as she looks out, she sees what the cat sees.

The person—if that's still the correct term—standing in the snow below the apple tree. Facing this way. Not moving.

She recognizes her boyfriend, and at the same time, she can tell it's not him anymore.

He's only wearing his boxers. His pale body is covered in dried blood. His arms and legs are too long. His posture is like that of a praying mantis. And even though his face is mercifully hidden in the darkness, she can tell his jaw is way too big.

"Leo," she breathes, not hearing the word herself.

It seems like Leo hears her, though. Because he cocks his head, lifts his hand in a greeting gesture.

Then he suddenly takes off running. And if Veronica had any doubts left that Leo was no longer human, the way he runs wipes away the last remnants of hope.

Within two seconds, he's gone from sight.

Veronica feels her throat close up. She's suddenly deathly afraid. Not for herself—Leo didn't run towards the house.

He was headed east. Towards his parents' cabin.

Towards Molly.

55

TIM

"I SEE HER!" TIM calls out to the commander. "Northwest. Two miles out. She's about to exit the airfield."

The cop asks Tim something, but he wastes no time listening. Instead, he runs to the back of the plane, jumps onto the pavement, and takes off running. As he comes at the soldiers, they part like the Red Sea, and Tim sprints right through the opening.

Now that he's on the ground, he can no longer see the woman. But he knows the general direction.

He runs as fast as he can, and it takes him less than a minute to reach the place he saw her. As he approaches, he sees two other people. Men, both dressed in fluorescent worker vests. They are standing by some minor building and were apparently doing some technical maintenance. Now, one of them is rubbing his cheek with a distressed look, while the other looks in the direction of the fence.

"Jeez, man," the second guy says, lifting his beanie to scratch his hair. "She jumped clean over the fence. Can you believe it?"

"What the hell was wrong with her?" the other guy asks, still touching his face. "I mean, did you see her eyes? You think she's got that disease they're talking about on the—"

He stops talking as he spots Tim come running at him.

"It's okay!" Tim shouts, holding up his hands as he grinds to a halt. "I'm trying to catch the woman you just saw. Did she touch any of you?"

"Yeah, she sure did," the guy with the beanie says. "Slapped John here like he insulted her or something. All he did was ask what she thought she was doing running across the tarmac. Can you believe it?"

Tim goes to the guy to check his cheek. As he steps closer, the guy suddenly screams out. "Bloody hell! Your eyes! You're like her!"

"No, it's fine," Tim tells him. "I'm here to help."

The guy doesn't seem to believe it, but he also doesn't have time to get away. Tim grabs his wrist and inspects his face. A clear, dark bruise from five thin fingers runs across his cheek.

Damnit. That wasn't just a slap ...

"Look, you're infected," Tim tells the guy. "Don't touch your buddy here. Or anybody else. Someone will come and help you."

Even as he's talking, he drags the guy to the building. The door is already opened, so Tim pushes him inside. He just stands there, staring out at Tim with huge eyes. "Will I ... will I die?"

"No," Tim tells him—adding in his mind, *But you'll wish you did.*

Then he slams the door, locks it and throws the key chain to the other guy—who has resorted to gaping at Tim, dumbfounded.

"Don't let him out whatever he says. Unless you wanna catch the thing too."

He swallows and nods his head.

Tim looks back and sees jeeps headed this way. "They'll take care of him. Now, tell me: Which way did she go?"

The guy blinks, then turns and points. "Uhm, that way."

Tim takes off in the direction and jumps over the fence. Outside is a highway buzzing with late afternoon traffic—it's the only thing separating the airfield from the city. On the other side of the road is a small residential area. Tim can't see the woman anywhere, but he assumes she crossed the road, because a car has stopped by the shoulder, and the driver is standing next to it, making a phone call.

Tim runs to him.

"Yeah, on the E20 ... no, she left ... I mean, she just ran away! ... Yes, I'm sure I hit her, damnit ... I'm looking right at a huge dent in my bumper, and I—"

Tim reaches him from behind and grabs him by the shoulder.

"Hey, what the—" He spins around and freezes as he sees Tim's face.

"Tell me what happened," Tim demands. "You hit her with your car?"

"Fuck, man!" the guy exclaims, recoiling. "What the hell happened to—"

Tim holds on to his jacket. "I don't have the time. Tell me what happened."

"Okay, look, I'm ... I'm really sorry, but ... she came out of nowhere!"

"Where did she go?"

He gesticulates wildly, unable to take his eyes off Tim's eyes. "I don't know, man! She just ... got back up and ran!"

"Where to?"

He looks across the road briefly, then points. "Over there, I think. By those trees."

"Did she touch you?"

"What? No!"

"Sure?"

"Yeah, man. I didn't touch her, I swear! I didn't even have time to stop before she was gone ..."

The guy has no visible marks, so Tim decides to take his word for it. He lets him go, then runs across the road, weaving between the honking cars. He reaches the patch of trees which is growing on a slight incline. Running up it, Tim soon gets a full view over the adjacent area. It looks like senior housing—typical of the government, placing the old folks right next to the airport—and on the nearest block he spots a couple sitting on the second-story balcony, both dressed in heavy jackets and mittens, but still insisting on enjoying their morning coffee outdoors.

He runs across the lawn and waves up at them. "Did you see a woman run by here just a few minutes ago?"

The woman gets up and leans over the railing. "Excuse me?"

"Did you see a woman?" Tim shouts. "She came by here a moment ago!"

"Oh, yes. She was limping badly. I thought she might have hurt herself. Was in a terrible rush, too. I told Bent, I asked him if he thought we should call someone, but then she was gone again, and he said, Bent said—"

"Where did she go?" Tim cuts her off. "Did she enter any of the houses?"

The woman frowns, clearly finding him rude. She probably couldn't make out his face from the balcony. "No. She just ran down the street. I couldn't tell you where was headed, but if you ask me—what's that, Bent?"

Tim doesn't waste time finding out what Bent has to say—he just runs on down the street. Passing one block after another, he checks every front door and every window, expecting to find one that's broken. But he doesn't. He also doesn't hear any screams or shouting.

Why is she just running? Does she know I'm chasing her?

There's another explanation, of course. One he cares very little for.

The woman could have a particular target in mind.

And that particular target could be Tim's daughter.

Helena's apartment is in the other direction, luckily, but then again, Lundbeck's colleague already confirmed that she's not at home.

But where is she, then? And why hasn't she returned my—

Tim turns a corner and stops abruptly.

In front of him, on the other side of the street, towers an impressive glass building. The name plastered over the entrance with huge letters reads, BESTSELLER.

Judging by the commotion in front of the entrance—a young guy sitting on the ground with a perplexed look on his face, rubbing his neck, while others stand around him—Tim is almost a hundred percent certain the woman just entered the building.

Bestseller is the workplace of nearly four hundred people.

But that's not why Tim feels his heart sink.

The reason for Tim's dread is that one of those four hundred employees is the only person left in the world that Tim truly cares for.

Bestseller is the place Helena works.

She's not at work today, he tries to assure himself as he runs across the street. *It's her day off. She's not here ...*

56

HELENA

"HELENA? SWEETIE? YOU SURE you're okay?"

Helena blinks and comes to. She finds herself with a blouse in her hands, as though about she's getting dressed, and for a moment, she wonders what Asta is doing in her bedroom. Then she realizes she's not at the apartment, but at work.

Her older colleague looks at her with a worried smile. "You looked like you were about to put that on." She nods towards the blouse.

"Oh," Helena mutters, folding the blouse and placing it on the table. "No, I just ... I was just lost in thoughts ..." She picks up the next shirt from the cardboard box and rips off the thin plastic wrapping.

"Of course you were," Asta says in a big-sisterly voice. "I still don't get why you even came in today. You shouldn't even be here. And with what's happening ... your father ... I mean, it's no wonder you're distracted."

"It's fine," Helena assures her, mustering a smile as a shopper—a big woman with earphones on, using her cart as a walking frame, supporting her weight as she consumes a greasy bagel—comes rolling by. Calm music is playing over the loudspeakers, and everything seems like it's any other day. She hoped the familiar work would help her take her mind off of things. "I just couldn't sit at home all alone," she tells Asta. "I'd rather be here, surrounded by people I know."

Asta smiles again. "I get that. If you wanna talk about it, I'm here."

"Thanks," Helena says, but she doesn't want to talk about it. For some reason, what's happening to her dad feels like a very private matter—although pretty much everyone knows about it by now. From what she's seen on Facebook, rumors are spreading all over the world about some "strange infection," which is "transforming people into monsters." It was all they talked about on the morning news, and they even advised people in and around Hornsted to stay home today and self-isolate. The policeman they interviewed kept assuring people that "everything was well under control" and that there was no risk of a "nation-wide situation."

Of course, Helena knows better. The policewoman she had talked to told a different story. A story in which they were playing catchup to something they hardly understood or knew how to handle. She didn't say it outright, but Helena got the impression they were grasping at straws. Which was also why they were desperate enough to try and reach her father through her.

Luckily, they didn't say anything about Tim Iversen on the news, and she hasn't seen his name mentioned on social media, either. She worries what will happen to him if the entire world learns he's half-alien. Surely, people won't believe he's still on mankind's side.

Helena knows her father is not only capable of killing people, but that he's done so already. Probably more than once. He never spoke about his time in the army, especially not his trips to the Middle East—at least not to her. But he confided in her mom, and in one of the last conversations

Helena had with her, she hinted at the fact that he was burdened with "what he'd done down there."

Helena didn't ask any questions, because honestly, she was horrified at the thought of her dad being a killer, and she preferred not knowing anymore about his past. She already found it difficult to love him—she didn't need another excuse to push him away.

Of course, their relationship had always been problematic, even before Helena learned about his former job. They had never seen things eye-to-eye. The only thing they had in common was that they both loved Helena's mother very much, and when she passed away, their fragile bond lost its last glue.

At least that's how Helena sees it.

Her father, on the other hand, clearly has a harder time accepting the fact that they have nothing to build on, and so he keeps embarrassing them both with clumsy attempts at pretending to give a damn about her life—something he never did when Helena's mom was alive.

But it's too late. Helena is sixteen now. She's basically a grown woman. She doesn't need a dad anymore. She did when she was little. All those years he had a chance to fill the role in her life that he's now auditioning for, and he never once stepped up, leaving all the parental responsibility to her mother so he could wallow in his own demons.

And yet ...

When she heard what had happened to him, all the resentment drained away. Like drops of water on a piping hot pan. As though it was always just a thin layer on top of something much bigger. And when she learned that he was probably going to die—or, worse, turn into something monstrous—Helena realized that not only does she still need a father ... she also loves the one she has.

Suddenly, she saw past all his flaws. Her image of him turned from a self-absorbed, immature klutz to someone who tried his best despite his shortcomings. Because the truth is, he has never stopped trying. He's never really told her outright that he loves her, but he's also never given her reason to believe otherwise.

At the same time, she is flooded with guilt, because she realizes now how she's carrying some of the responsibility, too. *She* has been the one denying their relationship a second chance. She could have let him in after her mother died. But she had been too scared of being disappointed again. Of more heartache.

It was much easier to just pretend there was nothing to lose, rather than running the risk of actually losing what little there was.

And so she'd kept her heart closed whenever he came knocking. And now, she regrets it dearly. Because it's probably too late to undo. She'll likely never get the chance to—

"What was that?"

Helena realizes she was once again lost in thoughts. "What was what?"

The noise comes again. A car honking outside the building. Someone is shouting.

Helena and Asta look at each other for a brief moment. It could be nothing. A cyclist who didn't signal as he turned, and a driver who almost hit him is now showing his frustration by honking at him.

But Helena can tell Asta thinks the exact same thing as her.

"Could it be ...?" she begins.

Helena runs to the windows facing the street. Looking down, she sees the normal afternoon traffic. With one exception: A car has come to halt in the middle of the street, turned at an angle, as though the driver had to lock the brakes. Pedestrians have stopped to look. Leaning closer to the window, Helena catches sight of a person—a woman—running into the building.

Five seconds pass. Then someone screams downstairs.

Helena's stomach turns to stone. *Oh, no. It's happening.*

She can't know for sure, and yet she does.

"Helena?"

She turns to see Asta looking at her, wide-eyed.

"What is it?"

"They're here," Helena hears herself say. "We need to get out."

They head for the rolling stairs, Helena leading the way with Asta on her heels.

Just as she's about to run down the steps, Helena stops abruptly, causing Asta to bump into her.

"What is it?" she asks. "Why are you sto—"

"Sssh!" Helena cuts her off.

From up here, they have a good view over the first floor, and Helena immediately spotted the woman as she came into the room. She's wearing sunglasses and a COVID-mask which hides her face, but it can't conceal the fact that something's terribly wrong with her. Her arms and legs seem too long, and the way she moves—it's more like watching a big insect. She's jogging along, weaving through the tables and racks of clothes, her head turning back and forth in a searching manner.

There are other shoppers down there, and the woman sees them, but she doesn't seem to care. A few of the closer ones notice the woman and immediately pull back or outright run away.

The woman pays them no heed—she just keeps moving, keeps scanning the room.

She's obviously looking for something—or someone—in particular.

"Oh, Jesus," Asta breathes, as she notices the woman too.

As though hearing her, the woman snaps her head back, and her eyes lock on them—Helena can tell despite the sunglasses, which the woman rips off just then. Seeing her eyes—even from up here—makes Helena's knees turn wobbly.

"God," Asta exclaims, backing away. "What's wrong with her?"

"Run," Helena says, turning around, just as the woman runs for the stairs. Helena shoves Asta along, almost causing her to trip. "She's coming for us! Run, Asta!"

"Oh, God, oh, God," Asta chants, stumbling away. Then she suddenly ups her speed. "The fire exit!"

"No, it's too far," Helena says, turning right. "Come with me, Asta!"

But Asta doesn't hear her, she just keeps running for the fire exit all the way down at the other end of the floor.

She won't make it, Helena thinks, headed instead for the much closer door to the break room. Reaching it, she rips it open, steps inside, then closes the door almost all the way. Leaving it open just a crack, she spots the woman coming up the stairs just then.

She stops to look around. Even from over here, Helena can hear her breathing. Just like Helena predicted, the woman immediately spots Asta who's still running. But to Helena's surprise, the woman doesn't take up pursuit—even though she could easily catch up with Asta. She looks the other way and sees the heavy woman, who seems not to have caught on to what's happening. But the woman with the mask doesn't head for her, either.

Instead, she does something which makes Helena's skin crawl all over: She points her nose upwards and sniffs like a bloodhound. Then, to Helena's horror, she slowly turns in the direction of the breakroom. Just as her eyes hone in on Helena, she closes the door as quietly as she can, and turns around.

The break room is empty. There are no other ways out—except for the windows, which would be suicide, since they're fifty feet above ground.

She's coming. Think fast. You've got like ten seconds.

To Helena's surprise, her brain is able to come up with a plan in a flash. She runs to the windows, opens one of them, then dives down and crawls into the cupboard below the sink.

Just as she closes the cupboard, she hears the door to the room open.

57

TIM

"DON'T TOUCH HIM! GET away from him!"

The crowd disperses as Tim runs towards the guy on the ground. The nearest people almost immediately notice his face and start freaking out.

Tim doesn't care. He just heads for the guy with the bruise on his neck. Grabbing him by his jacket, he pulls him to a bicycle stand next to the entrance. Holding on to the guy—who is by now squawking like crazy, demanding that Tim let him go—he rips the chain holding the nearest bike, and instead wraps it around the guy's leg. Opening one of the links of the chain like it's made of rubber, he pinches it shut again, linking it with the other end, effectively chaining the guy to the stand.

"What the hell are you doing?" he cries, swatting at Tim awkwardly—as though he's outraged but also afraid to start a real fight. "What's wrong with you, man?"

Tim ignores him and instead turns to face the few onlookers who haven't fled. "Nobody touch him! This man is infected with the Nigro... with the Nicrum... with the virus they're talking about. Stay clear! The authorities are on their way."

They gasp and groan and pull back even farther, and Tim runs through the glass doors and into the building.

People inside the store have clearly noticed the commotion outside, and most of them are standing by the windows. They reel back as he enters. Tim looks around. The place is big and decorated in a very modern fashion: concrete floors, glass walls and spotlights in the ceiling. Endless racks and tables of clothes, changing rooms, mirrors and chairs where tired husbands can sit down. Not too many people are here yet—either shoppers or employees—so he can pretty quickly surmise that the woman isn't among them.

"Where is she?" he asks loudly. "Where is the woman who just came through here?"

Most of the people in here are women. Which could explain why none of them answer. Tim figures it only makes sense. They just saw a young woman fleeing through a store. Then, a minute later, a huge dude comes bursting in, demanding to know where she is.

Tim adds, "She's very dangerous. She's come to hurt a lot of people. I'm working with the authorities. I'm trying to apprehend her before she can kill anyone."

Still, none of the women seem keen to help. Instead, most of them draw back or even leave the room, some headed into elevators, others slipping through the openings to adjacent rooms.

"Damnit, tell me where she went!" Tim roars. His frustrated outburst only causes the few remaining people to cry out in fear and scurry away.

Huffing, he scans every way out of the room. There are five from what he can see—not counting the front door he just came through. Tim has no idea which way the woman had gone. She seems to have been careful not to leave any telltale traces.

He's about to choose a random direction, when he feels an incoming call. Yanking out his phone, he sees Lundbeck's name. "Yeah?"

"Tim, where are you?"

"In the BESTSELLER building. Less than a mile from the airport."

"You got her?"

"Not yet. But she's here somewhere."

"We're coming. We'll evacuate the building, shut everything down."

"It'll be too late," Tim grunts, walking briskly through the opening to the next room. This one is even larger. Mostly empty of people. Shoes, boots, belts and hats.

"*The passengers are all being isolated,*" Lundbeck tells him. "*And we found the guy you locked inside the tech building. Good move.*"

"There's another one in front of the BESTSELLER building," Tim says, crouching down to scan under the tables. "And I'm pretty sure we'll have a lot more soon."

"Just hang tight. We'll be there soon. If you can—"

Tim disconnects the call and slips the phone back into his pocket. He's picked up a muffled scream from somewhere. Sounded like it came from above. He spots an escalator and leaps up it four steps at a time.

Reaching the second floor, he stares around at colorful kids' clothes. Even fewer shoppers up here. Tim is thankful for it.

He stops briefly to listen. No more screams.

Then comes another call. He pulls the phone back out. This time, he sees Helena's name, and his heart jumps.

With his throat all tight, he answers the call. "Sweetie? Where are you?"

"*Dad?*" Her voice is hushed, barely more than a breath. "*I'm at work ...*"

Tim's pulse rises. "Where?" he croaks. "Where in the building? I'm here too. Tell me where you are, and I'll come get you."

Helena pauses briefly, and Tim hears a bang. It sounds like something being tipped over. A stool or a small table. He hears it both through the phone and from farther down the floor. He begins pacing in that direction.

"I'm in ... a break room... upstairs ... one of them just came in here ..."

More commotion in the background. Tim spots a heavy woman leaning on her shopping cart while holding half a glazed bagel in one hand and a cup of coffee in the other. She seems to have noticed something, because she's staring in a certain direction with a worried look.

Tim rushes to her, zigzagging between the tables. Just as he's about to ask her if she's seen the woman, he sees the door she's looking at. It's marked, "Staff Only."

"*God, Dad ... please help me,*" Helena whispers, on the verge of tears—and now Tim hears her in stereo; both through the phone and through the door. "*I'm inside a cupboard, and—*"

Helena cuts herself off with a scream.

Tim drops the phone and sprints at the door. He hears his daughter cry out: "*You stay the hell back!*"

Then he throws himself at the door, breaking through it like it was made of cardboard.

58

HELENA

SHE HOLDS HER BREATH even though her lungs heave for air and her heart is pounding away in her chest.

The cupboard is just big enough that she can fit in here. It smells of stale water, dust and cleaning supplies. It's almost completely dark, save for a thin strip of light coming in at the bottom.

Listening intently, she can hear the woman close the door again—for a fleeting second, Helena hopes she left. But then she hears footsteps crossing the room.

Just like Helena expected, the woman seems to head right for the open window. She envisions her leaning out, looking down at the street, trying to figure out whether Helena jumped or not.

Then, suddenly, a hoarse voice says, "I know you're still in here. I can smell you."

Helena jolts and clasps a hand over her mouth so as to not gasp out loud. Her heart ups its speed even further.

The woman begins searching the room. Helena hears her tipping over a chair, and pushing aside the couch.

She's going to find me.

Not knowing what else to do, she slips out her phone—noticing five missed calls, her phone having been on silent mode—and calls up her dad.

It only rings once. "*Sweetie? Where are you?*"

Her father's voice is tense. He's slightly out of breath, as though he's been running.

"Dad?" she breathes. "I'm at work ..."

Just then, she hears the woman begin opening cupboards, starting with the one at the end. The one Helena is in is right in the middle. Her hand searches for something, anything. She finds a spray can of some kind.

"*Where?*" her dad asks. "*Where in the building? I'm here too. Tell me where you are, and I'll come get you.*"

Helena feels a tiny flash of hope.

"I'm in ... a break room ... upstairs ... one of them just came in here ..." She stares at the beam of light, expecting the woman's feet to step into view any moment. "God, Dad ... please help me. I'm inside a cupboard, and—"

The cupboard is ripped open, and Helena screams.

The woman crouches down so they're face to face. The sight of her up close is almost enough for Helena to lose her mind—there are hardly any human features left. And as the woman tears off the mask, she reveals a wide mouth contorted into a wicked smile. She reaches in a hand that's way too big and is about to grab her, when Helena screams out: "*You stay the hell back!*" and sprays the cleaning product into the woman's face.

59

TIM

BURSTING INTO THE BREAK room, Tim is afraid of what he'll find.

Please, God. Don't let her be infected. Anything but that.

There are no other doors, but a couple of windows facing the street—one of them is open. In the middle is a table full of coffee mugs, a dozen chairs around it, all of them empty. On the wall is a muted television showing the news.

He can't immediately see Helena anywhere, but the alien woman is right on the other side of the table. She's crouched down, grunting and wiping at her face with both hands, as though something is annoying her. She's much further transformed than Tim expected, looking more like Alan than a human being. What makes the sight of her even more awful is the fact that she was no doubt beautiful before. Not much older than Helena, she had her life in front of her. Now, she looks like something from a horror movie. Her hair reduced to ragged tufts, her body too big, her limbs too long, her fingers ending in sharp claws. And her face that of a predator.

Seeing her makes something fall into place in a flash at the back of Tim's mind.

The woman traveled by plane to the other end of the country. And not only did she happen to end up at the place his daughter works—she actually found her inside the building among hundreds of others.

Alan's warning wasn't a coincidence.

The woman was coming for Helena. And she knew exactly where to find her.

How?

Clearly, the aliens are somehow in contact with each other. Perhaps via telepathy, or maybe they simply tap into a shared, mental database—a cloud server, almost. And in that database is both their newfound, alien knowledge, but also some of their human memories. Including what Alan knows about Tim. Like the fact that he has a daughter. That she lives in the capital. That she works at BESTSELLER. Even what she looks like.

Which is most likely how the woman found her.

The next question is, why would they go for her?

The answer is obvious. By now, they must realize Tim is a threat to them. Probably the only real obstacle in their way. He could very well be mankind's last defense. The only one able to stop the invasion.

So what better way to crush his resolve than to turn the only person he loves into one of them?

And they are right. If Tim loses his daughter, he won't give two fucks about the rest of humanity.

Snapping back to, Tim notices a movement by the woman's feet, and he sees his daughter come crawling out from the cupboard. She hasn't seen Tim yet, so she makes a dash for the table.

The woman senses her, and, managing to open one of her blank eyes, she sees Helena and goes for her.

Tim leaps across the table with a roar and tackles the woman like a linebacker going for the takedown. She sees him coming, and her expression turns to surprise, but she can't get out of the way, and Tim slams her against the counter, bending her spine into an angle that must be painful. The woman is much more flexible than a human would be, though, and she's only momentarily rattled. Then she begins clawing and biting at Tim. He's ready for the onslaught and pulls back in order to take a series of heavy swings at her. Two of them connect, his fists landing on her jaw and temple, slamming her this way then that.

The woman staggers and goes down onto one knee like a boxer taking the eight count.

"Dad!"

Tim instinctively whirls around at his daughter's voice and sees Helena show him a butcher's knife she's apparently gotten from a drawer. She crouches down and slides it across the floor to him.

Tim is just about to pick it up, when the woman—having regained her bearings much faster than Tim thought she would—grabs him around the waist and lifts him off the ground. She wrestles him to the ground and lands on top of him. Tim manages to turns over as she immediately goes to work trying to bite into him. Tim grabs her hair with both hands and forces back her head, her wide mouth snapping and foaming inches from his shirt.

They're equally strong, and for a moment, it's a stalemate.

Then the woman digs her claws into his sides, and Tim screams out in pain as he feels her nails grate against his ribs. With a sudden burst, he pushes her head farther back and curls up his legs just enough that he can wrap them around the woman's neck, catching her in a perfect leglock. He crosses his ankles and tightens the grip as much as he can, his thigh muscles squeezing the woman's airways shut, causing her to give off a wheezing rattle.

She starts clawing away at his legs, ripping through his pants, tearing open his skin, but it's superficial damage—Tim can already feel her strength faltering, so he ignores the pain the keeps the leglock firm.

"Die, you fucking monster," he hisses, feeling a wild surge of elation as he realizes the fight is won.

Then, from the side, comes Helena. She acts so swiftly, Tim hasn't got time to react. She picks up the knife and stabs the woman in the back. The blade only goes in a couple of inches, but it's enough that the woman gives off a muffled scream and thrashes harder.

"No, Helena! Get back!"

Helena has already let go of the knife and is backing away, a mortified expression on her face, as though she can't believe what she just did.

The alien reaches back and grabs the knife. She yanks it out, and Tim is certain she'll go for his face or neck, so he blocks with both arms. Surprisingly, though, the woman instead uses her last strength to fling the knife away. Tim hears it hit something and fall to the floor.

The woman turns her eyes to Tim, and for a moment, it looks like she's smiling triumphantly.

"I told you to fucking ... *die*!" Tim grabs the woman's head—which he can do now because she's too far gone to try and bite him—and he twists it around violently, hearing and feeling her spine crunch. She goes immediately limp.

Tim kicks her off him and gets to his feet. Looking down at himself, he sees his shirt and pants in tatters. Blood is running from dozens of scratch wounds. But none of them seem serious. He'll be okay.

"Honey, are you all right?" he asks, turning towards Helena—and his gut sinks as he realizes that Helena is not all right.

At first, he can't grasp why she's just standing there, her back against the counter, staring at him wide-eyed, one hand on the side of her neck.

Then he sees the blood seeping through her fingers and dripping to the floor where the knife lies.

And it dawns on Tim why the woman threw the knife, and why she smiled at him like she'd won.

Oh, no ... Oh, no, she got her ...

He rushes to his daughter and catches her as her legs give way.

As he gently brings her down into his lap, he tells her, "It's okay, sweetie, let me see," and he pries her hand free.

What he sees makes everything inside him turn to water.

The cut is about an inch. It's right on the jugular. And the blood is pumping out rapidly.

In a flash, he recalls what they taught them in the military. Why neck wounds are so dangerous. Leave it, and the person bleeds out within minutes. Try to compress it, and the brain won't get any oxygen. Basically, with a cut deep enough, it's a death sentence.

And this cut is plenty deep.

"It's okay, it's okay," Tim hears himself chant, even though he knows it's a lie. He can't think of anything else than to cover the wound with his palm and apply a gentle pressure. Just enough to stem the flood. Not enough to save her, but maybe prolong her life with a few seconds.

"Dad," she croaks, reaching up to touch his face. She frowns as her fingers run across his brow, then down his cheek. "You look ... not as bad as ... I thought ..."

Tim bursts into tears. He pulls his daughter closer, inhaling the scent of her hair and her perfume, memories from her childhood flying through his head like sparks.

This can't be real. It's happening too fast. It can't be real.

But it is. All his senses tell him so.

"It'll be all right, honey," he whispers, licking away tears from the corner of his mouth. "You'll be fine, I promise."

Another lie. His last words to Helena will be lies.

She doesn't seem to hear him, though. She closes her eyes and breathes deeply. She's already pale.

Tim squeezes his eyes shut, and he does something he's never done before. Not when the IED almost killed him in Iraq. Not even when Anya was on her deathbed.

He begins praying. "Please, God, spare her. She's done nothing wrong. I'm begging You. This is all my fault. I should be the one to pay. Let her live. Take me instead. Please, take me instead ..."

Tim never really believed in God. And he certainly never believed in miracles.

And yet he keeps pleading for one, as he feels Helena's blood stop running through his fingers.

It's over, he thinks, feeling completely empty. *She's gone.*

He just sits there, cradling her, rocking her like he did when she was a baby. There are no more thoughts.

After what feels like an eternity, he opens his eyes.

And what he sees makes no sense at all ...

* * *

Or, check out the free prequel, *Blackout*, to find out how it all started.

Only available at

nick-clausen.com/blackout

Printed in Dunstable, United Kingdom

63536104R00163